STOLEN THINGS

For my agent, Clare, who believed in this story from the very beginning.

Stolen Things is a Fox & Ink Books book

First published in Great Britain in 2026 by
Fox & Ink Books
Part of the University of Lancashire
Preston, PR1 2HE, UK

978-1-917894-33-3

1 3 5 7 9 10 8 6 4 2

Set in 10/16pt Kingfisher by Amy Cooper.

A CIP catalogue record for this book is available from the British Library.
Printed and bound in Great Britain by Clays Ltd, Elcograf S.p.A.

Stolen Things

A. M. HOWELL

Fox & Ink Books

Chapter 1

My breaths cloud in the frigid December air as I watch the sleeping baby. It's lying in a navy pram parked outside the stationery shop. Taking a step closer, I notice the baby's knitted bonnet, and the blanket it's swaddled in, are soft pink. A girl, then. The wool is bobbly, a dropped stitch here and there.

Pulling my scarf more tightly around my neck, I stare into the shop, looking beyond the festive display of watercolour paints, oils, chalks and drawing paper. Lottie is behind the counter wrapping purchases for the baby's mother who swished inside a few minutes ago without a backwards glance.

The handle of the pram gleams in the late afternoon light; an instruction to draw closer still. My throat tightens as the baby stirs.

It would only take a moment. I imagine lifting the baby from the pram, holding her close and breathing in her sweet, milky smell. Curling my gloved hands into fists, I try to squeeze away the compulsion. I count to five, concentrate on the scent of roasting chestnuts being sold from a handcart outside King's College.

An elderly woman in a lopsided cloche hat bustles past, her shopping basket bumps against the pram wheel. The baby startles, lets out a jagged cry. People should take better care.

The woman turns, as if she has read my thoughts.

"Oh. I do apologise." She takes a step back, glances into the pram. "What a little dear you have there."

"Yes, she is." *Did I just say that?* I feel a strong desire to take back the words. Through the shop window I see the baby's mother place her purchases into a string bag. She turns and catches my eye, a frown puckering her weary face.

"You'll be looking forward to Christmas this year, then," says the woman, bending to pat the baby's blanket. Her cloth gloves are brown, the fingertips worn and frayed. Perhaps she has held the hand of a grandchild while wearing them, plump fingers grasping hers. "A new life. So important to keep looking forwards," she prattles on.

"Yes, she's a darling." Where are these words coming from? This baby is nothing to me. *But she could be.* The taste of my words and thoughts are like soured cream on my tongue.

The shop bell jangles a warning. The baby's mother is returning.

"Well. Merry Christmas, then," says the woman, giving me a quick nod, and a look tinged with compassion, before continuing along the parade of shops.

She must have seen the dark smudges under my eyes, the lank, grey-flecked hair peeking out from beneath my hat. My sallow cheeks, the red blemish on my chin that has hung about for weeks. I've an urge to call the woman back, tell her I haven't always been like this. But of course, I don't.

The baby's mother steps outside, adjusting the fur collar of her coat. Such luxury.

Feeling an ugly pulse of anger, I step forwards and gently tuck in the baby's blanket. A baby left outside a shop exposed to damp fog and the breath of strangers. It's not right. Then I lean into the baby's mother and whisper, lighter than a feather, "You want to be careful. Someone could take her."

The mother rubs her ear, takes a step back and gapes at me, perhaps wondering if she misheard. This is Cambridge after all, a place of scholars and intellect. Where respectable middle-aged women like me do not linger over strangers' prams.

Chapter 2

The familiar scent of paper, paint and the tang of turps helps anchor me, as I step into the stationers, black dots dancing before my eyes.

Lottie looks up, gives me a friendly smile. "Good afternoon, Mrs Pemberton. Just the usual, is it?"

"Yes, please," I say, loosening my scarf to ease the knot in my throat.

Lottie turns to open a drawer containing the rows of graphite pencils I come in to purchase once a month. The girl's dark hair is shorter than usual, cut into a flattering style that skims her shoulders. It's many months since I stepped inside a hair salon. It is not just the expense, although that's part of it now I'm no longer employed. More the thought of having to sit rigid in a chair while a stranger's hand snips and curls and primps at my neck. *Being trapped, unable to escape.*

Lottie seems distracted and I worry that her brother has worsened. More than once she's spoken of the deadly golden artillery shell which exploded at his feet last year on the front line, the oozing blisters of yellow fluid that broke out on his pale skin. He suffers the effects, the mustard gas still rattles in his lungs, which even now wake her from her sleep, make her think he's drowning in his own breaths.

When she tells me such things, I always make the

sympathetic noises expected of me, until all I see in my mind's eye is my husband Theo. Then I covertly guide my attention to something else until she finishes. The gleam of a nib pen in a walnut case. Or a pot of green ink – the type he used. Theo said the colour was kinder than black, less fussy than blue. Lottie knows about my husband, of course, but is sensitive enough not to mention him. For that small kindness my loyalty remains fierce to her and this shop.

I watch the mother with the pram through the shop window. She's hunched over the baby, and I soon hear the squeak of wheels on damp paving as she moves on.

While Lottie busies herself wrapping the pencils, I study the display of art materials on the counter. A travelling watercolour set in an opaque glass case, the rounds of paint like perfectly placed stepping stones. My heart thuds, the compulsion rising again.

Inching closer, checking I'm not being observed, I ease a roundel of poppy-red watercolour paint from its case before slipping it into my coat pocket.

"Will that be all?" asks Lottie, turning back to hand me my purchase.

"Yes, thank you." I take off my gloves and pull my purse from my cloth bag. My legs buzz, as if electricity is fizzing through my veins. A crushing swell of guilt and anxiety rises as I hand over payment, hoping Lottie can't see the tremor in my hand. I wait for Lottie's eyes to widen, fix on me with disbelief as she notices the missing paint. But instead, she looks to the door as another customer enters the shop, bringing with him a swirl of cold air.

Standing safely outside, I slip a hand into the pocket where the stolen paint lies, enjoying the cool feel of the roundel in my palm. Theo. What would he make of me now? How the angles of his soft face would harden with disappointment at my petty theft.

Heat gathers in my midriff and rises upwards, bringing a familiar surge of nausea as my heart palpitates. Pressure builds at the base of my skull as my armpits moisten. *Take a breath, Della. One minute and it will have passed.*

Chapter 3

My home is one of a pair; four-storey houses with matching beige bricks, tall rectangular windows and ivy snaking up the walls. This end of Barton Road is mostly undeveloped and for now these houses stand alone, like two front teeth in an otherwise gummy mouth.

Clattering up the six steps to the front door, I pull the key from my coat pocket.

Rabbit's paws click on the floor tiles as he comes to greet me. "Hello, old thing," I murmur, stepping inside the house and bending to scratch behind the terrier's ears.

Theo's dog never left his side. I sometimes sit on the stairs watching Rabbit as he in turn watches the front door. There are days though when Rabbit is diverted by other things, snuffling out sparrows in the garden shrubs, sleeping in front of the kitchen stove, waiting outside the old groom's lodgings. Then without any warning I'll come across the dog patiently front door-watching again. His loyalty is beguiling.

Rabbit whines. "Yes. Supper won't be long," I say, shrugging off my coat, unwinding my scarf and hooking them over the stand.

***

In the basement kitchen I place the drawing pencils on the

table, then turn to face the oak dresser. I run a finger over one of the pieces of blue and white porcelain displayed on it. Theo's favourite set, always used at breakfast. My finger comes away smudged with grey and I wipe it on my skirt. Agnes, my home help, will need to dust on her next visit.

Opening a dresser drawer, I move aside a pile of drying cloths, then carefully position the paint at the very back. It looks like a patty of dried blood next to the reel of navy thread from the draper's, the salmon pink pot rouge from the chemist's. A shade that would never suit my sallow complexion.

My fingertips rest for a moment on the pocket-sized leather-bound sketch book that lies beside my stolen things. Then I carefully cover all these items with the cloths, close the drawer and lean against it. My betrayal at the stationery shop momentarily steals my breath, this place where I've only ever experienced kindness. *I did not take the baby. That's all that matters today.*

The brown glass bottle sitting on the kitchen table next to my pot of pencils draws me over. Giving it a quick shake, the quiet glug tells me it is half empty. No matter, there are more waiting in the upstairs bathroom. Lined up like soldiers ready for battle, labels facing outwards. *Tonic for Female Disorders.*

Unscrewing the cap, I take a sip. Then another longer one. The liquid is viscous, herby and sweet, warms my throat nicely. Sinking into the highbacked armchair Agnes and I dragged downstairs from Theo's first-floor study, I rest my head, watch Rabbit watch me from his rug, his tongue lolling.

I should be sitting upstairs in the drawing room, a fire roaring in the grate, music on the gramophone. But I feel safer down here. This poorly lit basement kitchen is my haven now, its high window preventing prying eyes from watching me walk about with my blouse flapping open, or my dress unbuttoned to the waist when I'm overcome by a flash of heat. There's a door to the garden for the dog, a larder, icebox and electric lamps. We've everything we need. *No one to trouble us or poke their nose into our business.*

I think back to late summer, Agnes and me in headscarves as we shuttered up most of the other rooms in the house, throwing clouds of bed sheets over the heavy wooden furniture. We blocked up each fireplace with crumpled pieces of newspaper, our fingers blackened with soot.

Agnes had protested at first. "But the war's over. You don't need to limit yourself to living in one poxy room. You can light and heat the place as you wish. Arcadia House is your home. You should be living in it. All of it!"

For the first time in five years, things seemed normal. It's a stale and stiff word, one I haven't used for longer than I care to remember. But what I do know from reading the daily paper is that the majority of men billeted to the continent and beyond are home, the threat of influenza has mostly passed, and hope is threaded like gold through every written article. A chance to draw the curtains on the terrible war and march into a new decade with positivity and gratitude. But Agnes was never going to understand why I didn't take this view, a girl of twenty-one and less than half my age with no commitments and her whole life ahead of her.

The requests for the typesetting and printing of university periodicals at the firm I was employed at reduced in the war and I was eventually let go. But that hadn't seemed to matter much, not when I was newly married and there was ample voluntary work elsewhere. The man I loved was also bringing in an income enough for the both of us. Now, savings and my widow's pension pay for fuel and the electric, but I must be frugal. It's impossible to think about looking for new employment in my current frame of mind. Even the thought of it makes my throat tighten. The people, the small talk, the noise and responsibility.

Rabbit whines. "Supper, darling dog. Yes, I haven't forgotten." My limbs are languid and slow as I take horse meat from the ice box, chop and scrape it into the dog's ceramic bowl. I stumble a little as I bend to place it on the floor, feel a rush of dizziness. It's not an unpleasant feeling, reminds me of lazy days punting on the river when I would trail my hands in the cool water and watch mayflies flit about.

My arms begin to itch. A fresh wave of warmth begins. These flushes always worsen after the sun sets, as if the act of it sinking below the horizon lights a fire at my feet. I glance at the back door. Air, I need cool air. And it's also time I paid him another visit.

The cake tin is across the table, and as I prise off the lid the scent of cinnamon and ginger rises. Taking out a piece of flat gingerbread biscuit, I wrap it in baking parchment, securing it with a piece of grey twine.

Rabbit wags his stubby tail, is already waiting for me at the back door.

The harsh November gales and snow from the east have been replaced by this cloying mist, dampening everything in sight. I welcome the chill while Rabbit snuffles the flower beds. Vegetables grow there now in place of Theo's lines of beloved dahlias. The soil is newly turned over around the winter cabbages, their frilled leaves glistening.

It takes no more than forty steps to reach the old groom's lodgings at the end of the garden, where a gate leads out onto a narrow unpaved lane. Horses and carriages clattered down it once. Last summer a man would sometimes drive his motor car on the lane, his children squealing with delight as they bumped over the grassy ruts.

I sidle up to the gnarled wooden door of the single-storey brick building, trying to listen. There's no sound within, but a blade of light spills under the threshold so I know he's in. As always, the roughly sewn hessian curtain is pulled across the windowpane, the blackout lining I made now frayed at the edges.

My two knocks on the door are gentle. "Hello, are you there?" I swallow, waiting for the reply that I already know will not come. "How's work at the smallholding? I imagine it's busy with Christmas being near?" Still nothing, but I sense he's listening. "You've been digging the vegetable beds out here again too. Thank you for that."

I wait, my toes curling against the cold, just the planks of this door separating our breaths. "I've said this before . . . but please take anything you like. There's plenty of vegetables for the two of us."

Bending to ease the package under the threshold, I stand

and wait. Footsteps. Then a rustle as he picks it up. His sigh is as heavy as an anvil. Rabbit whines. Folding my arms around my thin blouse, I look to the sky and shiver as fat drops of rain begin to fall.

Chapter 4

The rain has let up, but the fog is thickening as I take Rabbit for his evening walk. The men on bicycles, the couple strolling arm in arm. They all look at me with either sympathy or concern, sometimes both. A woman out alone at this time with only a small and ageing terrier for company often provokes a response that I don't ask for or welcome. I'm not foolish though – I don't stray far from doors I could beat on should I encounter someone who means me harm. *While Rabbit is still alive, I must stay alive too. It's as simple as that.*

While the dog selects a railing for his nightly business, I stand for a moment watching a family inside their newly built villa. A boy is helping dress a Christmas tree with electric bulbs. Tiny dots of flickering blue and red light chasing away the dark. I know this boy's father, unlike so many others, came back. Mr Lloyd, a university fellow like my Theo.

The boy is around ten, the same age as my sister Mary's youngest. In four days, she and her family will arrive for Christmas. There's the ham to pick up from the butcher, gifts to purchase, the rooms to air and prepare. And I must venture into the attic to fetch down the decorations and bring some festive cheer to the house. I don't want to think of that now, the other things packed away in the trunks up there.

Rabbit nudges my calf, and we turn for home, the comforting

and earthy smell of woodsmoke accompanying us down the road. It's then I notice the person in the murk, waiting by the steps to Arcadia House.

I glance behind, but we are quite alone.

The skin on the back of my neck prickles as I watch this person climb my front steps, his shoulders rounded.

I click my tongue. "Come on, Rabbit." Drawing closer, I see the man's gloved hand reach into his coat pocket. He pulls out a key. The man looks about, then inserts the key into my front door.

Shock roots me to the spot, then I hurry forwards, Rabbit panting as he struggles to match my pace. "I say . . . excuse me. I believe you have the wrong house." My call is thin in the saturated air. *Silly woman.* I bend to scoop Rabbit into my arms and mount the steps.

The man half turns, a hand still grasping the key which is now wedged into the lock. Setting the dog down, I see he can be no more than thirty years of age, is wearing a dark frock coat that seems too spacious for his slight frame. A shiny silver pocket watch dangles and a top hat is jammed onto his head. *Strange.* Whiskery sideburns that seem too elderly for his years. A sheen of sweat glimmers on this man's forehead, and he holds his left arm protectively across his middle. "Have we met, madam?" His tone is cool and collected.

I shake my head. "No, sir." I gesture to the key wedged in my door lock. "You've made a mistake, I'm afraid. I live here."

The man blinks again, slow and steady, as Rabbit sniffs around his feet. "You. Live. Here?" He annunciates each word clearly and separately, as if their joint meaning cannot be possible. His hand drops from the key. Eyes narrowing, he scratches his whiskers. "But you are mistaken, madam. This is *my* house."

Rabbit barks gruffly, as if also alarmed at this blatant untruth. Arcadia House was Theo's childhood home, the place he was born and raised. The place we lived since marrying six years ago. "Please. If you'd kindly remove that key . . ."

Before I finish speaking, the man turns away. A quick click and a push and my door is unlocked and open to the night like a yawning mouth.

"Now look here, I don't know what this is about, but . . ."

The man steps into my house, pocketing the key. There's a swagger of arrogance about him, a fox claiming its den.

Rabbit trots in after him. "Stay, Rabbit," I command under my breath, but the dog just ambles along the chequered tiles towards the stairs to the kitchen and warmth of the stove.

My aging next-door neighbours are away, visiting family on the continent. On land opposite and to the right new buildings will soon be sprouting up. There are no other immediate neighbours to call out to, no help at hand. My side pinches as I think of the lodgings at the end of the garden. *I won't find help there either, must deal with this alone.*

Darting after the man, I switch on the electric lamp on the console table by the door. The bulb fizzes into life.

The stranger blinks, turns in a complete circle as he studies the hallway. Then he carefully places the palm of a gloved hand on the flocked wallpaper I so carefully chose after the wedding, delicate green and pink parrots sitting on twisting branches. Confusion creases his brow. "What . . . what has happened to the place?"

A chill ices the back of my neck. He speaks as if he has been here before. "Please. You need to leave."

Moving further into my home, his finger squeaks a path over the varnished wooden sideboard at the foot of the stairs. He stares at the photograph in a gilt frame, me and Theo in our wedding clothes. His brow furrows and he looks up, grey-blue eyes wide with alarm. "My furnishings . . . my possessions . . . where are they?"

He holds one arm across his body still, is hunched as if suffering from a sore stomach. He's sick then, and confused, perhaps running a fever? But how do I encourage him to leave, make the house safe? And how did he get the key? "Please . . . you must go now," I repeat, stiffly holding out a palm. "My house key. I . . . I don't know how you came by it, but I should like it back."

The man's frown deepens, and he steps closer. "Who *are* you? What are you doing in my home?"

The accusation in his voice makes me recoil. He is spouting nonsense, yet his fixed gaze bears the hallmark of self-belief. A faint but acrid stink is coming from this man. His odd clothes, the purple silk cravat and top hat, make him seem from a different time. Dizziness has me reaching for the wall to steady myself, closing my eyes for a second. Then I hear him bolt up the stairs.

"No! Wait!" Panic rises in waves, and I glance at the open front door. Leaning towards it, I push it shut. What if this man has a friend lingering outside? But then, he's also now enclosed with me. There is no telephone in this house, no other manner of seeking help. I silently curse Theo and his disregard for technological invention.

I've no choice but to follow him to my first-floor landing, where he now stands staring up at the longcase clock which strikes before or after the hour and never on time. I can't help hoping his expression in this half-light is one of bewilderment, not of malice. I've witnessed first-hand those men who fought in the war and returned but are changed. Often at sixes and sevens, occasionally liable to cause a fuss and a disturbance.

He peers down the landing. "Viola? Where is my child?"

"Viola," I repeat, wringing my hands together. "There's no one of that name living here. This is a mistake . . ."

He ignores me and carries on past the two guest bedrooms, then a bathroom, with its clawfoot tub and toilet that clanks and complains. Pausing outside Theo's study, he reaches for the doorknob.

"No! You cannot go in there. That's my husband's . . ." I begin, but this man is already inside, his shoes treading over a rug which my own soles have not walked on for more than a year.

The shutters inside are closed, a glow from the gas lamp outside throwing jagged lines of light across the desk. Tidy, just as my husband left it. Books, papers and periodicals in order on the shelf. A dust sheet covering his brass microscope and boxes of slides.

The intruder stands with his back to the two glass display cabinets containing my husband's insect collections; moths and butterflies pinned and recorded. His face contorts. "Where is my child? What have you done with her?"

My mouth is bone dry. That smell again. Milk gone off and something worse. My breaths are coming too rapidly; a high-pitched whine rings in my ears.

He turns and pulls the dust cover from the nearest display cabinet. An arm still held across his middle, he peers inside. "Dead things!" he exclaims. "In my daughter's bedroom."

"My husband's collection," I croak. A tap-tap-tap from upstairs. I turn, stare out onto the landing, heart hammering. *Someone else is inside the house!*

Frozen to the spot, I hear the man behind me, the rustle of his coat. Another tap-tap from above. *What is happening here?* Stumbling from the study I feel along the wall for the light switch, but before I reach it there is hot, stale breath on my cheek and an urgent whisper in my ear. "You are the imposter here, madam. This is my house, and I *shall* return."

My vision retracts to a pin prick, and I sink to the floor as this man hurtles past me, his feet thudding down the stairs. The front door opens and slams shut and the chandelier light fitting tinkles.

Every part of me trembles as I force myself to my feet. I switch on the landing light and listen. The tapping noise from upstairs has stopped and I hear Rabbit whine from inside the study. But that can't be right. The dog is downstairs.

Peering around the door, I notice a bundle of fabric beneath the legs of a wooden display cabinet that wasn't there when I looked in before. My instincts are telling me to retreat to the basement, lock the doors and stay there until morning. But then the cloth pushes upwards. *Something is inside.* Taking a step into the room, then another, I think of a hummingbird hawk moth, like the one pinned in Theo's cabinet, brown wings unfurling and taking flight.

A cry, then. Piercing and unmistakable.

The bundle wriggles and writhes and I tentatively, so tentatively, lean in and peel back a fold of greying muslin. *A baby.* Its tiny face scrunches and it begins to wail.

Chapter 5

A *baby.* The white cotton gown it's dressed in covers its length. The bib is darned with yellow-eyed daisies. A girl. The gown looks prettily made but, like the muslin the baby is wrapped in, it's frayed.

A stink rises. I'd assumed this smell came from the intruder, but I was mistaken. I think of the man's expansive coat, his arm held across his middle. *Concealing this child?* This thought snaps me from my shock and I run from the study, along the landing and past the clock as it chimes nine. "Wait! Come back!"

Half stumbling downstairs, I pull at front door. Locked! He has locked us inside. The baby is screaming now.

Rabbit looks pointedly up the stairs.

"The key. Where's my house key?" I shout, patting my coat pockets.

The dog's ears flatten.

Shrugging off my coat, I turn out each pocket. Dropping the garment to the floor, I shake the door handle again, desperation rising. I must exit via the basement to the garden, take the side passage to the street, find this man and make him take the child back.

Rattling shrieks drift down the stairs. A sharp realisation then. I cannot leave the baby alone here. Giving the door handle one last tug, I kick it hard with my boot, a ribbon of pain shooting up my ankle. Standing on tiptoes, I drag the top door bolt across, then do the same with the bottom. When he returns for the baby – and surely he will – he'll be forced to ring the bell. This man will not step inside my home uninvited again.

Rabbit barks twice as I hurry back up the stairs.

I stand for a moment on the study threshold, staring at this small bundle of fury, her arms and legs flailing. Saliva pools in the pockets of my mouth. Lurching inside, I kneel before her. "There, there," I say. The baby's wails soften momentarily. It gives me the courage to stretch out a hand, lay a palm on her heaving stomach. Her head moves from side to side, and she pushes a fist into her mouth.

I met Mary's boys, my nephews, shortly after their birth. Robust and healthy babies who announced their arrival with gusto. Remembering tiny fists between tiny lips, the sucks and slurps and all manner of other noises that came from their mouths, I understand at once. *This baby is hungry.*

Gently, I scoop her up. She is floppy, weighs next to nothing as I sit on the rug and place her on my lap, stroking her hot, wet cheek with the base of my thumb. Her skin is pimpled, tiny pinprick white spots flecking her nose and forehead. Thinking again of my nephews, I see this baby can be little more than a month old.

The intruder, the man who brought her into this house, this room. He said he was looking for his daughter. Could this be his child – left here in a moment of disorientation? *Where is the baby's mother?* I run two fingers over the soft spot on top of the baby's head. I recall Mary telling me if the skin was sunken here it could be a sign of dehydration. I devoured these facts once, actively sought them from my sister, certain they would prove useful. *But not like this.*

The skin is soft but firm on her crown. Feeling her arms and legs, she does not seem malnourished. The baby's cries weaken to a whimper as I run my careful hands over her. My thighs and calves begin to prickle with pins and needles and then numb. I'm rooted to this rug, too afraid to move in case she starts crying again.

In the quiet, I hear the same tap-tap coming from above. I click my tongue, recognising it at once. In the terror of the moment, I mistook the branches of the old oak tree brushing against a rear bedroom window for someone upstairs.

When the numbness becomes too much, I push myself to my feet, holding the baby in the crook of one arm. Careful to support her head, I open a window shutter and peer to the street below. The fog is too dense to see far, but there's no sign of the man now. No one lingering or watching the house. *This is my house and I shall return.* He said those words like a promise. Or a threat. The bolts are pulled across. I am safe. Yet at the same time the man *must* return. He cannot leave this child here with me.

The baby's mouth roots, opening and closing like a fish. I offer her a knuckle, and she locks her lips around it. She sucks furiously, as if her small life depends on it. I think of my sister again, the tins of powdered infant milk that used to sit in her larder. There's nothing like that in this house. I have a few tins of condensed milk though, perhaps those will do? I could warm some, dribble it between her lips with a spoon.

Rabbit is still waiting at the bottom of the stairs, my coat splayed on the floor next to him. The dog sniffs at it as I bend to pick it up and throw it on the coat stand.

By the feet of the console table I see the front door key. It must have fallen from a coat pocket when I turned them out after all. Tightening my hold on the baby, I bend awkwardly to pick it up. It's then I notice something resting on the table. A rectangular piece of card slightly larger than my palm. It sits next to the silver letter opener engraved with my initials – a gift from Theo. Turning the card over reveals a photograph, and it's one I don't recognise. Another thing this man left in my home – a calling card of sorts?

The baby throws her arms out, her face and lips purpling. Slipping the picture into my pocket with the house key, I hurry to the kitchen.

***

My back aches as I perch on the chair brought from the closed-up dining room. I've placed it next to the sideboard in the hall, where I have an unobstructed view of the front door. Dipping a spoon into the cup of warmed condensed milk, I dribble it into the baby's mouth. A slow and arduous task, with much of it wetting the bib of her gown, gathering in the folds of her neck and soaking into my cardigan and blouse too. She's blessedly quiet though, her lips smacking between sips.

He has a key. He has a key. This knowledge about the man who came into my house uninvited will not stop circling.

How did he come by it? All the keys to this house are in the kitchen on hooks above the sink.

He must be suffering from a type of madness. Shell shock. This war scarred people's minds as well as their bodies, and I know that better than most. There are men in this town with dazed and vacant stares, their shoes stooping and shuffling along the cobbles. Selling matches or lavender on street corners in best grey suits and hats, pretending to be something they are not. I imagine him lifting his grizzling child from its crib while his wife slept, buttoning it up inside his peculiar coat. Taking a feverish walk to this side of town. *But the key!*

Stretching out a slippered foot, I touch the wrought iron poker I took from the companion set by the drawing room fireplace. *Would I have the courage to use it if confronted with malice?*

The redness in the baby's cheeks is fading, and I wipe at her face and neck with the edge of the muslin, still tightly bound around her rear end to keep out the worst of the smell. I must deal with that situation next.

Nurse Crouch springs to mind, her instructions to us auxiliary nursing staff at the First Eastern General Hospital on the myriad uses for a triangular bandage made from a square of cloth. That would be just the shape to fashion a nappy of sorts. A year after the war began, I recall standing around a table with the other nine nurses in my cohort, the smell of disinfectant in my nostrils as the canvas hospital walls sucked in and out in the wind. That was one good thing about the place, the coolness to chase away ever-present germs and invigorate the wounded.

Mrs Crouch laid out an example bandage with printed instructions and illustrations on all the ways a piece of cloth like this might be used. We studied images of muscular half-dressed men, bandages protecting wounds to heads, thighs, hips and buttocks. The girl to my right tried to cover her sniggers with a cough. Later that week, after we'd started working on the wards, I saw her ashen faced and crying in the canteen. The week after that she was gone.

Rabbit lies at my feet, ears pricked as he silently watches. He is not used to babies, although is gentle with my nephews on the rare occasions they come to visit. I adjust position, and the child's mouth arches into a yawn. Eyelids flickering, she falls into a doze, any stiffness in her limbs loosening until she is no more substantial than a rag doll.

Standing to relieve the ache in my spine, the baby's head rolls from the nook in my arm. Such a delicate and small thing. The responsibility of keeping her safe and well until the man who left her here returns makes me watchful, making constant adjustments and readjustments in position until I'm certain she is supported. I feel for the door key in my pocket, thinking again of the intruder. It's then that I remember the photograph I slipped in there too.

The image is washed over with a brown hue, fading at the edges. A man and woman leaning over a white wicker baby carriage, smiling at the hidden occupant. I draw in a breath. The man is the intruder who came into this house and left this baby I'm cradling now. His whiskery sideburns, the wave to his hair and frock coat. The woman with him – his wife,

I suppose – has a dainty lace shawl around her shoulders. Her strong face and determined eyes gaze into the carriage with unbridled fondness.

As I stare harder at the photograph, I notice it's not just the man who is familiar here. The curve of the window, the unusual crisscross pattern in the brickwork behind them. This small family are sitting just a few short steps from where I am now, in my own garden at Arcadia House.

Chapter 6

The baby's legs twitch and jerk as she lies on a linen towel on the kitchen table. I glance at the sturdy back door and the bolts snapped across top and bottom. It was recently fitted and I'm certain I am the only key holder. *We are safe here.* Removing her soiled nappy, I drop it into the copper cooking pot by my feet. Reaching down to put on the lid, Rabbit sniffs at it. "You do not want to look in there," I mutter, and the dog grunts, shuffles back to his blanket.

I gently wipe the baby's red, pimpled bottom with a warm, wet cloth and carbolic soap. My insides twist as she screams, her face damp with tears, her arms flinging back over her head. "There, there," I say briskly, wrapping her in the flat nappy I fashioned from another towel. As I fasten it with metal pins from my needlework box she quietens a smidgeon, looks up at me. She becomes cross-eyed in her attempt, and I smile unbidden.

"Your mother must be missing you terribly." I give her nappy a quick tug to check it is secure, feel a burst of triumph at my resourcefulness. She turns her head to the right, and with little breathy gulps roots for her fist and begins to grizzle again.

More milk dribbles from the cup and spoon. It will never be enough to satisfy her. Afterwards, and pacing the kitchen, I sway with the baby in my arms. She weighs so little.

Picking up the tonic bottle from the table, I sink into the armchair and unscrew its cap. My eyes are gritty with tiredness, from the shock of the evening, and I carefully lay the baby across my lap and take a long draught of the liquid before lodging it down the side of the chair.

My eyes drift closed as I stroke the baby's stomach. She's calmer now, yawns periodically, and her breaths even out and slow. Mine are erratic as I think of the photograph. Who are the family standing in my back garden and when was the image taken? The man in the picture *is* the man who left the baby, but there's an oddness to this. The man's top hat and frock coat resembles the clothing of my long dead grandfathers. This thought makes me shiver. What would possess this man to take a child from its mother and give it to a stranger? *Viola. He was looking for a child called Viola.* My eyes flick open.

"Viola?" I whisper. My question goes unanswered as the baby drowses. As the heaviness of sleep loosens my own limbs, I decide that will be her name for now. I can't rest yet though, must first find a safe place for Viola to sleep.

I glance to the door leading to upstairs and my bedroom on the second floor. No. It doesn't feel right to take her up there, not after what happened here tonight. I must stay in the basement; my safe place and within earshot of the man in case he returns. But if I sit with her all night on this chair, she could slip from my lap to the floor, her skull shattering.

A small, dead thing taken away from this house.

Leaving Viola on the armchair, I take one of the larger dresser drawers, empty the contents and place it on the kitchen table. I pad the base of it with soft drying cloths. The baby begins to wail again.

"There, there. I've made you a nice bed . . ."

Rabbit lets out a gruff bark and I pivot. *No, no, no!* Viola's on the very edge of the armchair, the cushion I used to wedge her in kicked to the ground. In three strides I have her in my arms, her screams piercing as if she knows I'm incapable, a bad choice. *Yet in a fit of insanity that man chose to leave her with me.*

My hands are still shaking as I settle and soothe the baby into her new bed. She stretches, her limbs stiffening in a shiver. I tuck a cloth around her, a makeshift blanket that's usually tangled around wet crockery, not the body of a child. The baby yawns again, and her eyelids close.

Pulling the armchair closer to the table, I collapse into it. I scratch and scratch at my arms. Warmth glimmers and grazes at my skin and I unbutton my blouse, fan myself with a piece of folded drawing paper. Glancing at the wall clock, I sit waiting. When the scream comes from down the garden, it's as piercing as ever. I lean forwards, hoping that Viola won't wake. Rabbit's ears twitch, but he doesn't move from his rug, so used is he now to these nightly disturbances.

The screams cease, but I continue to sit quietly, the kitchen swimming in and out of view as my eyes open and close. *The doors are locked and bolted. We are safe.* I tell myself this again and again until sleep at last envelops me.

***

I awake with a start, a bluish dawn light pressing at the basement window. A corvid caws from the garden. Rubbing at the crick in my neck, I get up and stoke the stove, watch Viola as she dozes on. She's flung off her makeshift blankets, and her thin legs are mottled. Tucking her in again, I quietly set about warming some milk.

The baby slept for no more than two hours at a time throughout the night, her screeches dragging me from my short bursts of sleep with accompanying surges of nausea. My head is thick, my mouth vinegary.

After Viola wakes and has been fed twice more, I make my way upstairs, the baby's head nestled into my collarbone. Her breaths are soft as down against my skin. A dull headache threatens as I pause to look into the study. Sun streams through the half-open shutter, draws me inside. I frown. The walnut desk's dust cover is now neatly folded on the chair. On the desk sits a bottle of my Tonic for Female Disorders.

My insides hollow. I've no memory of bringing that bottle in here last night, of *being* in the study last night. Picking it up, I cast my eyes about the room, the memory of the man and this baby he left behind a splinter under my skin.

He said this was his daughter's bedroom. I've only ever known this room as Theo's and can picture my husband quite clearly the last time he sat at the desk, the smell of pipe smoke lingering.

I used to count Theo's lasts in the way I count sheep when I can't fall asleep. The last time I followed him to the train station, keeping myself hidden among the throngs of troops waiting for transportation. The last time I visited his place of work only to find him gone. *The last time he sat here at this desk, gripping my wrist so hard it hurt.*

The memories make me swallow and turn away, my wrist

throbbing as if the bruise that bloomed after that incident remains. I shake my head, turn my attention instead to baby Viola and the man who left her here under a cabinet of dead moths.

He hasn't returned, so I must visit the police station in town, see if they can help resolve this.

***

At the back door is a trug of vegetables. Two savoy cabbages, a tangle of parsnips and three golden onions. I glance at the groom's lodgings, before taking them inside. There's no sign of him, but I whisper a silent 'thank you' all the same.

Swaddling Viola in a blanket, I hurry to the brick outhouse. It sits halfway along the garden, between the lodgings and the house. In one side is the outdoor privy that he uses, in the other a storeroom of sorts, a place for rakes and spades, butterfly nets and pots of paint and varnish. There's something else in here I'm in need of today, an item I instructed Theo to sell or donate, I did not care which. He didn't listen though, or perhaps it was just too painful to contemplate. Whatever the reason, today I'm glad of it.

Stepping inside the outhouse, I look past the plant pots, and crates of seeds, all carefully labelled. A few seeds have fallen to the floor, scattering around the silver spoked wheels of the pram. A mouse perhaps, searching out winter sustenance.

The pram's silver handle is speckled with rust and rough beneath my fingertips. Giving it a pull, the contraption moves towards me and then we are all outside again.

Viola whimpers and I fold my arms around her as I stand looking at the pram. "I never thought I'd have reason to use this," I tell her. There's something quite comforting about talking to a baby. The conversations may be one sided, but the slight wriggle, the feathering of her eyelids, leaves me in no doubt she is listening.

Whisking off the two grey blankets covering the pram, I place a hand inside it. Only a slight dampness to the padded mattress, nothing a good wipe with a hot cloth won't solve.

The pram wheels squeak as I push it along the garden path to the house. Rabbit watches from under the oak tree, his tail wagging. So much upheaval for me and this little dog in such a few short hours. I'll report the intruder to the police, hand this baby over, summon a locksmith to change the front door locks. Normalcy will then resume.

Placing Viola in her makeshift bed in the kitchen, I clean, wipe and polish the pram, my mind darting back to a June evening more than two years ago now, not long after our loss. The open bedroom window carried in air heady with the perfume of flowers and cut grass. Theo must have assumed I was asleep after taking the draught prescribed by the doctor, but a sound woke me, a keening that had me stumbling to the window and drawing back the heavy drapes. There was my husband, hunched over this pram, his arms curved around it as he stood by the outhouse. I wanted to comfort him, but my stomach was still cramping, my legs too weak to carry me outside so we could share in our grief. We would have named our baby Emily if she were a girl, George if he were a boy. *Best not to think about that now.*

Swaddling Viola, I settle her in the pram. She's so small inside, barely fills the space at all. I think then of the woman with the fur-collared coat, her baby left outside the stationery shop yesterday. My vision blurs a little. The child must have been about the same age as Viola.

A sudden scraping like metal on stone has me turning on my boot heel. I see the man who lives at the end of the garden standing by his door, the gleam of a knife in his hand as he sharpens it.

Viola lets out a mewling cry, and he stares at us hard. Then before I have a chance to utter a single word his eyes flit away and he disappears inside, closing the door with a heavy thud.

Chapter 7

Theo told me this police station used to be a workhouse. Standing outside, I imagine small, dirty faces peeping out from the top floor windows to the street below, stomachs gurgling with hunger.

Viola has slept the whole way into town. Her cheeks are pink. I touch a hand to her forehead, worrying about chills, influenza and dehydration. She needs her mother's breast, or a feeding bottle and tin of infant milk powder. She needs more suitable clothes, warm knitted stockings, vests and cardigans and a hat. I think again of her father, swallow back a rush of anger at him abandoning her with me, a stranger. If I were her mother, I would be frantic with worry, and it's this thought which finally propels me to the door. A gentleman coming out holds it open, and I push the pram inside.

***

The fug of cigarette smoke is stifling. I park the pram against a wall, next to a table bearing a small Christmas tree decorated with limp red paper chains. Standing for a moment, I watch the young man with a neat brown moustache behind the counter. The brass sign before him says *Duty Sergeant*. He taps a foot on the floor as he pores over paperwork, a cigarette dangling from yellow fingertips. Ash spills onto the countertop and he absentmindedly sweeps it to the floor. There will be a woman who will come in and clean this up later no doubt, brushing up the remains of important men's cigarettes for a pittance.

"Excuse me?"

The sergeant looks up. "Yes?"

I clear my throat. "I wondered . . . has anyone been in this morning to report a missing child?"

The sergeant's forehead buckles. "A missing child?"

I nod, push my gloved hands into my coat pockets.

"No. There have been no reports of any missing children."

"You are quite sure?" I press.

"Yes, madam. Quite sure." He stubs out his cigarette. "Would you mind telling me what this is about?"

I gesture at the pram. "I need to report a missing baby. That baby over there."

His gaze sharpens; I have his attention now. But then I feel a curl of doubt. If there are no reports of a missing child, what will this man do with Viola? Will she be placed in a local orphanage? I think of the fearful stories Mary and I devoured under the bedcovers as children, when such places had draughts creeping under doors, mean spirited matrons and not enough gruel to go around.

I cannot help thinking of Viola's small and helpless form, the milky smell of the baby's skin as she nuzzled against me in between her nighttime spoon feeds.

"A man . . . came into my home uninvited last night and left. Left her, I mean. Viola. The baby is called Viola. At least, I assume that is her name." The words are fumbled, like a shambolic drawing.

Giving me a long look, the sergeant comes around the

counter and strides over to the pram.

He peers inside, then frowns at me. "I'm sorry. I'm not fully understanding. This isn't your child?"

The sergeant is giving me a stern gaze, and I feel my cheeks flush. "Yes. The man . . . her father . . . had a key. He let himself into my home and left the baby upstairs in Theo's . . . my husband's study. Beneath a cabinet of moths."

Why did I say that, about the moths?

"Moths, you say?"

"Yes. Moths. He collected them," I say weakly. *Silly woman.*

"Did you know this man, who came into your house and left this child?" The sergeant's gaze is arrow like, and he steps closer to me.

"No . . . but I have a . . ." I pause. The photograph, it was on the kitchen table. I intended to bring it with me but have forgotten. "I have a photograph of this man – it was taken in the rear garden of my home."

The sergeant gestures for me to approach. "Where do you live, Madam?"

My mouth is dry as I shuffle closer. My courage fades as I think of my drawer of stolen things. The small leatherbound sketchbook that lies beside them. To come here today is to invite scrutiny. *I've made a terrible mistake.*

I step closer, so close that I can see the open pores on the sergeant's nose, a silvery scar on his chin from a razor cut. "West. My house is west of . . ."

He leans in, sniffs, an exaggerated action that flares his nostrils. "I can smell it on you from here." His voice is low and confiding.

"I beg your pardon?"

"The drink," he says, folding his arms.

The shiny buttons on his uniform wink at me under the lights. "No . . . I . . ."

The sergeant walks to the door, holds it open. His eyes are narrowed, but it's not an unkind look he is giving me. "Look. My advice is to go home. Sleep it off before your husband returns from work and we'll forget this ever happened."

"But . . . but she's not mine," I breathe, panic winding inside my stomach like a vine.

The sergeant sighs, rubs a hand across his face. "It's nothing to be ashamed of, especially with Christmas coming. Seeing family, are you?"

"Yes . . . my sister . . ." I say, my teeth beginning to chatter.

The sergeant nods, seems pleased at me sharing this small fact. "Having a new baby can be tiring. Let your sister take care of you. Why don't you pop along to the chemist's, see if they have something that can help. Now, let me help you outside with this pram . . ."

My ears ring, the room spins, and it's as if this sergeant's words are being spoken under water. *He thinks the baby is mine.* He also thinks me a drunk.

The sergeant clumsily manoeuvres the pram outside, as I walk behind taking deep, gasping breaths which he must hear but studiously ignores. He wishes me a Merry Christmas and returns inside to his cigarettes and paperwork.

Viola begins to grizzle. I rub my lips until they sting. Tears threaten, and I stumble forwards with the pram.

A young man in a flat cap is calling out for better pay

for workers on the railways. He thrusts a pamphlet at me as I walk past, but I shake my head. Then I see his right arm is missing, and I change my mind, take it and stuff it down the side of the pram.

I push Viola onwards towards the market square where I know there is a locksmith. The movement of the pram soothes her, and she yawns, her eyes half-closing. Pausing, I tuck in her blanket, place a hand on her forehead to check her temperature. People hurry past, steering around us, conversations, light chatter and laughter filling my ears.

A young woman pushing her own pram, shinier and newer than mine, draws nears. The pram hood is up, and I can hear the baby inside mewling. The woman's lips tilt into a perky smile as she comes alongside and peers into my pram. "What a darling you have there. I wish my Alfred would sleep so peacefully when I'm out."

The woman is dressed fashionably, a belted navy coat with velvet collar and cuffs. My own coat is brown. Still smart but fraying at the hemline. On an ordinary day anyone this attractive and youthful would not give me a second glance. It's on the tip of my tongue to tell her this baby isn't mine, that her mother has not come forwards to claim her, that her father abandoned her. Instead, I say. "Yes. I'm very lucky."

The woman with the beautiful coat chatters on, about how poorly Alfred sleeps, how the nighttime disturbances drive her husband to sleep in the spare room. She asks where I shop for baby clothes, says her mother believes she should knit and sew everything by hand, but why should she when these days she can purchase everything she needs from a catalogue or

Robert Sayle & Co. department store.

My ears hum and I feel strangely light and outside of myself as I listen and take all the advice offered, where to buy the best priced infant milk powder, why taking an iron supplement is so important for good health after giving birth.

Is this what it is like for all mothers? Instant friendship and conversation on a street corner? Bonding over the simple fact you both have a child? This is what I hoped for, longed for.

But she's not yours.

Chapter 8

Sheltered between the wooden stalls and canvas awnings, I seek out the locksmith. He tells me he can cut me a new door key but can't come and change the locks until after New Year. He says every locksmith in this town is engaged in fixing locks for a factory, and the new homes springing up. He can book me in for mid-January. I shake my head in dismay, make the booking and push the pram deeper into the market.

I try and summon a credible excuse I can give my sister for why the front door to Arcadia House must stay bolted bottom and top during her visit, why we must exit via the basement if we leave the house. But all I can think of is the truth. *An intruder has a key. He claims my house is his own and that he will return.*

Viola is awake and fretful now. Small babies need feeding often and warm clothes, and I'm failing to meet those basic needs. Her survival is down to me. It's a frightening thought and I rub her stomach, utter soothing words as I watch a mother and a small girl at a market stall. They're examining handmade dresses with brass buttons.

A wicker basket of knitted vests, stockings and pram coats beckons. My stomach flutters as I stand quietly watching. I could reach into my purse and pull out the few coins to pay, but where is the thrill in that? The woman is engaging the stallholder in a lengthy conversation about sleeve lengths and then, while both of their backs are turned, I dart over, take a few knitted items and drop them into the pram, covering them with Viola's blanket.

My accomplice wriggles and cries, and my shoulders are heavy as I stride on, the rear wheels of the pram squeaking, my heart thumping out a too-quick beat. Aliveness runs hot through my veins. The cobbles are rough beneath my boots, the tang of roasting meat drifts through the air, while winter's chill curls down my neck. *I am here; I am here.*

***

Viola is making her hunger well known by the time I reach the chemist's shop. Inside, I sway with her in my arms as I consider the tins of powdered infant milk on the shelf, the glass feeding bottles and rubber teats.

A few people ahead of me wait to be served and the baby's wails make them turn and stare. I dip my head to breathe in her smell. Musk, warmth and comfort as sweat pools in the hollow of my back. She quietens as my nose touches hers, perhaps understanding that I'm doing my best.

A shop girl helps me select nappy cloths and pins, as well as the feeding equipment and milk. She coos at Viola; says how pretty she is. How alike we are. My face aches from the unfamiliar action of smiling.

***

Outside Arcadia House, there's still no sign of Viola's father, no ready explanations or apologies. "Never mind," I murmur to the baby, not that she seems to care one jot at her abandonment. Her cheeks are wet, and I dab them dry with my handkerchief. "Let's get into the warm and find you some milk."

I push the pram along the side passage, glancing back once, twice, three times to make sure I'm not being followed. The paving is damp and riddled with green moss and mould. A drainpipe drips, water pooling against the brick work. As I curve into the garden, I think of the photograph of Viola's father again. It was taken here outside the dining room window. Is it possible he told me the truth and did live in this house? That would explain his door key.

Taking Viola and the purchases inside, my brain aches as I try and recall how long Arcadia House has been in Theo's family. Theo was born in 1872, and I think I remember him telling me his father purchased the house around two years before that. If my calculation is correct then the family in the photograph could have lived here around fifty years ago. But that cannot be right, I think, as I read the instructions on the tinned infant milk twice before measuring it out. The man who left Viola was no more than thirty years of age. He looks to be that in the picture as well. By rights he would be old now. . . dead, even. It's a puzzle I cannot wrap my head around.

It's late afternoon and Viola is settled after suckling a full bottle of milk. She seems to have been fed this way before, instinctively knew what to do with the black rubber teat when offered. It makes me wonder about Viola's mother. Perhaps she was like my sister, milk drying up and nipples too chapped and sore to carry on the natural way. A darker thought occurs. *Unless the baby's mother is dead.* My throat knots. This could explain why no one has reported her missing, why the child's father was not in his right mind.

I cradle the baby to my chest, careful to support her head and neck. "You poor, little thing," I croon. She turns her head towards my breast at the sound of my voice and inexplicably, tears threaten. *Would having our own child have mended the things that went wrong between me and Theo?*

Viola gazes up, her eyes widening and narrowing as she tries to direct her focus. I stare back, trace a finger over an impossibly soft eyebrow, notice her cheeks are less pallid. The two of us are settling into new rhythm, like a song that hasn't been sung before. Placing her over my shoulder, I gently rub her back. Mary did this with her boys after they'd been fed. The baby's head flops onto my shoulder, and she belches. Then she vomits, a milky white trail down the back of my cardigan.

While Viola dozes, I scrub the wool at the sink, drape it over the drying line rigged over the stove. The kitchen smells of wet yarn as I make myself a supper of salted beef and pickles. Then it's back to work, swilling dirty nappy cloths in a metal pail of scalding water, washing and rinsing the glass feeding bottle and rubber teat with soap and laying them out to dry. The purpose of this kitchen is changing. *My purpose is changing.*

Through the window, I watch daylight fading to the colour of a fresh bruise. Three more days until Christmas Eve and my sister's arrival. There's still no tree or decorations up, no gifts bought for Mary and her family.

Taking a piece of gingerbread from the tin, I wrap it in parchment, my heart a contradiction of worry and weight at what my sister might say to find me here caring for this stranger's baby. Two years ago, and a few months after my own loss, I confided in Mary, a whispered conversation in a teashop over current buns and tea the wrong shade of brown.

I told her about our doctor's instructions to not try again, about my irregular bleeds, insomnia, the constant itching, and the jags of tears that confounded Theo and me both. My poor memory that left me sometimes leaving the house without my purse, and once or twice my key. I said I sometimes felt invisible, like a footnote at the bottom of a page. That the doctor said that with me being forty-four I was entering a decline and the change of life.

Mary was sympathetic, stroked my hand. But then she implied, kindly, I should add, that I must be stoical and grateful for the life I have; be thankful I was not in France in the trenches in mustard gas and mud. She was right, of course. I always took care to listen to any advice offered by my sensible older sister, adored her caring nature and mostly wise words. But sometimes being buried in mud seems preferable to this life I'm living now – widowed, childless and exhausted by symptoms which make my body feel not like my own.

I hurry along the path to the groom's lodgings clutching my small parcel. Rabbit barks, perhaps surprised at my haste, but I can't leave the baby alone and locked inside the house for long.

My boots slip and slither as I pass beneath the old oak tree. It shields the garden from the sky, lengthy branches flicking against the rear windows at the top of the house. My chest heaving from the short run, I rap on his door twice.

A cough from inside and the shuffle of feet. The light at the threshold flickers. He's there, listening. "Please . . . can I talk to you? Something . . . something's happened up at the house," I say. Glancing back to the house, I wonder if I can hear Viola cry. Something catches my attention then, a shadow at one of the two attic windows. I stare up through the encroaching darkness and the tree branches. The pane of glass stares back at me blankly. Slipping the parcel under the door, I hurry back to the kitchen, Rabbit panting at my heels.

As soon as we are inside, the dog trots to the internal door leading to the stairs and hallway above. His ears are flat, his stubby tail between his legs.

The shadow at the attic window. A shiver crosses my shoulders, and I creep past Viola who is sleeping peacefully, and over to Rabbit. Sometimes, lying in bed at night I hear this house groan and creak, the sound of what seems to be whisper-light footsteps.

Theo used to laugh when I told him these things, said his own father used to claim Arcadia House was alive, had a heart, bones and lungs just like the rest of us. But whoever heard of a house with a beating heart? Homes are made of bricks and wood and mortar. They have no feelings.

I pick up the poker and stand beside Rabbit, both of us looking at the door. *We are safe inside. We are safe. The doors are locked. The doors are locked.*

Rabbit lets out a throaty growl. My fingers tremble as I turn the key and open the door. A draught of cold air spirals down the stairs. I tread softly, hesitantly, to the hallway above. My palms are damp, and I wipe them on my flannel skirt.

At the top, I reach for the light switch. In the sudden glare, I see the front door is still closed and bolted, the doors to the dining room and drawing room shut tight. But there is something on the tiles close to where I'm standing now, a picture frame.

Me and Theo on our wedding day. Picking it up, the glass is cracked over my smiling face. I run a thumb over it, the jagged edges catching my skin.

Viola's father had paused to look at this picture on the sideboard, but that's at least five strides away. A well of dread sits heavy in my stomach. How did it smash and get over here?

The sudden prickle of being watched comes over me quickly, like a black cloak being thrown across my back. Stilling in fright, I quietly place the picture frame next to my feet, then raise the poker before me like a sword. I take small, sipping breaths until I wonder if I'm still breathing at all.

The quiet creak of a floorboard upstairs.

There's no one here. I am alone.

These are only the sounds of a house shifting and settling.

Another slow and distant creak has me turning on my heel and hurtling back down the stairs to the basement. I slam the door shut and turn the key in the lock. Rabbit stands watching me, his ears and tail still flat.

Chapter 9

My flushes and chills are worse than they have been for months, my hair limp, my petticoat damp and clammy against my skin as I wait in line at the butchers on Monday morning. The pram is parked outside, and I cradle Viola in her blue knitted cardigan and bonnet. Her cream footed stockings with their ribbon ties. They all drown her tiny frame. *There's no time to linger and choose the correct size when you are in the middle of stealing.*

The butcher's wife smiles at me and the baby with her rheumy eyes, her grey hair pulled back into a tight bun. "Got family staying for Christmas have you, Mrs Pemberton?"

I nod, smile back. I've thought long and hard about this necessary encounter, decided not speaking was safest. Nod and smile.

This butchery has served Theo's family for years. Always saves us the best cut of meat, even when I had to queue up for hours with everyone else during the meat rationing which finally ended this month. Placing the ham in my string bag, I pay and wish the butcher's wife and her husband a Merry Christmas.

I stifle a yawn as I settle Viola back in the pram outside. If only I could sink into oblivion too, just for a minute. The previous day and night have been an endless exhausting round of pacing the kitchen, my ears pricked for noises from upstairs, or the return of the baby's father.

My thoughts continually circled back to the family photograph taken in my back garden. "Is this your father? Is it?" I asked Viola gently, pointing out the man who left her here. She gurgled, and dribbled, her eyes fixing on me rather than on the picture I held.

I busied myself, warming milk, feeding the baby, wiping up her vomit and changing nappies. She slept for no more than a few hours at a time, and as soon as she settled, I lay my head back on the chair in the kitchen and closed my eyes, wishing for sleep too. But it evaded me no matter how many sips I took of my tonic, thoughts of Viola's family, and my own, running on an endless, wearing loop. The screams from down the garden came as usual, but I was expecting those.

My sketch pad and pencils provided some solace, and I studied Viola as I would one of Theo's insects. The pale blister that's formed on her top lip from her ferocious sucks at the bottle teat. The curve of her cheek, downy hair and feathery eyelashes. As my pencil scratched across the page and as the image of her solidified, I felt myself disappear outside myself for a short while, the minutes slipping by unnoticed. I'm an amateur, know full well that my work isn't worthy of any gallery wall. But the finished sketch is a good likeness of her, I think.

Glancing at Viola now, I slip a hand into my coat pocket, feel the tip of the photograph. I can't stay indoors waiting any longer and intend to visit the hospital today. The man who left this baby in my house was clearly not in his right mind. Perhaps someone will know of him there and be able to help.

I cinch in my coat belt. The skirt I'm wearing is the one I wore on Saturday, my underwear stale, my face unwashed. There's little time for caring about my appearance with a baby to look after, and this sends a strange thrill bouncing through me as I set off in the direction of town. *"My hair is unwashed? There's little time for anything when you have a baby." "What, no Christmas decorations? I've been so occupied with the baby it clear slipped my mind."*

I can't help the chuckle that flies from my lips, and a man in a greatcoat nods a greeting as he and his son amble past, a Christmas tree dragging behind them. Pine needles scatter across the pavement. The father laughs in response to something his son says.

I stare after them, thinking of Theo. We were out walking by the River Cam when I told him we were to have a child of our own. The look on his face, the delight and wonder in the creases of his smile. He would have been a good father. Patient and attentive, even if he wasn't with me during those final months. Letting these thoughts drift, I focus my gaze on the baby in my pram to stop myself from crying for the one who isn't.

Outside the hospital on Trumpington Street, a few people linger, cut heads, broken limbs and hacking coughs that make me want to not go inside at all. If Viola's father is known at this hospital, if by some chance he's a patient and there is no other family, what should I do about the baby? The nurses will care for her, I'm certain of that. But a hospital is no place for a child at Christmas. I decide to make delicate enquiries. *Don't reveal the truth of the matter too soon, Della.*

Leaving the pram outside, I hold Viola's face to my chest

to protect her from the air as I venture in. It's months now since I breathed in these familiar scents of disinfectant, boiled vegetables and worry at the war hospital.

A flash of memory, twirling around the drawing room in my crisp new nurse's uniform, Theo's eyes dancing with amusement at my failed attempts to pin the starched cap over my wayward hair. But the job itself was no laughing matter; relentless hours of tending to the sick and wounded brought back from the continent, stitching up broken faces, legs and arms, or what was left of them. My shoes soaked through with bodily secretions that refused to shift no matter how furiously I scrubbed them in the evenings.

A harassed looking woman at the reception desk, perhaps a few years older than me, looks up. "Yes?"

"I'm looking for a man. This man." I pull the photograph from my coat pocket and hold it out.

The woman stares. "Relative of yours?"

"No."

"And why would he be here?" asks the woman, glancing back at her paperwork.

"I think he's . . . unwell. Not sound in the mind."

"What's his name?" asks the woman, head bowed as her pen scratches on paper.

"I . . . I don't know," I admit, adjusting Viola in my arms to protect her from the man coughing incessantly at my back.

The woman puffs out a frustrated sigh. "If you don't know his name, then how can I help you?"

"He was out of sorts . . ." I begin, offering her the photograph again.

"I'm sorry, love. I need a name," the woman insists, shaking her head.

It's then I notice the faint opaque lettering on the back of the photograph under the glare of her spot lamp. "Never mind," I say, standing aside. Walking to a window, I turn the photograph this way and that, hold it up to the pale light streaming through the glass.

Nicholls Photo.

Post Office Terrace, Cambridge.

No. T00063

The stamp of a photography shop, the ink almost faded to nothing with age.

"Make way, please!" A young man in a tweed jacket, face bloodied and bruised, is being led past.

Two porters rush to assist. Blood from the man's wounds drips onto the floor. The heel of a shoe smears it across the linoleum like a slash of paint. I feel a wave of heat, followed by dizziness. Gasping, I'm afraid my grip on Viola will loosen and I hurry for the door, pushing past people, muttering an endless round of apologies.

***

Viola frets inside the pram. I tuck her arms inside the blanket, smooth a hand across her cheek. Not too cold or too warm, but she'll be screaming for milk again soon enough. I must also get the ham home and into the icebox. A visit to the photography shop will have to wait.

As I begin the walk along Trumpington Steet, I think of Agnes. She'll arrive early tomorrow to help me clean and open the rooms for my Christmas guests. She's been surly lately;

I suppose because she's back to a life of service rather than still working as a conductress on the buses. I'll have no choice but to trust her with the truth about Viola, but part of me is glad of that. Days can pass without company these days, my voice becoming unused and stiff. It will be better when my sister Mary comes. Her two boys dashing about and filling the place with clutter and noise. My fingers tighten on the pram handle. But what shall I tell Mary about the baby? I put that worry to one side. Viola will be gone by then, reunited with someone who cares for her. *Won't she?*

A newspaper seller drums up business on the street corner, copies of the Cambridge Daily News fluttering in the crate by his boots. I purchase one, decide to scour its pages later for reports of something, anything, happening to a mother. Something which drove Viola's father into a fit of madness causing him to abandon the child. But that still doesn't explain the key he had to Arcadia House, his claim that my house belonged to him, or the strange clothes he was wearing. The photograph he left behind on my sideboard of him and his wife in my back garden.

***

Something is different. Bile rises in my gullet as I approach Arcadia House. I see the drawing room shutters are flung open wide. I've not drawn them back like that since Agnes and I closed the room over two months ago.

The front door is bolted top and bottom from the inside. The back door is also locked. Yet someone has been into my house while I've been gone.

You are the imposter here, madam. This is my house, and

I shall return. He's made good on his threat and come back. I think of Rabbit all alone and I half run the rest of the way to the house, the pram bumping over the uneven paving, the ham rolling from side to side. A stuttering motorcycle drives past, a flock of birds chatter, the sounds dim and faraway beneath my clattering feet, my panting breaths.

A fir tree in the drawing room half fills the width of the window, bristly bottle-green branches grazing the glass.

I stare and stare at it. My ears are muffled as if stuffed with cotton wool. Viola is crying again, and I know I must push this pram along the side passage and take the baby inside and out of the cold, but my feet are leaden. Terror presses against my breastbone, and I rub at it furiously, fingertips needling through the fabric of my coat.

Reaching into the side of the pram, I pull out the bottle of tonic, unscrew the lid and take a drink. The liquid slips down my throat like molten silver. I wonder if I should just sink to the pavement here and wait for this situation to resolve itself, for someone to take Viola and for my life to return to what it was.

Viola's cheeks are red, her mouth a jagged line as she wails. I'm limp with lack of choice. Feeling for the back door key in my coat pocket, I push the pram forwards.

***

I hear Rabbit's familiar gruff greeting as I unlock the back door. It stands as it always has done, black paintwork and windowpanes grey with dust. There's no sign anyone has forced their way inside the house from here, and yet . . . the tree in my front window.

I glance back at the groom's lodgings. He doesn't have a key, refuses to accept one. It's absurd to entertain the idea he'd be capable of a grand gesture like a Christmas tree.

Rabbit sniffs around the bag containing the ham. If a stranger has been in this house, the dog is thankfully none the worse for it. "Is someone here . . . has someone been in?" I whisper. The dog looks up at me, licks his lips.

The baby squirms and whimpers. "Hush, hush," I murmur into her shell-like ear, as my eyes skirt over the stove, the table littered with my drawing pencils and sketchpad, the copper pan on the floor concealing the baby's soiled nappies. The larder door is ajar, tins, jars and bottles stacked haphazardly inside. There's no sign of an imposter and surely Rabbit would be bristling and alert if there were.

I glance back into the garden. A crow struts on the grass, its grey beak pecking at the loam. The vegetable bed nearest the house has been turned over, a garden fork sticking out of the soil. The oak tree tap, tap, taps against the windows above. Shivering, I pull the back door closed and lock it, snapping across the bolts.

Quickly settling Viola in her drawer on the kitchen table, I pick up the metal poker, head for the closed door leading to the stairs and hallway above. It remains shut with the key in the lock, but this only deepens my unease. *If someone did enter the house this way, they retraced their steps carefully, covered their tracks.*

Viola grizzles and wriggles in her bed, but there's no time to prepare her milk yet. I must go upstairs.

I lock Rabbit and Viola in the kitchen, then slowly walk

up the stairs, the poker held out before me. At the top I pause. The photograph of me and Theo is still on the floor where I left it, but the drawing room door is now wide open when last night it was closed.

There are no creaks or groans of floorboards, no sense that anyone other than me is here in this house. I hurry across the tiles and burst into the drawing room. The room is scented with pine and earth. The bare tree is perfectly placed in the centre of the bay window on a wooden stand. There's an object beneath the fir; a rectangular gift wrapped in crimson paper and bound in white satin ribbon.

A rash of fallen pine needles lie scattered beside the gift. I nudge it with the poker. It's flat, perhaps a book? There is no card to indicate the recipient or sender. Looking back at the door, I listen. Viola's cries echo from downstairs. Picking up the gift, I throw one last look at the tree and hurry from the room, closing the door behind me with a thud. Running downstairs, my palms are slick with sweat. A slam, click, and turn and we are safe again inside my basement kitchen.

I hurriedly measure out and warm Viola's milk and prepare her bottle. The gift, which looks handsome, is out of place on the untidy table.

When the baby is content in my arms sucking on the teat, I pace about. *The man with a key claiming this house as his own. The arrival of Viola. The tree. Now this.*

With Viola satisfied, I return her to her bed and approach the gift. Turning it over, I quickly unfasten the ribbon, let it drop to the floor. Rabbit sniffs at it, then whines.

Peeling back the red paper, I see it's a book of child's nursery rhymes. Opening the cover, a book plate is pasted to the inside.

For our darling Viola,

With fondest love, Mother and Father.

My leg's buckle and I sink to the floor, holding the book close to my chest. I know this cursive handwriting in green ink as well as my own.

Theo wrote this. But that's impossible, for my husband has been dead for more than a year.

Chapter 10

"What terribly awful luck," my sister whispered to me upon learning of Theo's death, just over a year ago and a few days after the war ended. Like so many women before me, my first thought upon receiving the telegram from the postboy on that bitterly cold November morning was that it was a dreadful mistake.

The previous day crowds had gathered in the town centre to celebrate the end of the war. I'd stood among them, while people balanced on top of walls, hung from windows. Music and dancing in the streets. So much relief, so much happiness that the suffering was over. Staring at that telegram, the words and letters blurred until they became meaningless shapes. It *had* to be a mistake. The war was over. And yet my husband had died the day before the fighting stopped.

The days following Theo's death became a hibernation of sorts for me, and Mary moved in to help. There was no body to bring home, bury and mourn over, no certainty that my husband had died at all. There was no child of ours to care for and console, a reason to look beyond my own grief. I lay shivering, then sweating, awake through each endless night, as if someone was shining a bright and painful flashlight in my eyes.

As I scoured the newspapers for information afterwards,

I learnt Theo wasn't the only man to have died in the days before the armistice. This knowledge did not make my grief any easier to bear. A grief that encircled me like the darkest of shadows, weighed down by the way Theo had changed in our final months together, and because of the secrets he'd been keeping.

Mary's stoic bravery was a constant source of guilty irritation to me. Her own husband William had weak knees and so hadn't been conscripted. She couldn't possibly understand the weariness I felt. Theo and I had only had five short years together.

I remember my fingers clattering across the typewriter keys as I prepared his research paper, reading all about the gypsy moth larvae and the havoc they had caused across Europe and in America. These small caterpillars stripped oak trees of their summer foliage, made their branches appear winter bare. In Crimea, they inched across railroad tracks so trains were delayed or could not run at all. In America, this pest had devastated crops. And yet for some reason, this had not happened in England and Mr Theodore Pemberton was intent on discovering why.

The bold images he depicted in his writing nagged at me, were all I thought of as I bicycled home to my lodging house and then returned to the printing press the following day. Such a small creature creating such chaos and then by some miracle forming a cocoon on the bark of a tree and emerging as a moth with wings, able to leave the scene of its devastation and lay a new clutch of eggs somewhere else. I was struck with an urgency to speak with this university man about his research, to learn more about this curious creature.

While the receptionist left her desk to eat lunch, I riffled through the work diary until I found the date Mr Pemberton was due to come in and collect his typed-up papers. For a reason I'm still unsure about I wore my smartest dress, washed and pinned my hair. While scrubbing the typing ink from my nails in the bathroom, I manufactured an excuse, so I was ready and waiting outside at the time he was due. An untied shoelace, I recall.

The things I noticed about Mr Pemberton as he approached: hair as black as crow feathers but shot through with grey; his back a little stooped; and middle aged, like myself.

"*Lymantria dispar*," I blurted out.

"Gypsy moth," he said, stepping towards me with a ready smile. "You know this species?"

I sidled closer, breathed in the smell of lemon soap. "Can you really hear the sound of the caterpillars eating in the trees?"

His gaze was warm. "Yes. You've read my paper, then."

"I typed your paper."

He pressed a finger to his top lip, eyes dancing. I felt an unexpected spark of something, and I wondered if he felt it too.

He gestured for me to go inside ahead of him. "You have an interest in insects and entomology?"

Turning, and taking in his bright and encouraging smile, I sensed that my answer had the capacity to alter the direction of my life. I was right.

***

There must be an explanation for this book of rhymes and the inscription inside, and the only possibility I can think of lies at the end of my garden.

The dog is reluctant when I call him, content lying on his side in front of the stove. I call him again and he rises at the impatience in my voice. *The three of us must stay close.*

The path is still damp, so I step on to the grass for safety. I must not trip or fall with this baby in my arms. Rabbit pauses to sniff at the base of the oak tree. Viola grizzles and I rub her back as I stride. Glancing back, the foggy imprints left by my boots lead to the house. There are no other footprints, no dropped pine needles, a sign that a person has come down this way to deposit the tree and book. But the fork stuck in the vegetable bed is evidence he was working out here while I was gone. *Did he see the intruder?* The tree and the book are not gifts. *There is malice behind these offerings.*

The wood stings my knuckles as I thump on the door. "I must talk to you . . . now." My voice is bold, forthright. I wish I felt the same.

Thumping on the door again, Viola fusses. I peep through the window, but the gap in the curtains is too slim for me to see inside.

At the door, I glance down at the flat stone he uses to scrape his boots. The edges are caked with mud. This stone has another use too.

Bending to feel around the back of the stone, my fingers soon grasp cool metal. A key. I'm about to break a promise I made to myself and to him, but that can't be helped. "I'm coming in," I call, just in case he's inside, cowering.

My breath catches as I remember the knife he was sharpening outside yesterday, and cautiously I push the door open. It lets out a long creak, and we're greeted with the smell of tobacco and the tang of onions.

Throwing back the curtains, daylight splashes over the small wooden table and high-backed chair by the stove, the grey blankets folded neatly at the end of the metal framed single bed. I recall standing and watching, arms folded, as the two men he'd paid carried the bed here from upstairs in Arcadia House. It scratched the wallpaper on the way down.

Occasionally I pause now and lay a hand over the gouged wall in that spot in the house, remembering another telegram I received on a day in November last year and this other man's return by train to Cambridge. Then much later the private tears I wept at seeing him wearing the painted copper face mask for the first time. A necessary but unwanted thing to hide his disfigurement. The unfairness of it.

Rabbit waits by the back door to the lodgings, panting as he looks in.

"It's all right, come on," I say, clicking my tongue.

The dog whines but refuses to cross the threshold. The strings of onions hanging from the wall on nails are perfect brown globes, assorted and strung by size. Too large to be from this garden, so from the small holding he works at. They swing and sway, like ornaments and I think again of the fir tree in my drawing room, and the gift for Viola and know that I must look for answers to those things here, in this room.

It feels wrong to be here, invading his space, but what if

he's been intruding on *my* space, *my* home? Will I find in here a key to Arcadia House, evidence that he comes and goes as he pleases? I think of his facial wounds, his injured mind too. The screams I hear at night. Living in this small gloomy space intended for a groom caring for horses, while the lights of his childhood home glitter down the garden in the dark. It would be enough to drive anyone to madness.

Unfolding one of his blankets and laying it on the bed, I carefully fold it around Viola. She seems happiest when she's swaddled, her legs and arms gently restrained.

I glance again at the door. Rabbit should give me some warning if he returns unexpectedly.

For once my head is clear and sharp – perhaps the additional sips of tonic I've been taking these past weeks are finally helping. My search is methodical and begins on a low bookshelf constructed from old planks, clumsily nailed together.

Burying my fingers inside tins containing earthy smelling seeds, I feel for the curve of a metal house key. The battered tin mug stained with tannin, and copper kettle blackened on its underside are both empty.

His bed pillow is indented with the imprint of his head. It's hard to tear my eyes away from the soft dip, and then I spy a wooden crate beneath the bedframe and drag it out. It's filled with notebooks. A stubby pencil rests on top of them and my throat thickens as I pick it up, feel the grooves of it between my fingers. The notebooks are well thumbed, and selecting one, the pages splay open like a fan. The words jump and dance in front of my eyes.

I'm sorry. I'm sorry. I'm sorry. I'm sorry. I'm sorry. I'm sorry. I'm sorry. I'm sorry.

I flick through each and every page, see these same words written. Reaching for another book, and then another, they're all identical and my breathing becomes heavier. He remains obstinately mute in here, refuses to engage. But now, there is this truth. He's done something which he is so sorry for, he spends his days and nights filling these books with written apologies.

There's something else to notice here too. His handwriting is markedly different to Theo's, the curve of the 'o' slightly off balance, like a ball that's been squeezed too hard, the 's' tall and straight. He could have copied Theo's writing of course, but there's no pot of green ink, no evidence to link him to the dedication in the book of rhymes. No hidden key to Arcadia House.

Viola gurgles and looking to the door, I see Rabbit has turned and is looking out at the garden. Hastily returning the notebooks and pencil to the crate and pushing it under the bed, I reach for baby and retreat to the house before he comes back and I'm discovered.

***

With Viola fed, I hunch over the newspaper, scouring each column for news of a baby missing, or a tragic accident befalling a mother that's left a child orphaned. A man in top hat and tails, seen roaming the streets asking for a daughter named Viola.

But instead the pages before me tell of performance times for a show at the New Theatre, a dinner announcement for old comrades of the Suffolk Eighth Regiment, and a bible reading by a Belgian professor. My eyes skirt over articles about the rising price of milk, a robbery at a golf club. There's nothing here that helps explain my predicament.

Turning my attention to the book of nursery rhymes, I wonder if the sender left some clue for me to find, bent the corner of a page that holds some special meaning. But the book's pages are shiny, stiff and new.

The bookplate, I turn this way and that as I read the dedication from every angle. These are my husband's words, yet that's clearly impossible. There is a sharp stabbing pain in my side. *What if he didn't die?*

Dragging in a breath, I shake my head. *In that thought madness lies.* The telegram confirmed his death. Theo's name was listed in the newspaper roll call in black and white. I had a letter from his commanding officer. But why would someone impersonate my husband's handwriting in this book, and to what end? It must be connected to the intruder and Viola, but how?

The photography shop, that's where I must try next.

I push against the swell of anxiety, this constant clenched fist around my stomach. The disappearance of the capable woman I once was still startles me. How is it possible to feel dread at being alone, and also in the company of others? The same dread if I'm perched on a chair reading or striding into town? I don't understand myself, or what I'm afraid of. Most days I'm too exhausted to try. Brushing a tear from my cheek, I think of Agnes. She'll be here in the morning; and I'm now desperate for her company. To talk openly about everything that's happening here.

Viola's chest rises and falls, her lips sucking on a phantom teat as she sleeps. When someone eventually comes to claim her, then my own life will be as it was before.

Quiet. Purposeless. Dull. Lonely.

***

Night settles over us. I'm beginning to wonder if I may keel over and die from this bone-aching tiredness. Is that even possible? Perhaps I am sickening. I've made a bed for myself next to Rabbit in front of the stove, but the tiles are hard and bruising against my spine. The tree and the gift, the noises upstairs and the broken picture. I cannot face going upstairs again until Agnes comes.

Holding the poker, I pace the kitchen, striding around the table, then lingering by the door to the upstairs, locked and closed. My longing to lie down and sink into my own mattress occupies my every thought, so I keep myself busy tending to the baby when she wakes, sweeping the floor, washing the bottle and Viola's nappies.

Occasionally the baby becomes inconsolable, and I feel a limp and rising frustration at my inability to interpret her needs as I sway with her in my arms, singing her nursery rhymes from the book I'm supposed to believe was gifted by myself and my dead husband.

Rabbit lies on his rug, watchful and awake, confused by our new sleeping arrangements, and weariness eventually forces me to the floor again beside him, bringing with me the baby in her drawer bed.

Something pulls me awake. I sit up, reach into the drawer

and feel the gentle rise and fall of the baby's chest. I can't have been asleep for long, for she hasn't woken screaming for milk.

A thud from upstairs.

Rabbit grunts.

My head spins and my eyes are gritty. Palpitations skitter in my chest as I sit, quietly listening. The poker lays at my feet, and I pick it up, its weight a comfort in my hand. The dark is oppressive, pushing down on me and making it hard to draw breath.

Rabbit whines and then I hear a scratching above, as if something's scuttling in the walls and ceiling. I try and slow my breaths, not think at all or else I'll be driven mad by it. Perhaps I am halfway there already.

The pram parked outside the shop; the baby cocooned inside. I see myself picking the child up, bundling her under my coat and carrying her home to Arcadia House.

Scrunching my eyes, I let the thoughts drift, for that is what they are, thoughts and not a memory. That baby's mother returned, and I went into the shop and bought drawing pencils and stole a paint roundel, not a living, breathing baby. I would never steal a child.

Blinking, I find myself standing at the kitchen table. My drawing pencils are scattered like matchsticks, my fingertips smudged with grey lead. Lips trembling, I open my sketchpad but there's no new drawing, only the single sketch of the baby I made yesterday. I stare at it in confusion, not understanding.

Pressing the pads of my fingers together, I wonder how I can have been drawing and not remember? Where is the picture? Circling the table, I pick up each sheet of drawing paper. The twisted oak tree in the garden I sketched last week. A sharp beaked crow pecking at the lawn. Rabbit lying on his blanket. There's nothing new here. My nerves jangling, I sip from the tonic bottle, the drawings now scattered about my feet.

The scratching from upstairs begins again, a mocking sound daring me to come and investigate. My stomach heaves and I make it to the sink just in time, vomit splashing down the front of my petticoat. After cleaning up the mess, I'm too weak and shivery to do anything but lie down again. I cover myself with the blanket and arch my body around Viola in her drawer bed.

Rabbit nuzzles against me, sniffs and licks my face once. The scrabbling sound again, little feet scuttling across wood, tails sweeping across the floor. Rats or mice? *Or something worse.*

Chapter 11

My body is lumpen and aching when I wake to a dull grey light outside. Nausea has me running for the sink again. When it subsides, I gulp down handfuls of water, my thirst suddenly insatiable. Viola is grizzling for milk, legs kicking in agitation, arms flinging up and over her head, fingers curled into fists.

After feeding the baby, I've the urge to crawl back under the blanket in front of the stove and wait for Agnes to arrive. I imagine my home help finding me like that, my petticoat stained with vomit and caring for a stranger's child, my drawings scattered across the floor tiles. That thought alone is enough to propel me to tidy up, peel off my petticoat and scrub it, then hang it up to dry. It drips steadily, and Rabbit sniffs and licks at the droplets.

I must go upstairs now; there's no choice in the matter. I need to bathe and dress. But the thought of the effort involved in that delivers me to the chair by the stove and I drop into it as heavy as a stone.

A knock at the door startles me and I realise I must have slept. Viola is screaming and the knocks are coming hard and fast. "Mrs Pemberton? Mrs Pemberton, are you in there?"

Agnes.

Leaping to my feet, I pull my coat off the back of a chair

and slip it on, hurriedly doing up the buttons. Picking up Viola, I stride to the door, unlock it and draw back the bolts.

"Oh," is all Agnes says. Her cheeks contract, her dark eyes are wide and fixed on the crying baby.

"Come in," I say, standing aside.

She steps in, still staring.

I swallow. "This is . . . this is Viola. At least, I think that's her name."

Agnes is watchful. "Where's she from? I mean . . . who does she belong to?"

Last night, with all the scratching and scraping and my mind spinning, I wondered for a moment if I had dreamed this up. The baby, the book, the tree. The intruder in my home. But Agnes sees Viola. She's staring at the book of nursery rhymes now as she walks across to the table. *These things are real, and Agnes is proof of that.*

Standing at the stove in my coat, nothing but pants and a brassiere underneath, I warm some cooled boiled water as Viola grizzles in my arms, the truth spilling from my lips.

Agnes leans back against the sink. "This man . . . Viola's dad . . . you've no idea who he is?"

I shake my head.

"And the police couldn't help?"

"I believe the sergeant I spoke with thought the baby was mine, that I was having a funny turn." I don't tell Agnes that the man thought me a drunk and unstable, advised a visit to the chemist's shop to buy a remedy for my nerves. *I already have plenty of that.*

Agnes frowns. "I saw the tree in the window from the street.

It's pretty. Thought you'd got it in for your sister's visit."

"No. It wasn't me," I insist, measuring out the milk powder. But I can tell from the way Agnes chews on her lower lip she's unsure. "None of this was me, Agnes. What I've just told you is God's honest truth."

"Well, if you're going to bring God into it then I have to believe you," she says with a small smile. This girl's mother is the most devout Christian I've ever known, Agnes often telling me of her daily visits to church and twice on a Sunday. Leaving Agnes to care for her younger brothers and sisters – all six of them.

Agnes folds her arms, looks thoughtful. "But, Mrs Pemberton, why would this intruder leave his daughter with *you*?"

She says the final word as if I'm the very last person on Earth someone would choose to leave a child with. *Perhaps that's fair.*

"You think this same man came back and left the tree and book of rhymes too?" the girl continues.

My shoulders lift as I mix the water and powder, test the temperature on my forearm. "I can't think of any other explanation. But he must have come in via the back this second time. The front door was bolted."

Agnes's eyes are unusually bright, eager to solve this mystery. "The intruder, the baby's father then. If he did live here, he could have a back door key as well?"

I frown, thinking back to the month after Theo left for war and some urgent repairs I'd had made to the house. "But this is what I don't understand . . . do you remember the back door was replaced after the previous one rotted away? The locks were changed then. I have the only key."

Agnes's expression changes as I make up the bottle, becomes softer. "Oh. What about *him* from the bottom of the garden? Could he have borrowed your key and had a copy made?"

Picking up Viola, I sit at the table and gently offer her the milk. "I went to the lodgings, searched for a house key and the green ink used in the book but found neither." The baby takes the bottle hungrily, is transfixed by something above her head, something that when I follow her gaze is invisible to me.

Agnes tilts her head. "He'd most likely keep the key on his person though."

"No. I think not," I say, dragging my eyes back to my home help. "I don't believe he's the capacity to be involved in whatever's happening here."

I slide the photograph of the man across the table towards her. "This is him. I found it in the hall after he'd gone. Do you see? It was taken here – in the garden."

Agnes frowns. "Look at the way these people are dressed. This is old, this is."

"It would have to be." I tell her that I believe if this man *had* lived here, it would have been around fifty years ago.

Her eyes narrow as she comes to the same conclusion as me. "But you said the person who came into the house and left his baby was a young man."

I nod. "He *was* the man in this picture . . . the same clothes, hair, whiskers."

Agnes barks out a laugh. "That's plain impossible, Mrs Pemberton. If he was young back then, he'd be . . .

he'd be ancient now. Or dead and buried."

We look at each other. It's a long and considered look. Agnes draws in a breath and places a hand to her lips. "A spirit, then?" Her words are whispered and muffled behind her fingers.

A burst of rain patters the window, startling us both. The girl's eyes burn with her idea that this man who visited me is not flesh and bone but an apparition. I swallow, stroke Viola's spindly legs. "The imposter was a living, breathing man, Agnes. Viola *is* a real baby."

Agnes has spoken of her belief in spirits before. How the manifestation of her dead aunt at a seance she attended with her mother made her weep with terror and joy in equal measure. Theo and I occasionally spoke of the rising Spiritualist movement, the belief that had people claiming to have seen or heard loved ones from beyond the grave. He thought it drivel and trickery, his mantra being, *there is an explanation for all things*.

I know this should be true and yet . . . the scrabbles and scrapes I heard last night. A bad dream, or wind rattling the walls? Something else? So many people dead after the war, so many hungering for contact with loved ones. Theo's writing in that book of rhymes. *A message from the afterlife?* I push that thought from my mind with all the force I can muster.

Agnes gives me a tight smile. "My aunt touched my shoulder. I *saw* her from the corner of my eye." She pauses and swallows. "Maybe the man in the picture came back in his spirit form to tell you something . . . to warn you . . ."

Shaking my head, I hold up a hand. This conversation is

at an end. I want to tell her that mediums are charlatans, extort money from the grieving and weak minded. This is what Theo would have said. *But I am not Theo.* "The baby needs changing," I say instead, pushing back my chair.

A sulky look crosses the girl's face, then she rearranges her features into something more pleasant. "There is a mighty stink coming from her rear end. Shall I change her for you? I spend half my life doing it at home."

Nodding my thanks, Agnes takes the baby from me as I fetch a clean nappy cloth from where it's been drying above the stove.

While I clear a space on the table, lay out the towel, soap and fetch a bowl of warm water, Agnes croons at Viola, stroking her face. My arms feel empty without her in them, as if a part of me is absent. *She's not yours.* I squash this nagging voice in my head, look back at the photograph of the man who delivered her to me. "There's a stamp on the back of this picture. Post Office Terrace. And a reference number. I could go there and ask if they have records. It will be easier to trace this man with a name."

Agnes makes quick work of changing Viola, the baby more compliant than she's been with me. Perhaps she senses she's in more experienced hands. "Why don't you go there, then?" she says, nimbly striking a pin through the folds of cloth.

"Yes. Yes, I must," I agree. All traces of the girl's previous surliness have vanished, and her soft smile and manner make my next words tumble out in a rush. "Perhaps . . . could I leave the baby here with you while you clean and ready the guest rooms?"

Agnes darts a look at the photograph still on the table, chews on her lower lip.

"I wouldn't be gone long," I assure her, my eyes drifting to the baby. It might seem foolish, but I worry the delicate bond building between Viola and me might tear if we're apart for long. It's cold and damp out though, and I don't want her exposed to the elements.

"I don't know, Mrs Pemberton . . ." the girl begins. I sense that Agnes's head is still cluttered with ghoulish thoughts.

Walking across, I place a hand on her arm. "There's nothing to be afraid of in this house." *If I say these words often enough, perhaps I'll convince myself of that too.* Her gaze back at me is trusting. *Too trusting?* "I'll put a little extra in your pay packet," I offer, knowing this is something she won't be able to resist.

Agnes tips her shoulders back, looks me in the eye. "Well, that's settled then. Thank you. I'll make a start on the guest rooms upstairs."

***

I've passed the entrance to Post Office Terrace many times but never had the need or curiosity to visit before today. The post office that gave the place its name has long since moved to alternative premises, and I believed this to be a row of terraced homes. But walking under the archway and through a short passageway, I see I was wrong as I emerge into a medley of houses and businesses.

The place smells of damp. Water drips from broken guttering. A small boy in a flat cap throws a rubber ball against a wall, while a girl sits on a house step quietly watching. Her legs are bare, mottled and scabbed at the knees. Was Viola born in a row of terraces like this, does she have brothers or sisters who are wondering why she's vanished from their lives?

At the very end of the alley there's a secondhand bookshop. Standing at the window, I notice a few of the books on display have fallen on their sides, revealing yellowing pages. It's dark inside and the sign on the door indicates the shop's closed today.

I look back along the street, then tut in irritation. There's no photography shop here. Taking the picture from my coat pocket I return to a bookbinder's where the warm glow from inside tells me it's open. The bell jangles as I step inside, the scent of paper and binding glue bringing a swell of familiarity and comfort.

"Good morning. How can I help?" asks the man behind the counter. He's examining the spine of the book, running a thumb up and down the bevelled gold font as if it's the most beautiful item he's ever handled.

I hold out the photograph. "Good morning. I am looking for Nicholls photography shop. I believe it used to be here on this terrace?"

Placing the book down, he wipes his hands on his apron. "May I?" He handles the picture carefully, turns it over and holds it to a lamp. "The shop closed at least ten years back when Mr Nicholls Senior retired. It was at the end of this alley, where the bookshop is now."

"Oh. I see." My throat constricts with disappointment. "Do you happen to know how I might contact Mr Nicholls?"

The man shakes his head.

Thanking him for his help, I leave and retrace my steps to the bookshop. I try the door handle, but as expected it's locked. Peering through the glass, I see the faintest hint of a light. My spirits lift a little. Perhaps someone is in there after all. Pressing the bell, I wait. When no one comes, I rap hard on the door.

Footsteps inside, then I see a young man approaching. He can be no more than sixteen and is bundled up in a thick sweater and a green woollen hat that makes his roundish head look like a pea. He unlocks the door and peers around it, holds a clutch of books to his chest.

I smile. "Good morning. I was wondering if I could speak with the owner of this shop?"

"Sorry. My dad's poorly," says the boy. "I'm trying to sort the place out, bring a bit of order to everything until he's well enough to work."

Looking beyond him and into the shop, I see books stacked haphazardly against the already groaning shelves that reach to the low ceiling. I wonder vaguely if Theo ever came here. He would detest this place, the clutter and lack of discipline. "I see. I imagine that's quite a task."

The boy grimaces. "Dad's eyesight isn't so good these days. Not since he came back."

There's no need to enquire where he's come back from.

"What did you want to speak with him about?" he asks, eying me with interest. He shifts position and one of the books he is holding drops to the floor.

A well-thumbed copy of a Dickens. Returning it to the

pile in his arms, I explain about looking for the photography shop owned by Mr Nicholls.

The boy's smile is broad. "Mr Nicholls. I remember Dad talking about him. He went to live by the sea, I think. Dad said he left this place in a right old state."

"Your father wouldn't have a forwarding address for him, would he?" I ask hopefully.

"I shouldn't think so." He gives me a long look. "Why do you want to speak with him, if you don't mind me asking?"

I show him the photograph. "I'm trying to find out more about this man. I hoped Mr Nicholls might have kept some photographic records. See here . . . there's a reference number on the back."

The boy's gaze is thoughtful as he studies the back of the photograph. He looks up. "I'm Arthur. You'd better come in."

Chapter 12

Arthur's nails are bitten to the quick. He sees me looking and flushes a little, sets down the armful of books by his feet. He then nods at the ceiling. "Mr Nicholls left some crates behind in the attic. Ledgers to do with his photography shop, my dad said." Throwing a quick glance at the stacks of secondhand books and the groaning shelves, he arches an eyebrow. "Dad couldn't toss them out."

A bead of hope unfurls at the information I might find stored here. *But the baby, home alone with Agnes. What if the imposter returns while I'm gone?* I reach for the door jamb to counter my dizziness.

"Um . . . you can take a look at the ledgers now if you like?" suggests Arthur. The boy is looking at me with concern.

Fixing a smile to my face, I nod and follow him inside.

***

"It's a while since anyone's been in here," says Arthur, opening the attic door. A musty, sour smell spills out.

I take in the grimy window, patches of dust on the glass dulling the light from the alleyway and a lone fly buzzing at the pane. The paintwork is peeling and silvery cobwebs flutter from the rafters.

Arthur heads to the first of several packing crates stacked around the edges of this small space. He prises the lid off with the screwdriver he thought to bring from his dad's bag of tools. Standing shoulder to shoulder, we examine the contents. Thick forest-green ledgers embossed with the words *A. Nicholls Photography.*

I feel a pinch of dismay. "There's . . . a lot to look through. I don't have long."

Arthur looks up. "I can help, if you like?"

"Thank you. My Agnes . . . I mean, my home help . . . she's at home. My home . . . I must get back soon."

Arthur bites on a thumbnail as he listens to my fumbled words.

My cheeks are hot as I reach for the first book and leaf through the pages. Arthur quietly looks at me still. Does he regret inviting me up here? A stranger old enough to be his mother who cannot speak in proper sentences. *It's the tiredness. Just the tiredness.* The ledger contains columns of dates, numbers and names all scribed in a neat hand. Arthur sidles over to look at it too. "This one dates to 1905. We need to look further back, I think," I say. If my assumptions are right, then the photograph was taken before Theo's parents purchased Arcadia House in 1870.

"Is the fellow in the picture a relation then?" asks Arthur, as we pull out the remaining five ledgers from this crate.

"Perhaps."

Arthur nods, and we begin to study each book in turn, but the dates are still disappointingly recent. Pausing to rub my hands against the biting cold up here, the boy offers to fetch us both a mug of tea, a small kindness I'm grateful for.

While he's gone, the need to return to Viola niggles as

I wonder how Agnes is coping alone in the house. She listened patiently as I gave instructions on how to make up the milk, tilt the bottle at the correct angle. The girl knows how to do these things, has been surrounded by children her entire life. It was like me telling a seamstress how to thread a needle. But what will she do if the man returns and forces his way in, claiming the baby is his? *Forces Agnes to hand Viola over?* The idea of being parted from the baby coils through me, jagged and unfamiliar.

A sudden insistent rapping on the shop door below pulls me from these troubling thoughts. Standing on tiptoes at the window I crane my neck, but the view of the shopfront is hidden from this angle.

The shop bell jangles, then I hear muffled voices. Minutes later, the bell rings for a second time as the door closes. Continuing to peer out, a man in a long grey overcoat comes into a view, a large umbrella obscuring his lowered head. He walks briskly away, retreating under the archway.

"Here we are," says Arthur a short while later, returning with two mugs of steaming tea. He passes me a teaspoon. "I put in half a spoon of sugar. You'll want to give it a stir."

"Thank you. Someone came to the door?" I ask, stirring the tea and placing the spoon on the window ledge. Taking a sip of the drink, I welcome the warmth it brings.

He nods. "A man. Looking for a book on moths. I said we were closed."

I peer outside again, but see no sign of the man, just a puffed-up pigeon on the guttering also trying to ward off the cold. The trapped fly bumps and buzzes the glass.

"Mrs Pemberton?" Arthur asks in a small voice, stepping over.

I turn to face him. "What was he like, this man? How old was he?"

Arthur blinks. "Um . . . normal looking fellow. Getting on in years . . . thirty, maybe."

My breathing slows. My husband is dead. *This is just a coincidence.* I manage a faint smile, gather myself. "My husband collected moths and butterflies. I drew them too – just for the enjoyment of it."

"Oh. Right. There are probably books on that type of thing downstairs, if you'd like a look?"

"Yes. Maybe I'll stop by another time," I say, placing my tea down and turning back to the ledgers.

As we continue our search, Arthur gives me repeated sidelong glances. *Make small talk. Try and put the boy at ease.* I ask him about his family, and he tells me how his mother's taken on work laundering other people's clothes to bring in extra money. His father is a proud man, dismayed at how their lives have taken such a drastic and downwards turn since the war.

"If I'd been old enough, I would have fought," Arthur says fiercely, draining his mug. "My brother says I wouldn't have been brave enough. He's wrong about that."

I look up from the ledger I'm hurriedly leafing through. "That would have been hard on your mother." *A boy, not much older than Arthur in the hospital and drowsy with morphine. His left arm amputated; the dressing darkened with dried blood. "But I'm left-handed," he whispered as I changed his dressing. "That arm can't be gone . . . please, nurse."* Warmth idles up my back, and I unfasten the top button of my blouse, try and blink away the images.

Arthur glances at me then away. "Yes . . . yes, I suppose she would have found it hard."

There is no air in here, no air at all. *Bandages damp and yellowing . . . the stink of it.* Pushing the ledger from my lap, I get up and stride to the window. The fly still smashes its body against the pane in its futile attempt to escape. *Sitting on the bed gripping his hand, willing the boy to live.* I grip the edges of the window frame, but it's painted shut, will be impossible to open.

Sucking in a breath, I turn to see Arthur; shoulders taut and a finger running around the inside of his shirt collar. *Breathe, Della. Just . . . breathe.* My fingers stray to my wedding ring. "My husband . . . he didn't come home. It's . . . difficult talking about that time." A small explanation for my behaviour. *The boy must think I'm mad.*

"I'm . . . I'm sorry." Arthur scuffs a boot against a packing trunk, can't look me in the eye.

"It's just me and Rabbit now. That's my husband's terrier. Do you like dogs?"

Arthur's face relaxes as he tells me about his grandparents' Jack Russell that sleeps on the end of the bed when he and his brother go and stay, licking their toes until they wake.

It's a good distraction and makes me quietly laugh, smothers any lingering tension in the air.

"Why's it so important you find the name of this man in the photograph?" asks Arthur.

More questions. I should have expected this, I suppose.

I feel a pinch of sorrow at his family's situation, how intent he is on helping both them and me. He deserves a portion of the truth. "The man in the picture let himself into my home with a key a few nights ago. He said that the house belonged to him, but I'd never seen him before."

Arthur draws in a sharp breath. He asks to look at the photograph more closely and I hand it over.

"Where'd you find this?" he asks.

"The intruder left it. It was taken in my back garden, connects him to my home. That's why I am here today, trying to get answers as to who he is."

Arthur's eyes narrow. "How odd."

What would he make of Viola? *A baby left in a stranger's home.* An image of the pram outside the stationery shop springs into my head. Walking away with the baby, feeling the weight of her in my arms. The surge of hot panic is piercing as a blade. *That didn't happen.*

"Have you told the police?" Arthur asks, pulling me back to the present.

I rub my eyes. "I did, but they were no help."

Arthur peers at the photograph again. "It's just . . . how can you be sure this was the man in your house? We're looking at pictures from the last century. This man who came in your house would be old by now . . . very old."

"Yet he wasn't. He was the man in the photograph," I say simply.

Arthur frowns but doesn't question me further on this. What else is there to say? He is either stuck in his shop attic with a mad woman, or I am seeing ghosts. *Which is what*

Agnes would have me believe.

We begin our search anew. The boy's eyes are focused, but I catch him giving me worried looks every now and again. As we start to look through another crate I hear Arthur blow out a breath and I look up. "What is it?"

"I think I've found it," he says quietly.

The year of the record he's looking at is 1852. Arthur has found the reference number that matches the one on the back of the photograph.

"Twenty-sixth of June 1852 your picture was taken," says Arthur. "The man who purchased it is called Emanuel Cleeve."

"Emanuel Cleeve." I roll the man's unfamiliar name around in my mouth.

Arthur points out the spidery writing in the address column. "Is this where you live, then?"

Arcadia House, Barton Road, Cambridge.

"Yes." The stranger at my door, this intruder. He didn't tell a lie. Emanuel Cleeve *did* live in my house. But to arrive on my doorstep the same age as his younger self in a photograph taken over sixty years ago is still an impossibility. Unless . . . of course . . . this man wanted me to believe he was Emanuel Cleeve? *But to what end?*

"Mrs Pemberton?"

"Della. Please call me Della."

"Della, then. Perhaps . . . do you think I could walk you home?"

"Thank you, but there's no need." This boy is concerned, thinks me troubled. *He's right.*

While Arthur tidies away the ledgers, I pick up our empty

mugs, eager to return to Viola. The fly lies upside down on the window ledge next to the teaspoon, having given up its fight. *Dead.* While Arthur's back is still turned, I pick up the teaspoon and slip it into my coat pocket. Rather than feeling my usual thrill, guilt burns like a hot coal in my chest.

Chapter 13

Back at Arcadia House, I press the bell three times just as Agnes and I agreed before I left. I hear Rabbit's gruff bark, then I clatter back down the steps and hurry along the side passage to the garden.

Agnes is already waiting at the back door, a linen cloth over her arm, Viola against her shoulder. The baby seems content, her cheeks rosy, but Agnes's features are drawn. "You've been gone ages."

Viola gurgles, a milky film trailing down her chin which Agnes expertly wipes away. "Did she take all her milk? Has she slept at all? Did anyone come to the house while I was gone?"

"Yes, yes and no," says Agnes, settling the baby into my outstretched arms.

The weight of her is a blessed relief. I dip my head to her neck, breathe her in.

Agnes is quiet as I tell her about the photograph, picking at her fingernails as she leans against the table.

"So, this Mr Cleeve lived here sixty years back as a young man with his family . . . the wife and baby in the photograph?"

"Yes. Yes," I say. "In my eyes that only leaves one explanation, doesn't it? The man who came here was mimicking Emanuel, wanted me to believe it was him."

Agnes gives me a long and considered look. "That isn't the only explanation."

"He wasn't a ghost, Agnes."

I wonder then why Agnes has dipped her head, won't meet my eye. "What is it? What are you not saying?"

"Nothing." A fierce blush erupts over her cheeks. "It's . . . it's only . . ."

"Only what?" I question, edging closer.

Agnes draws in a breath, then gestures to the tin pail by the back door I hadn't noticed when I came in. "I cleaned and tidied the bathroom and your bedroom, as well as the guest rooms today."

The pail is full of empty glass tonic bottles. "It's a herbal remedy. For . . . female disorders. I . . . I haven't been well."

"Yes, but today there were three empties under your bed," says Agnes. She bites her bottom lip. "Four more around the bathtub. I've never seen that many before."

Seven. My toes curl inside my boots. "I only take a few spoonsful a day." *This is my home. I don't need to justify my actions.*

Agnes throws a quick glance at the armchair by the stove, the blanket I slept under on the floor last night neatly folded, the cushions plumped up. "There were two more stuffed down the side of that chair too."

"No, Agnes. There was one there last night . . ." I let my words trail off, think of the sergeant's accusation at the police station. "This tonic is made of herbs, sugar and water. Contains a drop of alcohol as a preservative. It's available to buy at any of the chemist shops in town."

Agnes gives me a guarded look. "Some people have been known to take a remedy and see things . . . unexplainable things."

"Nonsense! What about Viola? What about the tree and book of rhymes? You think I . . . I dreamed them up?"

"No. Not dreamed up, Mrs Pemberton," says Agnes earnestly. "Maybe taking this tonic allowed you to see things. Things usually hidden to our eyes."

"I pay you to clean, not to snoop and offer your neurotic opinions." My words are whip sharp, and I immediately wish I could swallow them back. My burst of irritation fades into a hollow coldness. Could there be some truth in her suggestion? I shake my head, for my benefit not hers. *This is not me. I am not this person.*

Agnes's shoulders curl inwards. Tears burning behind my eyelids, I reach out and touch her hand lightly. "I'm sorry. I'm so sorry. That was unkind."

The girl sniffs. "I wasn't snooping, Mrs Pemberton. Honest I wasn't. I looked after Viola, made up all the guest bedrooms just like you asked, and cleared up the broken glass in Mr Pemberton's study."

"Broken glass?"

Her throat bobs as she swallows. "The picture frame that had fallen from the wall. Your sketch of the caterpillar."

I think back to the noises I heard the previous night, Rabbit's barks, my fingers cramping as they curled around the metal poker. "Please show me."

***

Fear nettles at my skin as I stand before the row of pencil sketches on the study wall, each frame the width of two palms. I know the order of them well, the ladybird, the lemon-yellow Brimstone butterfly, the bumblebee on a verbena, and finally the gypsy moth caterpillar, its furry body inching up the branch of an aged apple tree.

Yet now they are not in this order. They're back to front and the caterpillar sketch and its broken frame are on the ground. Leaning against the leg of the same display cabinet under which I found Viola.

"Did you rearrange these sketches?" I ask quietly, turning to face the girl. Viola squirms and I shift position, stroke her back.

Confusion crosses Agnes's face. "No, Mrs Pemberton. I saw the study door was open. The sketch of the caterpillar was face down on the rug, the glass smashed to bits. I went in to sweep it up."

I sense she's telling me the truth. But somehow this picture fell from the wall and the others rearranged themselves.

Agnes folds her arms around her middle. Any minute now the girl will be telling me this is supernatural. That it's a message from beyond the grave. *Flimflam.* That's what Theo would say.

The baby begins to wriggle and cry, arms flinging outwards, face scrunching. I force out a thin smile, the need to stamp out the girl's ghostly nonsense overriding all else. "Silly me. I remember now. This was my doing. A clumsy mishap." *Yet I remember nothing of this at all.*

Spots of colour stain the girl's cheeks as she stares at the rearranged pictures; she knows I am lying. Rabbit's bark echoes up the stairs and she shuffles back, glances at the landing. *She wants to leave.*

I fight the urge to retreat to the bathroom and spoon the sweet tonic into my mouth. The weight of the baby is a small comfort, but I suddenly doubt my capability of looking after this small, fragile thing while unexplainable things are happening in this house. I don't want Agnes to leave. I want her to stay until Mary arrives tomorrow. "Could you . . . could you stay a bit longer today? I'd welcome the company. Maybe we could fetch the Christmas decorations from the attic and dress the tree? I can make us some cocoa."

Agnes shakes her head. "Um . . . I'm sorry, Mrs Pemberton. I've already been here longer than usual. My mum'll be expecting me."

"Of course. Yes." I glance at the broken picture frame again, wondering how this happened. "Well, thank you for your help. I've left your wages in an envelope on the dresser, have put in the extra. I'll see you after the New Year?"

Agnes doesn't reply, just watches the baby suck on my knuckle.

The girl is scared, doesn't want to come back here. This fact makes me feel as if the floor is tilting, as if I am on a listing ship. If I concentrate on the perfect whorl of Viola's ear, I will not cry. Why did I not tidy away the tonic bottles, why did I confide in my home help? I'm her employer, not her friend. *Who might she tell?*

Agnes turns away to leave, and I step after her. "I will look after this baby well."

She looks back, stares. Her gaze softens and she gives me a small nod.

"But I'd be grateful if you'd keep this to yourself. What

I mean is . . . keep Viola to yourself and the circumstances of her arrival." This is the second person I've asked to keep a secret today.

"Yes. Of course, Mrs Pemberton." Agnes pauses, bites on her lower lip. "But what about your sister? How will you explain Viola?"

"I don't know," I admit. "But I will find the baby's family. You mustn't worry yourself about that."

She nods, her eyes fixed on Viola. "You might want to give her cod liver oil – just a drop each day. Mum gives it to all the little ones, swears it keeps colds and flu away. There's a bottle of it in the larder."

Smiling my thanks at this sharing of knowledge, the idea arrives in a jolt. Agnes is returning to a large family. This baby could easily be her younger sibling. That's what I shall tell Mary when she arrives tomorrow. I'm looking after Viola because Agnes's family is sick and they needed help over the Christmas period. An act of selfless charity on my part.

***

I stand at the drawing room window with the baby, the branches of the fir tree snagging at my blouse as Agnes heads off on her bicycle towards town. Her coat is belted, her hat pulled low on her head. Usually, she glances back and gives me a quick wave. Today she doesn't.

No matter. The girl has indirectly given me a solution to Mary's visit, a reason for Viola's presence that will allow me more time to resolve whatever is happening here. *To find a way to keep the baby.* A laugh bubbles up at this extraordinary idea. But is it extraordinary? No one has come for her. Not yet.

I'm about to turn away when a flash of green catches my eye from the building site opposite. A boy holding a bicycle. *A green woollen hat that makes his head look like a pea.* Arthur from the bookshop. He is staring hard at the house and must see me for he raises a hand in a tentative greeting. A greeting that has me heading to the hallway with Viola.

Unlocking the front door and throwing back the bolts, a swirl of cold air hits me in the face and I see Arthur at the foot of my front steps looking up, his eyes fixed on the baby cradled in my arms.

Chapter 14

"Why are you here?" I ask in bewilderment as Arthur walks up the steps to meet me. The brown satchel he's carrying bumps against his side.

The boy's gaze remains on Viola. "You've a baby." The air is freezing, his nose drips and he wipes it on the back of a navy woollen glove. It's the action of a child, not a man, and my heart squeezes.

I curl my hand around Viola's head, protecting her from the cold. "You shouldn't have come."

He blinks, and I see the tremor in his lips. Ungainly limbs and an earnest face. Seeking answers. I sigh. "I must get her inside before she catches a chill. Will you come in? Have some tea?"

He looks up, gives me a smile of gratitude.

Standing in my hallway with his hat in his hands, Arthur takes in the staircase that goes up and up, the dark wooden furnishings inherited from Theo's parents that seem to soak up the light, making it always appear a few shades gloomier than it actually is.

"We'll go to the kitchen, it's warmest there," I say, and the boy silently follows.

Hanging his satchel over the chair back, he sits at the table watching the baby's jagged kicks from her drawer bed as

I make a pot of tea. Rabbit sniffles around Arthur's feet and he bends to pat the dog, but the boy's eyes quickly drift back to the baby.

"Her name's Viola. She's the sister of my home help. Her family are sick, and I offered to take her in for a few nights." The lie flows off my tongue nicely, sounds convincing even to my ears.

"I saw a girl leave. Was that her?" he asks.

How long was he out there watching and waiting? "Yes. That was Agnes." I pass Arthur a mug and open the gingerbread tin.

"You told her . . . about the intruder? What we found out about Emanuel Cleeve?" Arthur munches a biscuit, crumbs scattering to his lap and the floor.

"I told her everything," I confirm, thinking of the pail of tonic bottles which I've transferred to the metal bin outside, and Agnes's assumption that these events might be something I've dreamed up because of drinking it.

"Communication with another world? Listen to yourself, Della."

Theo? I swivel to peer out of the window, for that's where his voice came from. Beyond the glass, muffled but also clear. The tap drips in the sink; rhythmic and grating. A cluster of leaves gust in the wind, whispering as they mingle and drop. *There's no one out there.* Turning, I press my spine against the sink until it aches with the promise of a bruise, watch the dog lick at the fallen crumbs by Arthur's feet.

The boy takes a gulp of his tea, is eyeing me carefully. The liquid is scalding, and he winces. "Um. Is it safe? For the baby to be here, I mean? What if . . . what if the man comes back?" His cheeks flush.

The boy knows a modicum of the truth, but the intruder leaving Viola here isn't a secret that should be shared lightly. "Arthur . . . you really shouldn't have come. I'm grateful for your help today, but what's happened is no concern of yours." My admonishment is gentle, yet he still does not look convinced.

Shifting in his seat, Arthur rakes a hand through his hair. "But this man who let himself in." He pauses, swallows. "Some men in the war . . . they didn't come back right. What if he's one of them?"

But war doesn't make all men into monsters – the man living at the bottom of my garden, his fractured face, he certainly isn't. That said, could my imposter, this person who pretended to be Emanuel Cleeve, be a man who is lost in his own head and is living the life of another? "We're quite safe here with the doors bolted. And my sister arrives tomorrow and will be staying over Christmas."

Arthur looks about the kitchen, and I see it through his eyes, the threadbare armchair, the smell of damp yarn from the washing strung above the stove. The ochre floor tiles that bear the marks and scars of people's feet. I'm ensconced in a cave down here, and the modernity of my electric lamps only serves to emphasise it.

"That's good. No one should be alone at Christmas," he says. His face broadens with a sudden smile. "My mum loves it. Starts dressing the house with holly and mistletoe at the end of November."

"You mother sounds like a nice woman," I say, thinking of the bare tree upstairs and the lack of effort I have made.

"Um. Well . . . I brought you something. That's partly why I came." Arthur pulls a small, flat item from his satchel, holds it out. An illustrated book of butterflies. Battered at the corners, it's been well loved by a previous owner.

"Thank you, but there was no need." A swell of compassion tightens my throat as I turn the pages, breathe in that papery, familiar smell that only old books can offer. He's written in the front. *To Mrs Pemberton. Merry Christmas. From Arthur.*

I think of the teaspoon I took from his attic, hidden with my other stolen things in the dresser. The urge to confess and give it back tugs at me. The need to apologise for my stupidity. A rush of heat warms my neck. *No, Della. Don't.*

"You said you drew pictures of butterflies. I thought you might like it," he says shyly.

As I pull at my blouse collar, a faint sound drifts to my ears from the floor above. A bump. Footsteps? Then music. I blink, glance at Arthur to see if he has heard these things too and notice his eyes have settled on the stairs. He looks back at me. "Someone else . . . is here?"

My mouth is dry; all the moisture whisked from it. "No. No . . . it's just us."

Arthur's eyes widen, and he scrapes back his chair, stands.

"Wait here," I instruct, placing the book on the table, my heart pounding. "Stay with the baby."

The fright in the boy's eyes must be mirrored in my own as his hands ball into fists. The music builds, staccato notes of a piano concerto. *The gramophone.*

Stumbling over to the stove, my hip glances against the table and I flinch. I grab the poker from the companion set, the remaining items clanking.

"Della . . . Mrs Pemberton . . ." Arthur croaks.

Ignoring him, I hurtle to the stairs, my breaths sharp.

Rabbit barks twice.

In the hallway above, the swell of the music lifts and lilts, staining the air. *There is no one in this house except us.*

The poker trembles in my hand as I creep forwards. Throwing a quick glance up through the stairs, I see nothing. Just the faint glint of the chandelier on the uppermost floor of the house.

The drawing room door is fully open, just as it was when Arthur arrived. *The front door.* I did not throw the bolts across after the boy came in, only locked it. *The imposter who has a key . . .*

Has he come back for Viola? *No, no, no. He cannot have her back. He cannot!*

My grip on the poker tightens further as I approach the drawing room, the music warbling. Gramophone records last but three or four minutes. It must end soon. "Come out . . . come out and show yourself," I command. My voice is too small, too weak. The man in my house will sense my fear. *I will not give him Viola. I will refuse.* This thought has me standing frozen now, wanting to retreat to the kitchen and gather the baby close, feel her nuzzle against my neck, breathe in the smell of her.

"Della . . . Della . . ." The whisper from behind makes me pivot, my nerves scattering. But it's only Arthur, and he's holding the baby. She lets out an almighty screech at the same time as the music comes to a stop.

My heart beats wildly as we make an exchange; I take Viola and Arthur grabs the poker. His jaw is set firm and I'm glad, so glad I'm not having to face this terror alone. "He can't take her . . . he can't have her . . ." I croak, as if this is the boy's decision to make.

These words are exposing, and his eyes are clouded with confusion, yet in four strides, Arthur is inside the drawing room.

I hold my breath, try and soothe Viola. There's no sound from within and wrapping my protective arms around the baby I step in after him.

The baby's cries fill the silence left behind by the music. The gramophone turntable is still circling, the needle scratching back and forth. But the room is blessedly empty.

"How . . . how did this happen?" asks Arthur, eyeing the gramophone warily. He reaches down and stills the turntable, lifts the needle.

I stand alongside him, run soothing strokes over the baby's back as she continues to fuss. "The front door . . . it was left unbolted. He must have come in again . . ."

Arthur pushes past the fir tree to stand at the window, the branches rustling, needles dropping to the carpet as his head turns every which way.

"Do you see anyone?" I rasp.

His shoulders stiffen. "A man. Further down the road heading towards town."

"Let me see."

Arthur stands back to let me through. Placing a hand on the cool glass, I let out a long breath. "You." He's exited the back lane to the rear of the house.

"You know the fellow?" Arthur is looking at me quizzically.

I nod.

"Could it have been him who came in?" Arthur's eyes are ablaze with indignation.

"No. He lives at the end of my garden. He's . . . he's family."

"Oh."

I sense the boy's curiosity, but he doesn't question me further. It strikes me then. This person who came in did not come back for Viola. He does not *want* her. He came back to scare me.

"I'll check the front door and the rest of the house," Arthur says thickly. "Wait here."

"No . . . I can't let you do that alone . . ." I begin, but he's already gone, his feet cantering up the stairs.

Chapter 15

When Arthur leaves, much later in the afternoon, pale faced and jaw clenched, I promise him I'll keep the doors locked and bolted, will stay inside until Mary arrives in the morning. I don't need any persuading. He promises to return, but I try my hardest to dissuade him. *I can deal with this alone, I must deal with this alone.*

***

With supper eaten and Viola fed and finally sleeping, I sit in the armchair, turning the key to the attic over in my hands. It's not a place I enjoy visiting, but tonight I must fetch down the tree decorations and find some of Theo's old toys I can gift to my nephews.

Old Mr Pemberton – Theo's father – is a man I never met. A few minutes in the attic of this house and anyone would get the measure of him though. I recall the flutter that darted up my back the first time I stepped into the hallway of this house with Theo.

Amidst the heavy furniture, the place was filled with the objects Theo's father had spent a lifetime collecting. A life-sized fairground horse with a red flank and golden hoofs, its eyes flared wide. Walnut music boxes and automaton sand toys that when tilted made the cardboard characters inside dance and twirl.

The house was cluttered and oppressive with curios and while Theo blanched at my tentative request these items must be stored elsewhere if we were to make the house our home after marrying, he accepted it none the less. Their migration to the attic was painless enough, men brought in and paid to do the job. The house afterwards seemed empty, so much space for the two of us to fill it with our own ornaments. *With our children.*

Pulling out the tonic bottle from the side of the chair cushion, I take off the cap. One sip, then another, and another, slowly gathering the courage needed to venture amongst the Pemberton family's relics.

My own bed is calling me tonight too – I cannot spend another night sleeping on the floor or in this chair with a cricked neck, my back cramping. The house feels safer knowing Arthur has entered and checked each room. Before my courage slips away, I push the attic key into my skirt pocket, pick up Viola and the book Arthur gave me, and head upstairs.

I switch on every light as I traipse through the house, and the place glitters and gleams as if preparing itself for a fine gathering. I feel a burst of fondness for Agnes when I notice she has prepared fires in the grates of each room. She's even laid the dining room table with the silver cutlery and crystal glasses that have been boxed for more than a year.

In the drawing room, the scent of pine needles pricking my nose, I look at the gramophone warily. Silent now, but the brass horn stares at me, an all-seeing and hollow eye.

Theo and I used to dance in here occasionally, his hand in the small of my back, guiding me around the room.

Laying Viola down for a moment, I select a record, wind the handle and drop the needle. The sound of Tchaikovsky's Casse Noisette – Theo's favourite – fills the room, grazes the walls, lifts to the high ceilings and gaps in the cornicing.

Viola kicks her legs, uncoordinated movements, but in pleasure, I think. My laugh fills the air as I watch. "See. There's nothing to be frightened of here."

Continuing upstairs with the baby, I pause outside Theo's study. I briefly step in to place the butterfly book on the desk and stare at the sketches on the wall. They are in the correct order now, with a gap for the damaged caterpillar picture. Picking up the broken frame I place it beside the book.

The glow of the streetlamp outside draws me to the window. Staring out into the dark, I stamp on the tremor of fear at who may be watching the house as Viola nuzzles against my chest. I push my shoulders back, see the dim outline of the stacks of building materials on the site opposite. "I'm not frightened of you. You have given me a gift. And look how well I am looking after her," I whisper, urging the words under the cracks in the window and out into the thickness of the night. I draw the shutters closed with a bump.

Settling the baby in my bedroom, I strike a match and light the wick of an oil lamp, head up the final staircase in this house to the attic. The music in the drawing room has come to an end and I try and ignore the silence, steel myself against the chill. I unlock and open the door and look in, breathe in the smell of wood and dust. Oak tree branches tap at the window, as if encouraging me inside. *There's nothing to be afraid of here,* I repeat silently as I stare at the clamour of objects in the dim light, trunks and boxes, and other heavy pieces of furniture I banished to the top of the house.

Towards the back wall, and between the two windows that look out onto the back garden, sits the fairground horse, its wild eyes watching, its golden hooves preparing to strike into a canter.

Mary found it mildly interesting up here as she helped me pack away Theo's clothes and shoes last summer, taking amusement from the automaton sandboxes, marvelling at the moving tableau powered by falling sand. I insisted she take one home for my nephews as gift, a garish court jester spinning on a trapeze. With Theo gone there is no need for me to keep these objects, I should arrange for an auction house to come and price them up and sell them. The money is needed now.

Turning my attention to the trunks and boxes, they are stacked neatly, each labelled with a cardboard tag. Mostly Theo's work, but mine and Mary's too. The wind judders the rafters overhead and I startle, glance back at the open door. I listen out for Viola but hear no cries.

Turning my attention back to the trunk before me and reading the label, I see this one is full of Theo's clothes, and I quickly move to the next and then the next, but there is still no sign of the crate of decorations, or trunk of playthings. I was certain they were close to the attic door when I came up here last. Perhaps Mary moved them, for there were times she was up here alone, when I had to retire to my bed when the sorting, rifling and packing became too much.

Shivering, I think of Mary pausing to hold up a ticket she'd found in one of Theo's trouser pockets as we prepared his clothes for packing. It had been warm then, the open window bringing in the smell of garden greenery.

The thing she held in her hand was a ticket stub from the Grand Cinema in the nearby town of Huntingdon. "I'm sorry. It must be painful bringing back these memories," she'd said, giving me a quick embrace.

I turned away then, did not want my sister to see the bewilderment on my face. Theo and I had never been to Huntingdon together. Had never been to that cinema. He didn't even enjoy going to the pictures, preferred his books and reading. Another shred of evidence that my husband had a hidden side to his life, a private part that didn't involve me.

The spring before he left to fight, I remember waking to a deliciously mild April day, my mood settled having slept better than usual. With a day's respite from working at the hospital, I packed the picnic basket, carried it across the backs to a fountain of birdsong. I anticipated Theo's eyes widening, his smile at my spontaneity. Yet when I'd arrived at his place of work, he wasn't there. His colleague had been bemused to see me.

"He's in London, Mrs Pemberton. Had urgent business to attend to. Didn't he say?"

My laugh hopefully covered my confusion. "Oh. Yes. How foolish of me to forget."

Over supper that evening I had brought the matter up.

"I came to see you at work today, brought a picnic. But one of your colleagues told me you were in London."

Theo's eyes remained fixed on his plate. "I was visiting my brother. I mentioned it this morning."

I quietly placed my knife and fork down. "No. No, you didn't."

Theo looked up, smiled. "I did, Della. I remember it clearly."

Sitting back in my chair, I'd thought back to his scrambled eggs, my toast and plum jam at breakfast, but the memory of my husband telling me about his London visit was absent. Theo's cheeks were strained as he continued to eat, and I knew with complete certainty he was lying. "How was your brother, then?"

"Fine," Theo mumbled, wiping his mouth on his napkin.

"What made you decide to visit today?"

"Oh . . . this and that." He looked up, a muscle ticking in his jaw. "I'm tired, Della. Please, no more questions."

As I cleared away the supper things, I'd stood at the kitchen window feeling a rising suspicion. My husband did not visit his brother often, and when he did it was planned weeks in advance. And never on a workday.

That evening, while Theo took a bath, I went through my husband's pockets for the first time. A train ticket stub. Not to London though. A day return to St Ives. I'd stared and stared at the stub, then slipped the evidence of his lie back inside his jacket.

***

At the far left of the attic, I finally find the trunk of playthings. Lifting the lid, I see a train set in its box, the picture of the red locomotive on the lid bringing a hint of brightness to the gloom. There is a bat and ball too. Pulling these items out, I close the trunk and look to the shelf behind it. On the topmost one sits a familiar crate, a limp gold-foiled paperchain dangling. *The tree decorations.*

Standing on the trunk, I test its weight. Balancing precariously, I reach up, but I'm still not tall enough. Pulling hard on the paperchain, it tumbles and drops, sprawls across the floorboards like a dead snake. It's clear I'm not going to be able to do this alone. Mary's husband William will have to help me tomorrow.

I'm about to step down when I notice a couple of large, scratched marks on the rafter closest to the crate. Theo or his brother, a bored boy with a penknife looking to make mischief? Standing on tiptoes again, my side pinching, I hold up the lamp.

Two letters, roughly carved. *E.C.*

My heart thuds. *Emanuel Cleeve.* It must be. He was here; in this very spot I'm balancing now.

A wave of dizziness threatens, and I breathe evenly until it passes. Peering at the initials once more, I see there's a small space behind this rafter, a triangle of cloth peeping out. *A hiding place?*

Sensing a presence behind me, I almost tumble off the trunk as I pivot, my heart pulsing wildly. There is no one here but me. I don't let my attention linger on those parts of the attic where trunks and boxes are stacked high enough to conceal a person. *Stop being so fanciful, Della.*

The back of my neck still prickles in unease as I turn

back to the rafter. Holding the lamp high, fingers shaking, muscles in my back and neck tensing, I pull at the cloth. It comes away but slips from my fingers and falls into the gap behind the trunk.

I reach for it, stretching and feeling around in the dark space. Something soft and sinewy brushes against my finger. Giving this thing I have found a sharp tug, I pull out a dead rat, its eyes blank and the flesh half rotted away.

Screeching, I fling it to one side, and losing my balance I tumble from the trunk. The oil lamp drops from my other hand, the glass ball-shade smashing and the flame extinguishing. I lie winded on the floor in the dark. *A rat, it was just a rat.*

Brushing myself down, I wipe my fingers on my skirt, but the sour smell of the dead creature lingers. Gritting my teeth, I clamber back onto the trunk and fumble about behind it for a second time, fingers poking and searching in the gloom. The cloth, when I pull it out, is folded around a thin item concealed inside, about the length of my hand.

Carrying it to the attic landing, I sink onto the top step of the stairs. The cloth is ordinary enough: a large and greying handkerchief with no distinguishing marks. Laying it on my lap, I gingerly unfold it, anticipation surging at what's hidden inside. *Something Emanuel has hidden up here?*

The wind whistles, rattling the roof tiles as if sending me a signal to hurry. I peel back the final fold of cloth. A thin bone. Belonging to an animal?

I think of the slim pock-marked bones Rabbit sometimes discovers on our walks – parts of long-dead foxes, badgers or hares. This isn't like that. It's a smaller imitation of the men's bones I saw in textbooks and on operating tables while working at the war hospital.

Turning it this way and that I run a finger over its inward curve, the slight rounding at one end. A femur bone. A thigh bone. So small it will have belonged to a baby. And it fits neatly in my palm. *As if it belongs there.*

Chapter 16

Who did the bone belong to? Why was it in my attic? I glance at Viola, sleeping soundly again after her last bottle of milk. My eyes skirt over the dim outline of her legs, as I study the femur. There is no one in this house to ask these questions to aside from myself, so I do so repeatedly until I'm dizzy with the thought that muscle and skin once bound around this bone. *A real living thing.* I take a sip of tonic, then another.

The day of our loss comes tumbling into my head. The cramps that came with no warning at all eight weeks before our baby should have been born. My naivety convinced me that all would be well, and I remember the doctor's careful fingers examining me as I lay on this bed I sit on now. I took slow, slow breaths, trying to calm my racing heart, willing this baby we had longed for to arrive alive and healthy.

But the look on the doctor's face was grim, and he called Theo in. I knew immediately, didn't need to be told. A midwife was sent for, a thin faced but exceedingly kind woman who smelt of rose water and held my hand and wiped my cheeks as I wept.

Afterwards I squeezed my eyes shut against the sound of a small thing being wrapped and bundled out of the bedroom door. Afterwards I drank the sweet tea offered to me.

Afterwards I agreed that I would take the sleeping draught, that I would rest in bed for at least a month.

But then . . . the endless questions about how and why this had happened. Theo was an intelligent man; usually had a ready answer or theory to anything I asked. On this topic he remained mute.

In the following days I grew stronger, began to press him about what had happened to the bundle whisked from the room so fast I did not even know whether I'd given birth to a boy or a girl.

"You must try and put this behind you. I dealt with it," my husband said, his voice stiff and sad as he stroked my hair. *Dealt with it how?*

I'm somehow unafraid as I race downstairs to the kitchen, quickly seeking out my sketchpad and a drawing pencil. Returning to the bedroom and sitting cross-legged on the bed, I place the bone on the quilt and concentrate on sketching its curves and lines. My limbs vibrate as if ants are crawling through my veins. The insides of my ears itch and no amount of scratching will ease it. *The bone. Who did it belong to? Who hid it in my attic? Was it you, Emanuel Cleeve?*

When I'm finished, I carefully rewrap the bone in the handkerchief and shuffle across the bed to Viola. Her breaths are feather light. *Theo would have loved you. He would have cherished you.* She's so insubstantial on this bed, so fragile. Yet I will keep her safe. Grief swills inside me, but not the all-encompassing kind that has me in fits of weeping. Tonight's anguish is softened by the presence of this real, living baby.

Viola snuffles in her sleep. The thought of having to give her up takes my breath away.

***

I'm pulled awake by Viola's cries. The bed covers are damp with her urine. Peeling off the baby's wet clothing, I wash and dry her in the bathroom. It is five-thirty and there will be little point in going back to bed after the baby has been fed. Christmas Eve yawns ahead of me, the day of my sister's arrival when I must be bright-eyed and welcoming to her and her family when all I wish for is for sleep to pull me under. *And to not dwell on the bone.*

My head thickens with worry again as I think of reasons to explain why it was hidden behind the rafter bearing Emanuel's carved initials. This thigh bone belonged to his baby? *A small and cherished thing.* The photograph of Emanuel and his wife, their baby in the wicker carriage – perhaps there wasn't a happy outcome to his family life and his child died during infanthood? *He came to this house in distress, looking for his baby Viola.* I shake my head, nausea rising again. That man was not Emanuel Cleeve's ghost. He was an imposter, a pretender. Yet everything that man did was intentional. A key to my house in his palm. His close impersonation of Emanuel in the photograph, a man who lived here years ago. The bold claim my house belonged to him. A baby hidden within his coat and deposited here. *Where did he get her from? Who does she belong to?*

Viola squirms as I pin her nappy cloth. The imposter's premeditated actions make me think the name Viola was not plucked from his imagination. There will be a reason he spoke it out loud that night, why the book of nursery rhymes is so dedicated.

***

Switching on the lamp in Theo's study, Viola gurgles and grunts. Since finding her in here, I'm increasingly drawn to this room. I tentatively sweep my eyes over the desk, cabinets and shelves, recalling the tonic bottle left in here, the discovery of the rearranged pictures on the wall. To my relief there's nothing different or changed today. This morning only memories of the past linger. A flash of violence that had taken me by surprise, as if Theo had cracked open like a fissure in rock. It was June, almost a year after our loss, and Theo's fingers wound tight around my wrist like a bandage.

A letter from a London solicitor's office had arrived that morning, the company stamp on the back. I'd dithered over opening it, but curiosity got the better of me. It was a request for payment following three telephone calls and a meeting with Theo. Calls and meetings I'd known nothing about.

In the past months a chasm had opened between us, Theo retreating to a guest room on the first floor. He'd also taken to breakfasting earlier, the thud of the front door as he left for work each morning startling me awake. Then at supper his face would be carefully blank and so unlike the husband I knew and loved. He was grieving our loss too, that much I knew, moving further apart from me, just as I was moving away from him. I was on the shoreline, watching as he drifted out to sea without a compass, not able to pinpoint his destination, only knowing it wasn't the same as mine.

I was too weary to make gentle conversation, at bridging

the distance. Every evening Theo ate quickly and then retired to his study. Sometimes I took to quietly standing outside the study door in the evenings, listening to the creak of his chair, the shuffle of papers, the scratch of his pen. Recalling the times I had sat on his lap, arms wound around his neck, his breath warm on my cheek as our child grew in my womb. I wanted those times to return, yet we'd both changed. There didn't seem any way back for us.

"A solicitor sent an invoice," I said, as soon as he came through the front door that night. Rabbit had ambled over to meet him, and he'd bent to fondle the dog's ears.

"Did you hear me, Theo?"

He shrugged off his hat and coat, hung them on the stand. Then with his head lowered he'd wordlessly taken the letter, stepped around me and disappeared upstairs. "This should have been sent to my office," he muttered.

I'd set off after him, suddenly determined to get answers. He was leaving for the continent the following week and we were short on time. The sensible part of me knew it was a poor decision to push things, but I could not let him go with this unknown thing sitting between us.

Theo had been exempt from enlisting at first, to ensure teaching was maintained at the university. But the conscription rules changed that April and men older than him were being called up. Theo had decided he had to do his bit. Couldn't sit by any longer while his colleagues and students fought for our country while he wielded only a pen. I told him I was proud, keeping the rock of dread settling in my stomach to myself.

"Not now, Della. Please," my husband said when I entered the study without knocking. He sat low in his chair, rubbed at his temples. His brown eyes were like dark tidal pools, the furrows on his forehead deeper than usual.

"Why do you need a solicitor? What is it you're not telling me?"

Theo dipped his head. "It's nothing to concern yourself with."

My irritation morphed and twisted into anger. "You're keeping secrets."

His face was creased with weariness, but I prodded him again, like a tongue worrying at a loose tooth.

"You didn't visit your brother in London a few months ago, you went to St Ives. I found the train ticket. And now you're speaking with a London solicitor."

Theo's eyes flashed a warning. "Please, Della. Don't ask me about this."

"You disappear for afternoons; telling me you are doing one thing when it's plain it's another."

Spots of colour stained my husband's cheeks.

I stepped closer to the desk, my desire to extract an explanation increasing. "I followed you to the train station last month. You told me you were meeting a work colleague at the library. Where did you go really? St Ives again? Or to see this solicitor?"

The sudden feel of my husband's fingers bound around my wrist made me gasp.

"You must stop this, do you hear? No good will come of it." His voice was tight and thick.

I twisted away, but his grip was too firm. "You're hurting me."

He dropped his hand like I was hot pumice, watched in

silence as I rubbed at the band of red erupting. He looked stricken, regretful. He reached for me again. "Sorry . . . I'm so sorry . . . Della . . ."

As I strode from that room, I recall thinking that I wanted nothing more than my husband and his secrets gone from Arcadia House. Felt a shocking spike of gladness that the following week he'd be at war. Then after he'd left, I cried on and off for the entire week.

Back in the kitchen with Viola, water for the milk powder warming in the pan, Rabbit at my heels, I think again of Emanual Cleeve, his carved initials in the attic, and the baby's bone that nestles in the pocket of my dressing gown. My sister would think it horribly macabre of me to keep the bone close, but I feel the pull of a connection. Perhaps because I would not want any part of *my* child's remains to be stuffed between the rafters of a draughty attic. The 'why' of that is another piece of this mystery. I'm like Gretel from the fairy tale, following a trail of breadcrumbs and I wonder where it will all lead.

Our parish church will have records, dates of marriages, births and deaths – perhaps of the man who lived in this house and scored his initials into the roof support. My sister will surely want to attend the crib carol service with the children this afternoon. I must find an opportunity to slip away and search out another breadcrumb, something that will throw some light on Emanuel Cleeve and his life in this house.

Chapter 17

From the front step, I watch Mary take an armful of gifts from their new motor, tastefully wrapped and bound in silken ribbon of course. I wince internally at the lack of presents I have bought.

Their journey from Suffolk appears to have been a fractious one; Fred is snivelling, and Bertie, his older brother, pinches the back of Fred's neck when he assumes no one is looking. He sees me watching though, throws me a brazen look. Thirteen years old and I sense Mary and her husband William will have some difficult years ahead.

"There you are!" Mary cries rushing up the steps, bringing with her a wave of lavender cologne. It is the same scent that our late mother wore, and always brings a heady rush of nostalgia. She's wearing a maroon woollen belted coat, the fabric so thick I long to run my fingers over it. "Oh. You look quite peaky, Dell. Are you ill?"

I smile. "Just tired, that's all." My ears strain for the sound of Viola who's lying on a sofa in the drawing room wedged in by cushions. I thought it best not to greet them with the baby in my arms. My explanation for her is not something to be handed out on a chilly doorstep.

Mary clicks her tongue as she looks back at her family. "Will you stop fussing over that motor, William. Come on

Bert, Fred. Come and say hello to Aunt Della."

I grimace. "Must they call me that? I would rather it was just Della."

My sister raises an eyebrow. "They may only see you a couple of times a year now, but they need to remember your position in the family."

Do not rise to this thinly veiled dig. My sister writes often, invites me to visit. But the thought of the journey, the smile I would have to fix on my cheeks for the duration of my stay. It's all too much to contemplate.

"Fred! Come and say hello," I say, as the boy runs up the steps. He's three years younger than Bertie, is full of sunshine and smiles and barrels into my embrace.

Bertie follows, his face glowering and I immediately sense he's not happy about leaving his comfortable country home and coming here for Christmas. His willowy limbs seem too long for his frame, and there's also a sly look about him that was absent the last time I saw the boy. "My, you've grown," I say, trying to inject some cheer into the situation.

Bertie looks at his shoes, scuffs them on the concrete.

"William, do hurry!" calls Mary again. She leans in "His new motor car rattled my bones half to death, would have much preferred to have come by train now they're not full of troops and running to time again." She stands back, appraises me again in that frank way only sisters can. "You *do* look exhausted. Your hair is limp too . . ."

Ignoring my sister's observations, I fold my arms to ward off the cold and watch my brother-in-law unload two brown leather suitcases from the back of the motor. They've brought enough luggage for two weeks, rather than three nights.

I feel a tug on my sleeve and Fred looks up at me shyly. "Where's the dog? Where's Rabbit?"

"He's in the kitchen. You can run along in and find him, if you like? He'll be glad to see you."

"Are you coming, Bertie?" the boy asks.

Despite the pinches and slyness, Fred still wishes to be his brother's shadow.

The boys disappear into the house in their hunt for the dog.

My shoulders soften a little. The fire in the drawing room is lit, the room warmed through. The baby is sleeping, and I hope she'll stay that way until I am able to quietly and calmly explain her presence without interruptions.

While William stows the luggage in the guest bedrooms on the first floor, I lead Mary into the house. Wiping my palms on my dress, I turn at the threshold to the drawing room. "We have another guest this year. It was all rather last minute, I'm afraid."

Mary's eyes widen and a slow smile arches across her cheeks. "A man?" she whispers conspiratorially.

I pull in a breath. "No. Nothing like that. Please . . . come in and meet her."

Mary stands staring at Viola, her jaw slackening. She kneels at the foot of the sofa. "A baby?"

My fingers worry at a hangnail. "You remember Agnes, my home help? She and her family are sick. Her baby sister Viola is well though, and I offered to take her in for the Christmas period. Just for a few days until the family are recovered enough to look after her again."

"Influenza?" Mary's voice is razor sharp.

"No, no. Nothing like that."

"But . . . Della. This is preposterous. You know nothing about babies!"

Viola stirs, eyelashes fluttering at Mary's reaction. In disagreement I like to think, and this causes me to smile. "I know more than you assume. And Agnes provided me with a list of instructions."

Mary stands up, smooths her dress. Her eyes are bright. "This baby's mother was happy to hand her over to you? She's . . . she's so little."

"She's six weeks, smaller than she looks." This might be a lie, or it might not. I clear my throat. "The family had no choice. They were desperate, have six other children to care for. And you know the price of tinned milk . . . how high it is. I can feed her up while she's here."

Sighing, Mary stands and walks to the fireplace. Her shoulders are taut as she holds out her hands to the flickering flames. My sister is as slim as ever; her navy dress cinched at the waist. Unlike my own waist which is thickening and aching under this corset which I'm wearing today to appear respectable.

Mary shakes her head again, places a hand to her neck and worries at the string of pearls that used to belong to our mother. "It's just rather a surprise. You could have warned me."

"There was no time to write or send a telegram. I only took her in last night . . ." I counter, taking a breath. Enough with the explaining. The lie has been told; the seed sown.

"Shall I go and make tea? I've made cucumber sandwiches for lunch."

Mary glances at Viola again. "Oh, Della. I do worry about you."

"Don't fuss! I'm perfectly well."

In the kitchen, Bertie and Fred are rolling a cricket ball across the floor, laughing as Rabbit attempts to pick it up. It's too big and cumbersome for his small jaw.

As I make up the tea tray, I imagine for a second what Arcadia House might have been like if it had been filled with the laughter and calls of my own children. Pausing to watch the boys, I place a hand to my stomach. It's rounded now, but empty. The memory of the swell of a new life has never left though.

Back outside the drawing room with the tea tray, I catch the edge of a whispered conversation, and I linger.

"It's very peculiar. Asking your employer to take in your baby sister at Christmas time." Mary.

"Perhaps it's a good thing. You're always saying Della needs something more to occupy her time." William.

"If she'd only had her own children . . ." Mary.

William is quiet but sighs heavily, as if this topic has been discussed many times before.

Taking a few quiet steps back, I cough to alert them to my presence and walk briskly into the room with the tray and place it down.

Mary is cradling Viola, rocking her back and forth as she stands before the undecorated Christmas tree. "Tea. Lovely!"

"Yes, lovely," echoes William, helping himself to a plate

and a triangle sandwich. He nods at the tree. "That's a splendid looking fir."

"No decorations though?" Mary's gaze is appraising as she takes in the bare branches.

I think of the attic, my failed attempt to fetch down the crate. *The baby's bone hidden up there, now in my bedroom tucked inside a chest of drawers.* "They're on an attic shelf out of reach. Perhaps you could help me fetch them later, William?"

"Of course," my brother-in-law replies through a mouthful of bread.

Mary arranges the presents they've bought under the tree. The paper and shiny ribbon bring a new air of festivity to the room.

"I must apologise in advance to you both. My gift buying this year . . . well it didn't quite go to plan. I'll send something through the post in the new year. But there are some things of Theo's I hoped to pass on to the boys," I say, pouring the tea.

"That's very kind. Yes, they'll like that. Won't they, Mary," says William, wiping crumbs from his thin moustache. Not a question, but a statement. Giving my sister no room to comment or judge my failings. My brother-in-law is well practised at soothing Mary's occasional sharper edges.

"How's business?" I ask, passing around the sugar bowl. William helps to run his family's jam factory. I'm hopeful the parcel for me beneath the tree is several jars of his finest.

He takes a sugar cube from the bowl, holds it up. "It's expensive with the hike in sugar prices."

"Things aren't too difficult, I hope?" I ask. William pops

the cube into his teacup and stirs, the spoon tinkling. My skin prickles as I think of the spoon I stole from Arthur. After I'd left, did he search for the spoon in the attic of his father's shop? Did it occur to him I might have taken it? *I'm sorry, Arthur. I'm sorry.*

"We're turning a healthy profit," my brother-in-law says, pulling me back to the present. "But since the munitions factories closed people are lining up outside and asking for work. Becomes a little tiresome."

I feign a sympathetic nod. William has no sense of the hardships being faced by so many, how ex-servicemen are failing to regain the jobs they left to fight in the war. Him at the foot of the garden comes to mind and I feel a ripple of unease.

"Della, don't scratch like that. You'll mark your skin," Mary admonishes briskly.

Smoothing my blouse sleeves, I clamp my jaw and breathe through the itch that feels like beetles crawling up my arms.

Viola yawns, her legs and arms stiffening and then relaxing. "She's a dear little thing," croons Mary, and I see that my sister has that same familiar look of affection in her eyes from when her own boys were small. "Will we take her with us to church this afternoon?"

"I was expecting to," I say, thinking again of my intention to inspect the church records and try and find out more about Emanuel Cleeve.

There is the rumble of a vehicle outside, and moments later the thud of feet up the front steps, the trill of the doorbell.

"More guests?" asks Mary, arching an eyebrow, as she pats Viola's back to ease a rash of hiccups.

At the window, I peer around the branches of the tree, see a van at the kerb. "I'm not expecting anyone."

Opening the door, I'm confronted by a delivery man dressed in brown overalls. He looks up from a notebook in his hand. "Mrs Pemberton?"

"Yes?" I watch a second man in a flat cap open the rear doors of the van parked up outside the house and ease out a large object wrapped in grey felt.

The overalled man at the door passes me a docket. It's marked with the stamp of a furniture warehouse on Mill Road.

"No. There must be a mistake. I'm not expecting a delivery," I say. Standing in the doorway, I clutch the docket as the man in the cap carries the item up the steps. "Please . . . you've made a mistake."

The overalled man gestures at me to stand aside.

"Is everything all right?" Mary is at my shoulder, the baby in her arms, her hand cupped around her head to protect her from the cold.

"Delivery," the second man says, and I have no choice but to step back as they carry this object into my house. They unfold the felt covering to reveal a baby's crib; painted white wicker, with a cream lace hood and valance. Inside is a parcel wrapped in tissue paper; sheets and blankets by the looks of it.

Frigid air sweeps through the front door and a tremor rattles through me. I sense Mary's deeply inquisitive glance as she stands in the hall, quietly watching. "I did not order this," I say again.

The man in overalls sighs, pulls out the notebook from his overall pocket. Licking a thumb, he quickly turns the pages, stabs a finger at the book. "Says here you paid extra for delivery on Christmas Eve. To Arcadia House. Mrs Pemberton. It's all here in black and white." He says this as if anything written in this small book must be the truth. "Shall we leave it here in your hallway?"

This is a battle I won't win today, and I feel weighed with weariness and confusion. "Please . . . just take it upstairs. The bedroom at the back of the house, on the second floor."

The men do as I ask, as Mary and I stand watching.

"Della . . . I . . ." begins Mary in a low voice.

"There's obviously been a terrible mix up," I cut in. "I'll have to sort this out after Christmas." My words are light, but inside dread gathers. If I did not order this crib, then who did? *Sent here as a gift for Viola? Just like the book of nursery rhymes.*

Once the men have gone, and the door is locked, I snap the bolts across. Mary steps closer, Viola against her shoulder. Her face is tight with concern. "You don't seem yourself." She reaches up, tucks a strand of my hair behind my ear. A gentle gesture.

Sinking onto the bottom step of the stairs, I stare at the door. "Like I said, I'm tired. Not sleeping well."

Mary sits beside me, lies the baby across her lap and plays with her tiny fingers. "Still? I thought you were feeling better?"

Swallowing, I turn my attention to the wallpaper, a lone green parrot sitting on a branch. Theo used to walk through the door each evening and say 'good evening, birds' as he took off his coat and hat, as if they were alive and had been waiting all day for him to return, just like his beloved dog. And me. He could be tender like that, once. "I find things difficult sometimes. Being in this house . . ." I pause, an urge to tell my sister everything rising like an errant weed.

Mary gives me a careful look. "Sometimes I find things difficult too. The boys are demanding, and William is often late home. But . . . you need to resist the temptation of things that might make you feel worse rather than better."

"Such as?" I say, giving her a bemused glance.

She strokes Viola's leg. "I couldn't help noticing the sherry decanter in the drawing room. It's . . . nearly empty."

I shake my head. "Theo was the last person to use it. I . . . don't have a taste for sherry."

Mary purses her lips but doesn't offer any further comment. "Have you thought any more about looking for work? The twenty shillings a week your widow's pension brings is hardly generous, and Theo's savings won't last."

Oh, the irony, I think as a headache nags at the base of my skull. My sister had never been especially happy about me moving to Cambridge to work at the printing press, then volunteering at the war hospital. With William unable to enlist and working at the jam factory in the war, and their children so young still, Mary stayed at home. Did her bit by knitting an endless supply of men's fingerless gloves and hats in scratchy grey wool to be shipped to the front.

"I'll think about it," I say. This is at least a small truth I can share with my sister. It seems impossible that I can stay in this state of limbo for much longer, roaming the Cambridge streets, thieving small items to fill my days. I'm living simply on my war pension, but it does not go far enough and she's right about Theo's savings – they're dwindling fast.

"Good," says Mary, her expression settling into one of satisfaction. "I know things haven't worked out how you'd hoped. But you have this beautiful house . . ."

"Yes." My voice is dull, and she gives me a sidelong glance.

My sister is quiet then, and I sense a new line of questioning about to spill from her lips. "Has *he* said any more about his intentions? He surely can't be intending the groom's lodgings in your garden as a permanent living arrangement."

The boys' footsteps thunder up the kitchen stairs. "Please can we not talk of this now."

Viola frets and squirms on Mary's lap; her mouth roots for the bottle teat. Mary rubs the baby's stomach. "You've been so kind to him, Della. And he's given you nothing in return. You don't owe the man anything."

"The baby needs feeding," I mutter, as Fred charges past into the drawing room.

Mary sighs. "The bottle and tin of milk powder are in the kitchen?"

I nod.

"I'll feed Viola. Why don't you rest for an hour?" My sister's tone is conciliatory and kind.

"Are you sure?"

"Yes. I worry about you. Please rest."

I sink into her words like a pillow; feel a gratefulness I cannot put into words.

***

Light at the bedroom window is fading when I wake. I lie quietly for a second or two, hear the sound of gramophone music from downstairs, laughter and conversation. A game of charades perhaps. Glancing at the carriage clock, I sit up at once and switch on the lamp. I've slept for almost three hours.

Pushing back the quilt, I ease myself onto the side of the bed and yawn. The threatening headache has vanished. Then I see the baby's crib and remember the peculiar delivery, the men's insistence that I made this purchase.

I admire the carefully woven wicker, trail a hand over the frilly lace valance. The mattress is soft and stuffed with down. Whoever did buy this item spared no expense, has excellent taste. *It's just what I would have purchased myself.*

Unlike the pram, the crib I did choose for our unborn child is long gone. A charitable donation to the orphanage. Hearing the boys' voices downstairs, I push that thought away. I refuse to allow space in my head for it, will take pleasure from having this beautiful bed for Viola to sleep in tonight.

Lifting the tissue-paper wrapped package inside, I notice a flash of white beneath. An envelope. It is blank – no address on the front.

Carrying the envelope to the window, I stifle a gasp as I look out. He's there in the garden, his spade chipping away at a vegetable bed, a cigarette dangling from his lips. He's not wearing the flesh-coloured face mask. His hollowed cheek, the half a nose is exposed. A mash of mangled flesh. I lift a hand to wave, but he turns his back as if anticipating my move.

My heart thuds an irregular beat, with the urge to charge downstairs and invite him inside for drinks this evening and for lunch tomorrow. But then I imagine Mary's pinched face, her concern that his appearance may frighten the boys and provoke unsolicited stares and questions. That's the last thing he'll want. It will be a kindness *not* to invite him, I tell myself, drawing the drapes firmly across.

Another burst of laughter from below. Then I hear Viola cry. Looking back at the envelope in my hand, I quickly open it. I struggle at first to understand the meaning of the typed-up words on the single sheet of white paper.

Notice for printing in The Cambridge Daily News
Murder in Cambridge at New Year

Mrs Della Pemberton, a war widow living in Newnham, has been arrested for a wilful murder committed at her home on New Year's Eve. The name of the deceased has not been released, yet Mrs Pemberton has made a full confession to the crime. It is understood she is also facing allegations of petty theft, although further details of these offences are not yet known. Mrs Pemberton will be charged at Cambridge Assizes at the end of January.

Chapter 18

Murder, murder, murder. The words reel repeatedly around in my head like a clutch of marbles as the boys dawdle behind Mary and me as we walk to church in the gloaming light of the late afternoon.

As I push the pram, I sense my sister's occasional sidelong glances, her concern to see me with this contraption which was supposed to carry my own baby.

While previously I might have dwelt on it, this now seems inconsequential. I'm instead consumed with thoughts of the newspaper notice – that I'll take someone's life this New Year. *Impossible!* My eyes burn at the mere thought of it. Yes, I'm a thief, but I do not have it in me to kill or even wound another. Who would write this, make such a wicked assumption about my character?

I've seen such things reported before in the Cambridge Daily News, murders, and untimely deaths. My first urge was to crumple the note; toss it on the fire and watch it burn to ash. But instead, I slipped it into my chest of drawers next to the bone. Hidden under petticoats and ready for taking out and examining again later. Maybe it will be gone when I get home, maybe I hallucinated this out of sheer exhaustion. *Wishful thinking, Della.* I'm chilled and shivering as we walk, the relentless heat I've been feeling drowned out by this fresh panic.

Someone means me harm. My boots stumble with this thought. I'm being told of an event that has not yet happened but will. A fortune told. A spool of thread, a pot rouge, nail clippers, paint, knitted baby clothes. A teaspoon. Many other small stolen things too. I was careful, oh so careful. Never seen, never accosted or accused. Yet someone knows.

These items I took are not jewels, diamond, rubies, or pearls. They are trivial. Inconsequential things stolen on a whim, daring myself to be dangerous, to use my middle-age invisibility to my advantage. Daring myself to feel something in that moment when most of the time I did not. It seems foolish as I think this, but the worst of it, the absolute worst of it, that causes the lump in my throat to thicken to the size of an onion, is this; I've been secretly watched and surveyed as I thieved and never knew a thing of it.

"Della. Did you hear what I said?"

I throw Mary a sidelong look, the pram wheels splashing through a puddle that soaks the hem of my skirt. "Sorry. I was thinking . . . about the ham."

"Yes, yes. We'll prepare it tonight," my sister replies impatiently. "I was telling you about Bertie's handwriting. He's so lackadaisical, puts in no effort at school." Mary sniffs and I gesture that we should turn right up the path leading to the church, follow the families already heading inside.

Hanging on to the pram handle, I let it bear my weight. It's on the very tip of my tongue to tell my sister about this note. To unburden myself with it all. Her face would startle; her nose would wrinkle. And I'd have to explain everything.

Confess the truth about Viola, the intruder impersonating Emanuel Cleeve who left her in my house, and the key he still has in his possession.

If she knows the whole truth about me and this situation I find myself in, she may decide to leave early, return to Suffolk, when already I'm making plans to encourage her to stay longer. I need to surround myself with people, family that I care for and who care for me. *People I would not murder.*

"Such an interesting looking church," remarks Mary. "It's a shame William didn't come with us; he would have appreciated it. He has a fondness for good architecture."

I make a small noise of agreement. St Marks's mellow red brick and squat appearance is in stark contrast to the surrounding streets of beige villas and terraces. But my brother-in-law feigned a headache, when we both knew full well he will likely put his feet up in front of the fire and have a thimble or two of sherry while we are gone. *Better he drinks it all so Mary won't worry about me becoming a lonely drunk.*

Beyond the church lies a public house, a motor van outside offloading beer barrels. There are distant thuds as one by one they roll into the cellar, like falling bodies.

Who?

Who would I possibly want to harm?

How?

How would I commit such a crime?

"We should leave the pram at the church door," states Mary. "There'll be no room for it inside."

I eye everyone who passes. Well behaved and rosy cheeked children in woollen coats, families talking and laughing and greeting friends and neighbours. Everyone enjoying the festive season. A few acquaintances pause and wish me a merry Christmas, their gazes drifting to the pram. I force a smile and nod.

My breaths shorten. I *cannot* go inside and risk anyone asking me about the baby. I cannot perch on a pew and sing and listen and pretend with this weight hanging over me. There's also the matter of the parish registers I need to find. A clue that will hopefully help me unravel what is happening here.

I force out a smile. "I'm feeling a little nauseous. Why don't you take the boys in. I will join you."

"You *are* sickening. Do you have a fever?" asks Mary, eyes narrowing.

"No . . . no. It is my . . . We don't need to speak of it here."

My sister gives me a knowing look. This is the only helpful thing about women's complaints. They're private matters, not for discussion in the open. Although I often think it would be better if they were. Experiences shared; lessons learnt.

"We shouldn't leave Viola out here in the damp though," I say, looking into the pram.

"Mother, we're cold," whines Bertie, stamping his feet. Fred grins and mimics his older brother.

Mary's jaw tics in irritation. "I'll take the baby. Come and find us inside as soon as you're able, Della. We'll take a pew near the back."

I watch the four of them enter the church, quickly swallowed up amongst the others thronging inside. My sister knows no one here. Nobody will question seeing a baby in her arms. Eventually the door thuds closed, and I can hear the low hum of the vicar's voice as he begins the sermon.

Wind ripples the grassed area that curves around the church. It's void of gravestones, this church being a daughter to the one in Grantchester where Theo's parents worshipped and are buried, and the place we married. According to my husband, an old wooden church once stood on this site. I wonder if this is where Emanuel and his family came to worship.

The organ strikes a chord, and the congregation belts out 'O Come, All Ye Faithful'. My nerves are like frayed pieces of paper as I think of the person who knows about my thieving, their steady surveillance of me.

I snap myself back to my intention to search the church records. Theo and I occasionally attended services here, and closing my eyes for a second I picture the vestry situated beyond the organ. That is where the registers will be kept. There is a rear door to the church, and with any luck I may be able to slip inside unnoticed.

Pushing the pram along the path that hugs the church wall, I step through pools of light spilling from the stained-glass windows. As I approach the side door I look around. I am still quite alone. The lights in the neighbouring rectory are off, everyone inside the church attending the crib service. A small and familiar thrill tightens my stomach. The door latch opens easily without even a squeak. Not that anyone would have heard above the pounding of the organ.

It's cool inside, an aura of papery prayer books and polished wood hanging in the air. Positioning myself behind a pillar, I peep around it to see the rows of pews and bobbing heads as people sing, mouths wide and inelegant, heads held high.

A bored girl fidgets and her mother flashes her a disapproving look. It brings back memories of Mary and me attending morning service every Sunday with our parents. The tedium, the talk of heaven and hell that Mary and I would sometimes debate in private. A secret opinion of my own which I once shared with my sister when we were tucked up in bed and the lights were out.

"You'll go to hell for not believing in God," my sister remarked. I could well imagine her face as we lay there in the dark, stony and disapproving.

"But there's no proof," I'd said quietly. "No one has ever seen or heard God."

"You don't have to see or hear something to believe in it," my sister had quipped.

But I did. I had to see, taste and feel things to believe in them. I've wished hard over the years for my sister's belief in something bigger, something all seeing and all knowing. A guiding light. In the end, my belief is that all we have is ourselves. Yet Agnes, she is devout but believes in something she can't always see. *Dead loved ones watching and waiting for an opportunity to make their presence known.*

Lowering my head now, I slink around the back of the church, never straying far from the walls. If I pretend to be invisible, maybe I am. The vicar's voice rises and swells as he speaks of the glorious hope a new century will bring. A century in which someone is saying I will appear at the Cambridge Assizes and be charged with murder.

It doesn't take me long to locate the vestry and the cupboard where the books containing records of baptisms, marriages and funerals are kept. There are two; the first with a green cover cracking at the edges, and a newer one bound in black leather. Choosing the older register with the disintegrating cover, I quickly open it and riffle through the stiff, yellowing pages. The book dates back to the last century and the wooden church that would have stood here when Emanuel Cleeve lived in Arcadia House. Turning to look about, there's no one here to witness what I am about to do.

Unbuttoning my coat, I take the register and press it to my blouse, feel my heart quicken beneath it. *Stealing from a house of God.* Pulling my coat around the book, I hurry back to the door and the waiting pram.

Chapter 19

"Well, that was perfectly awful," says Mary in a clipped tone as we make our way home after the service. While Viola slept through most of it, my nephews were not so well behaved. Bertie dug his nails into Fred's hand, drawing blood and making him cry out which, according to my sister, resulted in a wealth of disapproving looks. She sent him to wait by the door until the service had finished.

As I push the pram, I think of the parish register lying beneath the mattress. I held my breath as Mary lay Viola inside and tucked her in, afraid that she would comment on its lumpy appearance. I suppose I have my nephews' poor behaviour to thank for her distracted state.

My sister comforts Fred who is still snivelling, his shoulders rounded. Bertie trails behind and I pause, waiting for him to catch up. We walk in silence for a few steps, our breaths steaming in the frigid air. I give him a sidelong glance. "Your mother's upset. It would be nice if you could apologise for what you did in the church. To her and to Fred."

He kicks at a stone. It hits a pram wheel, goes spinning off into the gutter. "Why should I?"

I blanche at his poor attitude. He used to be such a sunny natured boy, always cheerful. "You hurt your brother. Made him cry. Doesn't that make you feel sorry?"

"No." He looks up, lips curling into a sneer. "I saw you."

"Pardon?" I say, steering the pram around a puddle.

"I saw you in the church, near the front." My nephew's eyes are sly. "What were you doing?"

Marching on, my cheeks flash with heat. "You're mistaken. I was waiting outside."

Bertie's shoes clatter behind me. "No, you weren't. You were hiding something under your coat too. What was it?" His eyes rake over me, as if hoping it will reveal itself.

"Come along, let's hurry home," I say, pursing my lips.

"Mother says liars go to hell." The boy is giving me an imperious sidelong look.

Pausing, I place a hand on his shoulder. He tries to squirm away, but my fingers have a talon-like grip. I lower my head until we are eye to eye. "Boys who pinch their little brothers and make them cry go to hell." My words, my harsh tone have sprung up unbidden. *This is not me. It is not me.*

"Hurry up you two!" calls my sister. Mary is watching us, as Fred blows his nose on a handkerchief.

I grit my teeth and smile at my sister, then release Bertie's shoulder. "Run along and apologise. Now."

Bertie's eyes are sullen. Head down, he strides on to his mother and younger brother, and I am glad to hear his mumbled apology.

***

Approaching the house, something catches my eye in the dark. A flicker of movement on the building site opposite, amidst the stacks of bricks and planks. I blink and it has gone. The memory of the imposter who must have been hiding and watching the house, waiting for an opportune moment to let himself in again and start up the gramophone, flies into me.

"What is it?" Mary asks.

"Will you wait here for a moment – watch the baby?" Before there's time for her to question me, for me to question myself, I dart across the road and stride towards the piece of vacant land that will soon be occupied by our future neighbours. I'm emboldened by the thought of Mary watching me, the children next to her. "Hello. Is . . . anyone there?"

The bare trees behind the site rustle and tremble, and around my feet shadows seem to dance. I rest a hand on some building materials covered in tarpaulin, my boots squelching in the mud underfoot.

A small cough comes from behind a pile of bricks.

I curl my hands into fists. "Come out. Come out and show yourself."

Another cough and a shuffle. My heart careens in my chest as I prepare to dart back across the road. It could be a vagrant, a war veteran. *It could be Emanuel Cleeve.* In his top hat and tails, his pocket watch ticking. The image of him is clear in my head, bright and illuminated. "Emanuel?" I have the sensation I'm about to fall, down and down into a place I cannot come back from.

"Della."

The whispered voice startles and, as he steps out, I immediately see this is neither a vagrant nor Emanuel. My heart slows. "Arthur. What in heaven's name . . ."

"Della? Is everything all right over there?" Mary's call is threaded with concern.

"Yes. Quite all right," I say, turning to wave. "It's a . . . friend. I won't be a moment. You take the boys and the pram around the back."

Arthur is looking at his boots; his green hat pulled to his eyebrows. Even in the dark I can see his cheeks are pinched with cold.

"You should be at home," I say softly.

He scuffs a boot against a plank. "I'm sorry. I couldn't stop thinking about you. Worrying he might come back again."

Reaching out, I touch him lightly on the arm. "It's Christmas Eve, Arthur. You should be at home with your family. Not watching my house. My family is here . . . and I can take care of myself."

The boy looks up. "I saw that delivery van earlier. A crib, wasn't it? Was it . . . from him?"

"You've been here all this time?" I say in dismay, the air misting between us.

He nods.

"Yes, it was a crib but delivered to the wrong address. I'll put it right after Christmas." The newspaper notice nestling inside, that was no mistake. That was intentional. Placed there for me to find, but I can't share that information with Arthur who clearly thinks himself something of a detective. That will only fire his curiosity further.

"But someone sent it, for the baby. They knew you were looking after a baby," he persists, the whites of his eyes shining.

A horrible thought occurs. The person who knows about my thieving, who's been watching me, just as this boy is hiding and observing me now. *Is Arthur involved?* "Do you . . .

do you know anything about this? If you do, I need you to be truthful."

He blinks. "What do you mean?"

I lift my hands. "The man . . . the delivery of the crib." The photograph led *me* to this boy's family's bookshop, the ledgers in his family's attic. It's led him to my house twice after that.

"No. Of . . . of course . . . not," he stutters. His expression is both honest and wounded.

There's a scuffling sound deeper in the building site. A pair of yellow eyes watch us warily. A fox. It scarpers, its feet pawing through the mud and grass. "Look. I must go inside. It's getting late. Promise me you'll stay away from here."

Arthur gives me a long look. He sniffs, then nods. "I promise."

***

At supper, Mary and William are doing their utmost to lift the boys' mood, but it's clear the incident at church hurt Fred's feelings, and he's studiously ignoring his older brother.

Bertie eventually slinks off to bed early, claiming a sore throat. He won't meet my eye when I say goodnight. Mary fusses, fetches him warm water and honey, worries again that Viola might be passing on the same illness that has infected her own family.

Thankfully, with Bertie upstairs the atmosphere lightens, and Fred asks for the tree decorations. While Mary watches Viola, I take the attic key from the hook by the back door and William and I traipse upstairs with a lamp. The shock of finding the baby's bone caused me to leave behind the gifts

I found for the boys. I must bring these down too and wrap them, place them under the tree.

The air that greets us in the attic is peculiar, scented with the faint tang of something sweet above the rancid smell of dead rodent. "Do you smell that . . . something like apples?"

"I can only smell that darned rat," William replies, looking about. I forewarned him of the animal, and he's come prepared, brought an old cloth and a tin pail to help dispose of it.

The lamp in my hand flares over the fairground horse, barbs of light causing its flank and hooves to glitter. Its eyes seem to follow me as I retrace my steps to the rodent, to the pile of sinewy, rotting flesh. All traces of what I thought I smelt are extinguished and I fight the urge to retreat to the warmth of the drawing room and Viola.

William makes swift work disposing of the rat. Wrapping it in the cloth, he places the bundle in the pail. "Rat poison. That's what you need." He wipes his hands on his trousers with disgust, picks up the pail and hurries downstairs with it.

While I wait for him to return, my eyes are drawn to the rafter and the bone's hiding place. I sweep to one side the remains of the lamp shade which shattered when I fell from the trunk. Thoughts run through my head again of why that child's femur was up here. *And who it belonged to.* Staring hard at Emanuel's carved initials I think of the parish register still hidden under the pram mattress, and what it might reveal about this man.

William returns. His eyes also flick to the carved initials as he lifts down the decorations, clutching the crate to his chest. "That's curious." He stretches his neck a little, peers into the space behind the rafter as if half-expecting to find something hidden.

I look to the items belonging to Theo on this attic shelf – household tools and such like. For William to notice the initials has me thinking it's likely my husband would have seen them while up here too.

William eyes the toys in my arms as we retreat from the attic, and I lock up. "Are you certain you don't want to keep those? Don't they hold sentimental value?"

My stomach twists. "I'll have no children to pass them on to. It's better they go to your boys."

William pauses halfway down the stairs ahead of me, turns. "What about him living at the end of the garden? Will he mind?"

I shake my head. "He's not interested . . . and everything in this house belongs to me. I'm free to do with it as I please."

Continuing on behind my brother-in-law, I see him glance up at the chandelier hanging from the second-floor landing. "This is a lovely place, although rather large for just you alone." He coughs, adjusts the weight of the crate and waits for me. "Do you think you'll ever . . . sell the house on, perhaps? If you ever did, I would . . ." William's eyes dip, as if embarrassed then. "I'm sorry. That was inappropriate."

"You would want to . . . purchase this place?"

His jaw ticks. "Well . . . it's just that Mary . . . she likes the house. Speaks fondly of it and I know she'd like to move closer to you . . ."

"My sister would like to live in *this* house?"

William's cheeks spot with colour. "Only if you found

somewhere you preferred to live."

"But I haven't," I retort.

He shifts position. "I see that. It's just that this house is so big for you alone . . . and the boys seem comfortable here. We enjoy Cambridge and good schools are plentiful. Please . . . forget I mentioned it."

Uncertainty bristles across my shoulders. "Has Mary asked you to approach me about selling?"

William looks remorseful, and more than a little desperate. "No, she hasn't." His laugh is short. "I've made rather a hash of this, haven't I? But if you ever do decide to move on . . ."

"I'll let you know," I cut in.

William nods, runs his tongue over his teeth as he glances at Theo's study, then carries on downstairs, leaving the last part of his sentence hanging between us.

***

Mary and I spend much of the remainder of the evening in the kitchen, studding the ham with cloves, then placing it on a shelf in the larder. Peeling potatoes and carrots and storing them in copper pots ready for boiling and roasting tomorrow.

Whenever my sister casts her eyes over Viola in her drawer bed she clicks her tongue. I ignore her disapproval. Viola will sleep like a princess tonight in her pretty crib.

While Mary is busy at the sink, I nip into the larder under the pretence of fetching the lard, take a sip or two from the bottle of tonic I've wedged behind the tub of flour. My stomach warms and my limbs loosen. Rabbit stands at the door watching, tongue lolling.

After we've finished washing and drying the supper dishes,

Mary yawns, wipes her hands on a cloth and looks at the clock. "It's after ten. There's no more we can do until tomorrow."

She has tidied and cleaned all evening; the kitchen is gleaming, and Agnes would approve. Some of the anger I felt at Mary meddling in my affairs has faded, as is often the way. I take my sister's hand, look at her short nails which are the mirror image of mine, and our mother's. "Thank you. I'm glad you are here." We smile at one another.

"I am glad to be here with you too. Although . . ." Mary begins.

"Although what?" I press.

Releasing my hand, she pulls out a chair and sits at the table, gestures for me to do the same. When we are sitting opposite one another, she pulls in a breath. "Bertie said . . . you had cross words with him on the way back from church this afternoon."

I reach across and tuck in Viola's blanket. "He treats Freddie terribly. Shows little respect for you and William."

Mary splays her palms flat on the wood, leans in. "You told him he'll go to hell for pinching his brother."

"Mary . . ."

My sister's gaze is steely. "Bertie's only thirteen. You were too harsh on him."

Heat rises. At Bertie and his insolence, and Mary and William's inability to recognise his nature and deal with the situation. "Maybe it's you who should be harsher. Maybe then he wouldn't pinch his brother and make him cry. He has all the makings of a bully."

Mary sits back in her chair, her jaw slack. "You think I don't know how to raise my own child?"

I shake my head. "If he were mine . . ."

Mary barks out a laugh. "But he's not yours. And this baby lying on the table before us isn't yours either. You shouldn't be purchasing fancy cribs, pretending this child is something it isn't."

Her words further fan the flames of my rage, and I curl my shaking hands into fists on my lap.

"You've changed, Della." These words are quiet and soft, shot through with sadness.

"Yes. Perhaps I have," I snap.

My sister's face contorts. I know this look well and that tears will soon follow.

"I feel like you are far away . . . somewhere else. Living in the past. Look at you . . . your clothes are out of fashion. You take little care of your appearance. I don't know you in the way I used to." She pulls her handkerchief from her pocket, twists it between her fingers which are pink and chapped from all the peeling and preparing. "Bertie also said . . . he saw you inside the church. Why did you lie about feeling sick?"

"He's the one who's lying," I counter. I imagine climbing the stairs and hurtling into the room Bertie is sharing with Fred tonight. Telling him exactly what I think of him. I will not give him the train set tomorrow, I think meanly. I will not. *Smother these horrid thoughts, stamp on them.*

Mary's lips pinch. "I think it's best if I go to bed. It's been a long day."

When my sister was a child, she would clatter up and down the stairs at home, was often reprimanded for it by our parents.

Now my sister's feet thud wearily up to bed, and I ache for those past moments, when things were simpler and carefree, when there was not so much space between us. When I was a better person than the one I am now.

***

Viola sleeps peacefully in her new crib. Her face is free of creases and worry, as if she has let out a long sigh. She's safe and content under these soft new sheets and blankets, with my family sleeping on the floor below. The house seems more settled with them in it, as if it has been longing for a larger family.

Maybe I should think on this. Find a small cottage somewhere, by a river or a babbling brook. Somewhere peaceful. Then the newspaper notice and its warning crashes back into my thoughts.

Poor Rabbit has missed his evening walks for the last few nights, and so have I. My body thrums with a hidden energy as I stride several times around the dark garden, the dog contentedly sniffing at the vegetable beds. Then I turn to the outhouse to retrieve the parish register hidden in the pram.

Emerging from the outhouse, I see a light on in the groom's lodgings. I've reminded Mary, William and the boys about the noises they may hear in the night, said that they should not concern themselves with his screams.

Whistling for Rabbit, he ambles back to my side. We return to the house, the dog nudging against my boots. Looking up, I see the twitch of the drapes in the guest room on the first floor. William peering out into the dark. Half turning to conceal the register, I watch him stare at me for a long moment, then he loosens the drapes and is gone.

***

Newnham is not a large parish, and I'm glad about that as I sit in bed turning the pages of the register of baptisms, marriages and funerals. The book is separated into three parts, reflecting the order of our brief lives.

I think of what I already know.

That the photograph of Emanuel Cleeve was taken in 1852.

If he were around thirty years of age then, he would have been around fifty when Theo's parents purchased Arcadia House in 1870.

Picking up the child's bone from where it rests beside me, I turn it over in my hands. Will I find the answers to this in the register? Fear ties a knot around my neck.

I begin with baptisms, search for the baby concealed within the carriage in the photograph. Running a finger down the pages, I skim the entries. There is no Cleeve listed in 1848, or in the year after that. But halfway along the next page I note an entry that causes me to pause.

Surname: Cleeve.

Parents' name: Emanuel and Sophia.

Child's name: Viola.

Date of baptism: Twenty-third of May, 1851.

Their abode is listed as Newnham and Emanuel's profession is listed as banker.

Viola was the name of Emanuel's daughter. She lived here, in this house. My eyes flicker to the bone again and I swallow. Was this man's grief the reason it was hidden behind his carved initials? A fragment of his child he was unwilling to let go? The thought is both morbid and horrifying.

I barely breathe as I turn to the latter pages of the register, to the lists of funerals. As I study this section, my eyes are unable to keep pace with my galloping thoughts. As the pages turn, as years are left behind, my tension eases. There's no sign Viola died as a child in this parish. Or as a young woman. And then . . . the year of the entry is 1870. There is Emanuel again, his age now fifty. The date of the man's death was the thirty-first of December. *New Year's Eve.*

Spots dance in front of my eyes. I close the register and push it away, thinking of the notice for the newspaper that arrived in the crib. *The declaration that I will be arrested for murder on that very same date.*

Chapter 20

My uneasy sleep is punctured by screams. I rub my eyes, reach for the crib which I've moved to the side of the bed. But then I realise the baby is quiet, still sleeping deeply after her last feed, the empty bottle resting on the bedside table. The screeches are coming from downstairs. There are barks coming from the garden too – Rabbit's barks.

Flinging back the bed covers, I shrug on my dressing gown and bolt for the door. Mary is already coming up the stairs, her hair net askew, face drawn and pale in the shadows. "What's happening . . . what is that dreadful noise outside?"

My nerves jangle. "Are the boys all right?"

"Yes. In bed but awake."

"Fetch William," I call, running past her, and downstairs. At the threshold to the kitchen, I am speechless at the scene before me. The back door is open wide, the air icy. A fox stands by the larder door, chewing on the Christmas ham. Meat and cloves are flayed across the tiles, the empty pan on its side.

"Get out! Get out!" My voice is shrill and breathless, and I sense William alongside me. He pushes past and into the kitchen. The fox gives him a brazen look, then with the ham clamped between its jaws it trots out of the back door as if it's been here by my invitation.

Rabbit's barks from the garden are insistent, and I'm filled with a gut churning terror for the dog. Did this fox attack him?

I stumble into the kitchen after William who is now standing by the back door beating two copper pots together. They clang-clang-clang a warning into the dark.

My bare feet slip on the strips of meat, cloves stabbing my soles as I run outside and into the night. "Rabbit! Rabbit!"

There is no sign of the fox, but the dog still barks from down the garden. My feet sink into the damp grass, and I ignore William's calls to return. I find the dog cowering under the oak tree. He's shivering, his tail and ears flat. Dropping to my knees, my nightdress and gown flare about me, the damp quickly soaking through the fabric to my skin. "Come on, dear thing. The fox is gone. Come here."

Rabbit's eyes are bright as beads as he approaches, and I gather the dog onto my lap. He whines, smells of the garden and alarm. Trembling and panting, his paws streak my nightclothes with mud.

William places a hand on my shoulder. "Della, come on inside. You'll catch a chill."

Another voice then, croaked and unused. "Della."

I look up, see him standing there. The oil lamp in his right hand illuminates the blade of the knife in his left. His fingers hold it tightly, his knuckles white.

William quickly pulls me to my feet, places a protective arm around my middle, his eyes flickering to his face, the knife. "Steady there, old chap."

He throws a dull glance at his hand, his eyes widening as if surprised to see the silver-tipped weapon there.

"A fox. In the kitchen. It ate the Christmas ham," I gabble.

"I thought it had attacked Rabbit."

The look he gives the dog in my arms is one of affection. Rabbit wriggles and I wonder if he wants to go to him, whether his familiar scent is compelling the dog to draw near.

"We should go inside," mutters William, throwing an anxious glance to the house where I see Mary's taut form illuminated in the doorway.

A touch on my arm, and he passes me a handkerchief. It's soft and greying, clean. Then he turns on his heel and strides back to the groom's lodgings.

William's grip on me is firm as we walk back along the garden.

***

After the boys are reassured and settled in bed, Mary, William and I sit at the kitchen table nursing cups of sweet tea.

"I don't understand how the fox got in," William says again. Steam from his tea dampens his moustache, tiny beads of moisture clinging. "You are certain the door was closed and locked when you went to bed?"

I stare at the whorl of hair on top of Viola's head as I cradle her, thinking hard. I'd gone to fetch the parish register from the pram, was certain I'd closed the back door. But is it possible I forgot to lock and bolt it in my haze of tiredness? The last thing I remember is seeing William watching me in the garden from the guestroom upstairs. Perhaps I did forget. It would not be the first time I've thought to have completed a task, when I have not.

"Even if Della did forget to lock the door, how did that fox get in?" Mary is ashen faced, gripping her cup with both hands.

"Foxes and dogs have paws. They cannot turn door handles."

"I don't know. I don't know." My voice is limp as a dishrag. I've no answers to these questions, but I do have questions of my own. My sister is right; Rabbit or the fox could not open a door or take the ham from the larder shelf. Bertie, then? He's angry with me after yesterday, may have been looking for a small and petty way to get back at me. *I must keep this thought to myself though; no good would come of mentioning it now.*

"We've no ham, nothing to eat on Christmas!" declares Mary, her cup clattering on its saucer. She presses her fingers to her wan cheeks.

William gives her a lopsided smile. "We will make do."

"With just vegetables?" she quips.

My brother-in-law yawns, wipes his hands across his face. "Bread and jam and a helping of roasted potatoes. The boys will be delighted."

***

The house settles into a slumber again, but my brain is too consumed by thoughts to sleep, slipping from one to another like a fast-flowing stream. I linger in the kitchen, stoke the stove to ward off the last of the chill, change Viola's nappy, comb every inch of Rabbit's fur for a fox bite.

Emanuel Cleeve lived in this house and drew his final breath on a day it's said I will commit murder. I'm being tormented by someone. These are not the actions of one of Agnes's ghosts. A living, breathing person went to great lengths to manufacture a costume to make them appear the spitting image of Emanuel in the photograph, then enter my house. And for a reason I still cannot comprehend, leave a baby.

Arcadia House connects us but holds its secrets close. Just like Theo. I think of my husband's private meetings with the solicitor, his mysterious disappearances and lies. The threads of all these unknown connections dance about, frustratingly out of reach.

Theo's study was his domain. A place of work and refuge he would retire to every evening. It was a place I wasn't welcome in our final week's together and so I had no qualms about shutting the door to the room after he died, drawing a veil over that terrible time. Yet now I'm regretting that I didn't find an inner strength to poke and pry amongst his private things, dig around for answers to his secrets. Could there be something in Theo's study about Arcadia House that will help explain all this?

Dawn finally breaks and Fred appears at the kitchen door, sleepy eyed. I busy myself making plates of buttered toast and jam, listen to his excited chatter about the watercolour paint set he hopes is waiting for him beneath the tree upstairs.

Then Bertie arrives, his brown hair at right angles and his face sullen. He slinks over to the stove and pets Rabbit. While making mugs of cocoa, I explain again about the fox and having no ham for lunch and watch Bertie's face for any sign of guilt, that he is responsible for opening the back door, taking the ham from the larder. But he doesn't even seem to be listening as he rolls the cricket ball across the tiles. He encourages the dog to try and retrieve it again and again, even though each time he fails.

After the boys have eaten, I settle Fred with some drawing paper and pencils at the table, while Bertie curls up in the armchair by the stove with his book.

I pick up Viola. "You two will be all right down here alone? I must go and get dressed."

Fred nods but Bertie is silent, lowers his head. Unhappiness flows off the boy in waves. Crouching beside the chair with the baby's head cradled against my shoulder, I lightly touch his arm. "I am sorry if I upset you yesterday."

His Adam's apple bobs in his throat, but still he says nothing. I remember holding him as a baby. Time would slow as I studied his delicate features, wondering whether I would see them echoed in any future child of mine. Even back then, before Theo, the yearning was strong.

"Bertie? Please look at me." His gaze is inscrutable, and I place a hand on the chair, willing him to let me in. He carefully rearranges his limbs until he is angled away from me. Standing up, I see there is nothing to be achieved by pursuing this conversation.

***

Settling the baby for a nap in her crib, I half pull back the drapes in my bedroom, am confronted by a day of grey, low light. There's not even a frost or a sniff of snow this year. The garden is quiet, no sign of him this morning, or the wretched fox.

Hearing the murmur of my sister's voice in the bedroom below as she talks to William, I quickly wash and dress, then go downstairs to Theo's study, pulling the door almost closed behind me. Where to begin looking for answers? The desk, I suppose.

Sitting in his chair, I push the broken picture frame

and Arthur's butterfly book to one side, then pull out each of the four drawers and examine the contents. Household bills, bundles of notes for his research papers. A compass, paper clips and book receipts. Pens and pencils, his ink pot.

I turn my attention to the bookshelf; the periodicals and journals carefully filed in order. Pulling out the box files, I riffle through them. I eventually find the house deeds, but they reveal nothing unexpected.

I think back to my visit to the solicitor's office in town for the reading of Theo's will. Mary accompanied me, commented on how fortunate it was that women could now inherit property from their husbands.

But all the while we sat there in the office that smelt of coffee and cigars, I could not help worrying that Mary was in for an awful shock. That Theo had left his possessions to someone else. An 'other' whom he cared for more than me.

It was a natural conclusion I suppose, for what causes a husband to lie to his wife about his comings and goings? From the novels I'd occasionally read it always seemed to hark back to money or another woman.

My foot tap-tap-tapped on the linoleum floor as I watched the solicitor's eyebrows furrow as he read the document. But it was simple. Everything had been left to me. The house and the entirety of its contents.

Mary patted my hand and smiled, pleased at my good fortune.

I recall turning to look out of the window to the street below, watching the blur of bicycles go past. Yes, I was fortunate, but there was no getting away from the fact our marriage had disintegrated. It was natural to wonder if this was because my husband had found someone else, especially as I'd failed to provide him with a child. I'm also fully aware that men have needs, urges. Theo never once pressured me to lie with him . . . but I occasionally wish he'd cajoled me into it more often. Perhaps that would have helped mend things.

If he was having a liaison, had taken a lover, did that woman know Theo was dead? Had he written to her, as he'd written to me from France? His letters were always scant but factual, an echo of the man he was. Always signed with fondest love though. I remember ripping up the first letter he sent, tossing it into the fire. Wishing he'd not signed off his correspondence with affection. Is this other woman still grieving his death, perhaps wishing for some small token to remember him by? I'd watched for her out of the drawing room window for days. An elegant hat, the sweep of a coat coming up the steps. But she stayed away, or perhaps she doesn't exist at all.

A tentative knock at the study door pushes the memories aside. Fred looks in. He's holding a drawing which I assume to be of Rabbit. "Do you like it?" he asks shyly.

I gesture for him to come inside, and he places it on the desk before me. "It's marvellous, darling."

He looks about. "What are you doing?"

"I'm looking through some of your Uncle Theo's things."

Fred walks over to a display cabinet, stands on tip toes to study the contents. "Why?"

"I . . . well, I suppose I'm having a tidy up."

"I like this blue butterfly! Mother says you don't want to clear anything out, but you should."

"I see," I say with a small smile. "I suppose your mother is right."

Turning my attention back to the picture of the dog, I feel a tightness under my ribs that a child of my own will never draw for me like this. I would have treasured each offering, kept every single one. Mary barely pays Fred's pictures any attention, only keeps the best while the others line crates of fruit in their garden shed.

Fred's sudden exclamation is sharp. I spring to my feet, see him stumbling backwards from the second display cabinet.

"What is it? What's the matter?" I say, taking his hand in mine.

He points. "It came alive. It came back alive."

It's then I hear the fluttering, whisper light and persistent. Still gripping Fred's hand, I draw us closer. A fat brown moth, wings beating against the glass. It is mesmerising.

Fred twists from my grasp, and I hear him run from the room excitedly calling for his mother.

Footsteps thudding, a garbled conversation between Mary and Fred on the landing. I sense these things, but all I am capable of is studying the moth, its body vibrating as it seeks a way to flee the cabinet. Then my sister is standing beside me peering through the glass, her eyes as wide as moons. After what could be a minute but might only be seconds, she turns to me. "Did you do this?" Her voice is low.

Her voice brings me back into myself and to this room, which is suddenly too cold, filled with a strange pressure that pushes down on my scalp. I moisten my lips, give a brief shake of my head.

"It's alive, Della. This is a cabinet of dead moths, yet this one is alive," Mary hisses.

The moth's wings are frantic.

I reach for the lid. "We must let it out."

Mary places a hand on my arm. Her fingers are tense, knuckles white. "First the fox and now this. I don't know what's happening, but I don't like it. Neither do the boys. They heard noises last night before the fox incident. Creaks. Footsteps. Someone walking about the house after you'd fed the baby. Was that you?"

"No!" I answer truthfully. "I settled Viola and then went to bed."

My sister's gaze is probing and like the swirl of a paintbrush in water, I feel some of my resolve at keeping my secrets fade. I swallow. "Things occasionally happen in this house. Things I can't always account for."

Mary frowns. "Such as?"

I tell her then about the pictures on the wall rearranging themselves and the one that fell. The wedding photograph that flew along my hallway and smashed. The thuds and bumps I sometimes hear in the walls. What Theo's father said about this house being alive.

Mary shakes her head, fiddles with the string of pearls around her neck. "What you are telling me now. How do you explain it?"

Placing my palms flat on the glass, I shield the moth from the light to try and calm it. "I . . . I can't." My throat constricts. *Theo was wrong. Not everything can be explained.*

Mary pulls in a breath. She leans in close, conspiratorially.

It reminds me of when we were small and had a secret only the two of us were privy to, taking an extra piece of fudge from the tin, or staying out too late in the woods making paper boats to float in the stream. "What about him? William said last night in the garden he had a knife . . ."

I think of that blade, how easily it could slice into flesh. I stamp on the thought. "No. I refuse to believe that. This isn't the work of *him.*"

My sister looks doubtful as I ease up the lid of the cabinet, guide the moth into my cupped palms. Upon closer examination I understand what species it is at once. It's the one that brought Theo and I together on that fateful day at the printing press. *Lymantria dispar* – a gypsy moth. A moth which destroys lives, decimates apple trees and crops. A species that does not even reside in this country. *Another impossibility.* It flutters softly against my skin like a distant heartbeat.

Mary opens the window, cool air rushing in to greet us. I release the creature as my sister stands watching in silence. It settles on the ledge, as if wanting to retreat back inside.

A whisper of a voice then. *"It will die in the cold, Della."*

I turn swiftly, stare in the direction of Theo's voice. But the only person here in the room besides me is Mary. My sister gives me a long and considered stare, then leaves the study, while I continue to stand at the window watching the moth which still refuses to fly away.

Chapter 21

"Anyone for another potato?" asks William at lunch. The mirth in his voice is forced, and I notice Mary glance at him, an eyebrow arching as she pushes a carrot around her plate with a fork. Her eyes flicker away to the window and the garden beyond. She's watching for him, and I hope he doesn't show himself. My sister's thoughts on the matter are clear, that I've been too kind and accommodating. *Perhaps I haven't been kind enough.*

Viola will not stop crying as I hold her to my chest. Breathy, jagged wails which catch in her throat, her head bumping against my collar bone. Picking up my wine glass, I take a sip, enjoy the warmth as it slips down. When only the dregs remain, I ask William if he'll pour me another glass from the decanter.

Now it is my turn to be on the receiving end of my sister's shrewd gaze. "That is your second glass."

"And what of it?" I reply stiffly. "William has had three, and a sherry before lunch."

My sister shakes her head in poorly concealed irritation, and it makes me want to put the rim of the glass decanter to my lips and drain the whole lot in front of her. Closing my eyes for a second, I take a deep breath. *I must try harder to be pleasant.*

"May I play with the bat and ball in the garden after lunch?" asks Fred, seemingly unaware of the tension between us.

"No." William and Mary speak in unison, and I recall the conversation I'd overhead this morning after gifts had been exchanged and opened in the drawing room.

Mary and William were talking in hushed tones in the hallway, and I'd lingered by the door, quietly eavesdropping while the boys set up Theo's old train set on the carpet. Bertie was pleased with his gift, even gave me a small smile of thanks. I think, and hope, the bad feeling between us is thawing.

It was clear from Mary and William's conversation however, that *our* relationship was taking a turn for the worse.

"This baby she's caring for, then the back door being left open and the fox getting in. A live moth appearing in Theo's cabinet. Something peculiar is happening here, William," said Mary.

"Hmmm. I admit Della doesn't seem herself," mumbled my brother-in-law.

"Yes, but this is different. I think . . . I think my sister might be turning to alternative methods to . . . soothe herself."

"Such as?"

"Isn't it obvious? Liquor, of course!"

Silence from William then and my nails bit into my palms.

My sister cleared her throat. "Anyhow, whether she's turning to drink or not, I'm worried for the boys. Della didn't recall wandering about the house last night, but Bertie's certain he heard someone. Is it him from the bottom of the garden, letting himself in and causing mischief?"

"Della says not. The fellow doesn't have a key," said William.

"He has a knife though."

"Mary . . . I . . ."

"It's not safe here, William," hissed my sister.

Hearing her voice a truth I also felt constricted my throat into a knot.

There was a tug on my sleeve then. "Aunt Della, a piece of the train track is twisted. Please can you help straighten it?"

"Of course, Fred." As I sat pressing and straightening the track into the carpet, I knew one thing for certain: I did not want to be here alone in the house with Viola in the days leading up to New Year. I had to do everything to make my family want to stay.

"I can take Fred into the garden," I say now, as we sit at the table with its empty platters of bread and roasted vegetables. "It's perfectly safe. William can come with us. The baby also needs air, so she'll sleep better later."

Mary's fork clatters on her plate as she places it down. "You're still speaking as if Viola's yours."

"Mary," says William. His voice is a warning.

"Not mine, but I'm caring for her as well as if she were," I reply mildly.

"I like the baby," says Fred, sopping up the gravy from his plate with the remains of his bread. "Will she be here when we come and visit next time?"

"No. She will not." The words expel from my sister's lips as quickly as if she's snuffing out a candle.

***

Rather than letting Fred play in the garden after lunch, Mary and William take him for a walk and Bertie retreats upstairs with his book.

With Viola settled in the crib, I quietly pace my bedroom, pain knocking at the base of my skull. I think about the noises my nephews heard in the house last night, and the moth that somehow found its way into Theo's display cabinet. The fox and the ham. Was it my footsteps Bertie heard echoing through the house? But Theo's voice . . . I heard it as clear as day in the study. And before when Arthur was here.

I rub at my ears, pull and tug at the lobes. A high-pitched ringing makes me feel off balance, as if the room is on a tilt. A sob of quick terror rises in my throat. *There is no such thing as ghosts.*

Pausing in front of the crib I watch the rise and fall of the baby's stomach, gently place a palm on her blanket and anchor myself to the present. Time moves differently when I'm with her, seconds, minutes and hours easily lost in the small moments we share. A fierceness rises in my gullet at the thought of the murder notice. I would never harm this baby, would rather die than that.

While Viola rests, I decide to distract myself by tidying away the lunch things, determined to prove to my sister that I'm a good hostess, that my home is a place of calm and order rather than fear and chaos. Somewhere they would welcome staying on for a few extra days. But stepping into the kitchen, I find Bertie facing the dresser, his shoulders hunched. I drag in an unsteady breath when I see the open drawer. "What . . . what are you doing?"

He whips around at the sound of my voice, cheeks flaming. In one hand is my leatherbound book, in the other a spool of stolen thread and the pot rouge. "I . . ."

"Put those things back." Fury steams inside my head as I stride across and take the book. Snapping it closed, I shake it at him. "You read this, looked inside?"

Eyes lowering to the floor, he nods.

My book of stolen things – that title boldly scrawled at the top of the first page. Small sketches of the items I've taken, dates and places too. Proof of my bravery, and my stupidity. Proof that a person can have a purpose even when considered invisible. "Don't you ever tell anyone about this. Ever." The boy's eyes widen at the malice in my voice. "If you tell anyone, Bertie . . . bad things will happen."

He sucks on his bottom lip. "To me?"

"Perhaps." My heart canters, and sparks flicker at the edge of my vision. How foolish I've been to leave these items hidden down here.

Bertie shuffles away to the stove; the walk of the guilty. Rabbit sits on his haunches watching, ears flat. The boy looks over his shoulder. His expression is sly. "There was . . . a picture of the baby in the book. Did you steal her too?"

Outside a bird calls, the wind whistles and tugs at the window frame. I let these sounds fill my mind, steady my breathing. He's wrong. The only drawing of the baby is in my sketchpad and that's upstairs in my bedroom.

Leafing through the pages of the book, my eyes sting as I take in the final drawing. There is Viola, alongside the date she arrived in this house. *A stolen thing after all?* The pencil work is clumsy, but it was clearly done by me. And yet . . . when? A memory flitters back. *The night I woke up standing at the kitchen table, my fingers smudged grey with pencil lead.*

Taking a string bag from the larder door, my hands tremble as I remove my stolen things from the drawer and stuff them inside. The pot rouge, the paint, thread, tweezers, Arthur's teaspoon and other items too. I place the book on top. "You should go upstairs and wait for your parents to return."

Bertie gives me a long, slow blink, then thankfully does as I ask.

As his feet thud up the treads, I stride over, place a hand on the door jamb and watch his retreating back. "Remember what I said, Bertie."

The front doorbell jangles. My sister is back early.

***

"We've decided to leave today." William's tone is apologetic as he takes off his hat, hooks it on the stand.

Mary is helping Fred out of his coat. "Go and gather your things. We'll be leaving shortly."

The boy scurries off upstairs.

"Now? But it's . . . Christmas Day, and will be dark soon. You have a long drive."

"The new motor eats up the miles. Don't worry about that," says William, forcing a smile.

I take Mary by the arm and lead her into the drawing room. The tree lights twinkle behind her. "I don't understand. You were intending to stay here until the twenty-seventh. I would like you to stay longer than that."

"Our plans have changed. William needs to get back to the factory."

My sister's excuse is weak, and she knows it. I shake my head in dismay, take her hands in mine. "Please stay. Please."

Mary pulls away. She kneels and begins to uncouple the train track, each length coming apart with a loud snap. "I'm sorry, Della. This visit hasn't worked out as we'd hoped. Perhaps you can come and visit soon. It would be nice to see you away from here . . ."

I crouch beside her. "Away from here? What do you mean?"

She looks up at the cornicing, then at the fireplace I laid and lit, flames licking at the coals. "You're more disagreeable, sharper. William sees it too. Perhaps . . . you should take some time away from the house."

I think back to William's words on the landing yesterday, his inquisitive question about my future intentions. "So that you can purchase Arcadia House and live here?" My voice is woven with an icy current, but I can't help it.

My sister winces as she finishes returning the train set to its box. Leaning back on her heels, she picks a spot of lint from her skirt. "William mentioned that?"

I nod.

She sighs. "That was something we intended to talk to you about at a later time. We only have your best intentions at heart."

"If that's the case . . . if you want my house, then why leave? Are you afraid of being here?" My sister's expression tightens, and I know I have struck a nerve.

"It is not the house I am afraid of, Della," she replies quietly.

I know precisely what she means by that, and my stomach churns. "You think him responsible for the things happening here?"

Her shoulders lift. "It's a sensible . . . the only . . . conclusion to make. You shouldn't be living in such close proximity to a man like that. You're too soft on him, too accepting. If we bought the place . . . well, he would have to go."

It's my turn to sigh now. So that is where her interest lies. She wishes to force him from his home. "I made a commitment to him. I won't go back on our agreement. The groom's lodgings are his for as long as he needs them."

Mary clicks her tongue. "He's dangerous!"

I grit my teeth. "Not dangerous, Mary. He was wounded. Badly wounded. He needs . . ."

"He doesn't need *you*. He's made that very clear. Why are you so stubborn about this?"

Why am I so stubborn? It's a jolly good question. Perhaps because I feel a sense of loyalty. That I'm unwilling to give up on him and that I hope one day he seeks out my company. And I shall be here ready and waiting when he does.

"There's something else. We also . . . *I* also . . . feel you should see a doctor," Mary continues.

I leap to my feet, blood rushing to my scalp. "I'm not ill."

Mary shakes her head, lips thinning. "You say that, but Theo's death and your . . . health is affecting you still. Your cheeks are sallow, you've little appetite. I've seen the flushes that cross your skin, the constant itching. There's no shame in seeking help. Liquor is not the answer."

"For goodness' sake, it was just a little wine with lunch,"

I retort hotly. Curving my arms around my middle, I walk to the window and look out. William is by the motor car, checking the engine, wiping condensation from the windshield. He glances up and our eyes meet momentarily. He looks troubled, as if he can well imagine the turn our conversation in here has taken. I pivot, turning my back on him. "I'm perfectly all right, Mary. You're wrong about my drinking habits. Take every bottle of liquor you can find in this house if it makes you feel better. And *I* won't be leaving."

My sister stands, reaches out to me. Her face softens. "Come with us, Della. I could take you to see Doctor Broughton in Ipswich. You can have your own room at ours. I'll bring you breakfast on a tray."

I give her a stiff shake of my head. "I've the baby to look after."

Mary's eyes brim with tears. "She's not your responsibility. You've done a kind and compassionate thing by caring for her, but I fear she's too much for you . . . bringing back memories that are . . . painful and difficult."

Picking at a hangnail, I imagine packing a suitcase and climbing into the motor car with my sister and her family. Locking up Arcadia House and watching it retreat to a pinprick as we drive away. But the secrets here are compelling me to stay. This house is not done with me yet, nor I with it. I force out a smile. "I'm sorry this visit has not turned out well. I will make it up to you."

My sister's back is as straight as a metal rod as she leaves the room.

Chapter 22

The house is too large, too empty without my family. I'm back to sleeping in the chair in the kitchen, a rug over my knees and Viola in her drawer bed on the table. His screams from the end of the garden come at the usual time, and I stare at the back door. My limbs are weak and leaden as I take small sips from a bottle of tonic, thinking of my sister and her concern for me. A gurgle comes from my stomach, and I press a hand to stave off the cramp which I know will follow. I'm in no mood to eat, my appetite vanished like a stone down a well.

There are no scuttles or creaks within the walls of the house tonight, and I feel a vague hope that my sister's visit snuffed them out. I sit quietly, with just the ticking clock, Rabbit's snores and the baby's gurgles and grunts for company. The creamy thigh bone from the attic is warm in my palm. Its curved edges are so familiar now I would know this bone amongst a pile of others. A new parlour game – find the femur and win a prize. I draw in a shaky breath. *I'm descending into madness.* Just like the woman who lived down the street from us when I was a child, Mrs Holway.

Mary and I would sometimes wake in the night to see Mrs Holway meandering down the street in her billowing nightdress, barefoot and weeping. While this ghostly vision, with her long, blonde plaited hair, had Mary running back to her bed, it transfixed me. My hot breath would steam against the windowpane as I watched Mrs Holway's husband beg and plead with her to come home. The woman must have been around my age now but seemed ancient to my younger self.

"She's not well in the head," Mother would say, her lips downturned when I asked her about it.

One autumn day when Mary and I were playing outside, a pony and trap arrived at the Holway's cottage. Mary scrimped an apple to feed the pony, while I stroked its straggly mane.

Mrs Holway was led out by two men, her arms constricted by a peculiar white jacket. Her eyes were dull and listless, her body limp. It was as if her soul had left her body and that caused my breath to hitch in my chest.

"Run along home, children!" a grey faced Mr Holway barked, when he saw us watching.

Mary did as she was told, but curiosity made me linger by the old yew tree. My sister must have told our mother what was happening, for moments later she was alongside me, dragging me back to the house. "What's wrong with her? Why are Mrs Holway's arms tied?" I cried.

Mother's reply was whispered. "Don't fuss, Della. It's just the change. It's badly affected her nerves."

I didn't understand what Mother meant at the time. We never saw Mrs Holway again.

The lamp beside me flickers. Rabbit whines. Viola stirs, arms jerking above her head. It's as if they both hear a sound that my own ears do not. It's claimed I'll commit murder in six days. A new plot needed in a church burial ground. A corpse under the earth, flesh rotting in the soil. A life taken by my hands. Holding my fingers out, I see how they tremble with a will of their own. I curl them into fists. My nerves are shot, just like poor Mrs Holway's. I imagine she lived the rest of her days in an asylum. I begin to cry, wondering if I'll do the same.

Blink the tears away and there is Emanuel Cleeve standing by my back door in his top hat and tails, a mild look upon his face. I leap to my feet, wipe my face with my hands. *It's a figment. He's not real.* In my mind's eye I see shadows gather at his heels. He's beckoning me to accompany him to the churchyard where he now rests. He wants me to kneel before his gravestone, press my fingers into the grooves. *Tick, tick, tick, tick.* Every second, every minute is taking me closer to the truth. My stomach cramps. Weaving around the table to the sink, I lean over and grip the cold porcelain until the dizziness and nausea fades.

***

The burial ground for Newnham parish church is in Grantchester, a pretty village I visited often with Theo. Summer walks through the river meadows, fields of wildflowers and cow parsley that set off in me fits of violent sneezes. There is no chance of that today though as I push the pram along the muddy track, the wheels soon thickening with soil.

The river meanders coldly, two paddling swans beside a naked willow tree the brightest things for miles. I hunch into my scarf and coat, tuck in the baby who drowses despite the jolts and sways as I navigate the ruts.

I greet the other people out for a Boxing Day walk with

pleasant nods, families with young children carrying new balls and hoops, red cheeked and laughing as they skitter about. Viola will be this age one day. There is a sudden pulse of pain in my chest that I may never get to witness it. I watch the baby rather than my surroundings then, drinking in every last delicious drop of her.

Breathless, I eventually enter the village, passing thatched cottages where smoke spirals from chimneys, the post office and the painted wooden sign to the tea gardens where Theo and I sweetened our tea with honey as we sat in the orchard.

The church stands on a bend in the road, the grey chancel and tower at one with the sky. Gravel crunches as I press on through the gate and up the path, pausing for a moment to study the burial ground which wraps around the church. It's quiet, only the sound of a horse and cart on the street, the splutter of a motorbike and the clatter of crows in the bare-branched trees for company.

The gravestones lean towards each other like old friends amid the lumpy grass, and I see there's no hope of pushing the pram through there; I shall have to carry the baby.

Tucking Viola inside my coat, I watch my step as I set off in search of Emanuel's resting place. *Fathers, mothers, sons, daughters.* Reading each headstone, I see locals, fellows and dons from the university mingle here in a way they never would in reality. Death is a great leveller at the end. All that is left of these lives is a stone in the ground, riddled with moss and engravings worn away by the elements.

After ten minutes of wandering, I'm losing all feeling in my toes and my nose drips steadily. Viola grizzles a little, but I carry on weaving my way through the stones, pausing to study each in turn, thinking of the bones that lie beneath my feet. *Just like the femur nestled in my coat pocket.*

Heading past the east window of the church, there are yet more gravestones around the corner. I'm away from the road now, out of sight. Ahead of me a large yew tree stands against the boundary wall, shading the ground below. Beneath it I can just make out three graves, tucked away from all the others. Two are overgrown, but one is well tended and a flash of white on the scrap of grass in front of that headstone draws me over. A posy of white hyacinths bound in twine.

In memory of Emanuel Cleeve, husband of Sophia, who died Dec 1870 aged 50 years.

I bend and reach for the flowers. They're fresh and fragrant, from a hothouse. *Placed here by whom?* As I run a finger over the bulbous petals, I have a feeling of being watched.

The hair on the back of my neck prickles. There's a rustle behind me. Still holding the flowers, I quickly turn. A laurel bush twists in the wind, leaves fluttering. "Arthur?"

There's no reply. I feel sure if the boy had followed me here today, he would make himself known. My breathing steadies: Viola and I are quite alone. A gloomy day, a churchyard, and my imagination. It's not a happy combination.

Turning my attention back to the flowers, my fingers dance over the stems, are careful in their selection. The one I choose is more wilted than most, won't be missed. I slip it into my coat pocket, a clue of something yet to be discovered.

I wind my way back through the headstones, glancing over my shoulder every now and again, still unable to shake the feeling I'm being observed. Settling Viola in her pram, I see a man walking towards me from the church, a flash of white at his collar, a large key in his hand. The reverend, a man I don't recognise from the times I've visited this church before.

"Good morning," he says, tipping his hat. "I saw you from the porch. I must say, I didn't expect to see anybody else here today."

I gesture at the pram. "We both needed a long walk . . . after all the festivities."

The reverend pats his stomach. "Yes, it was a rather overindulgent day yesterday."

I think of our carrots, potatoes and bread: not the meal he feasted on, I'm sure.

His eyes stray to the imprints my boots have made across the damp grass. "You came to pay your respects?"

"Well, yes. I suppose you could say that," I say, thinking quickly as I smooth Viola's blanket. "I've been looking into a distant relative. There's a gravestone under a yew just past the east window . . . a posy of flowers on it."

The reverend smiles. "Ah, yes. Mr Cleeve. His daughter visits religiously."

My pulse floods my ears. "His . . . daughter? Viola?"

"Yes. Miss Viola Cleeve. A wonderful woman."

"Oh!" Surprise gives my voice a shrill edge. I swallow. "I would very much like to speak with her. Do you . . ."

"Goodness," he cuts in, his brows lifting. "She's not . . . is she the relation you're looking for?"

I press a hand to my chest. "Yes, I believe so." I hope

that my thoughts on God are right and that lying to this reverend doesn't mean eternal damnation.

The reverend clasps his hands together. "Well, this is quite marvellous. What a happy chance encounter this is. Your name is . . ."

"Mrs Pemberton. Della Pemberton."

"Well, Mrs Pemberton. It would be a pleasure to escort you to Miss Cleeve's cottage."

My cheeks are tight and flaming. "She lives here in this village?"

"The white cottage – a thatched place. You must have passed it on your walk in."

Viola has been living only a few miles from Arcadia House. My head swims as I recall all the occasions I've walked here, past her cottage, unaware of our connection and the reasons that would one day bring me to her door.

Chapter 23

We stand outside Mulberry Cottage waiting for the reverend's raps on the brass door knocker to be answered. As we walked here, I had to think on my feet as I fielded his endless questions, told him Viola Cleeve was a distant relation of my husband. That the war had prompted us to seek out relatives he'd lost touch with as a boy.

The reverend listened soberly as I spoke, commenting that the only positive thing about the war was the way it was bringing some fractured families back together again.

The person coming to the door is slow on their feet, and I stand with the baby, the pram parked at the gate. The door opens to a woman wearing wide legged navy slacks, a russet-coloured jumper, and a thick gold chain around her neck. Her grey hair is pinned stylishly, loose strands framing her lined cheeks, and a shimmer of rouge lifts her complexion.

"Can I help you?" Her tone is soft and inquisitive, and the reverend babbles out my lies. I introduce myself, and when her eyes settle on the baby, it's then I admit her name.

Viola Cleeve's laugh is like a warm burst of sunshine on this bitter day. "What a remarkable coincidence. You must come in, tell me everything."

I bite my lip, glance down at the baby who is becoming

fractious. "I've been out walking for a while. She needs feeding again."

"Do you have infant milk with you?" she enquires.

"Well, yes, in the pram but . . ."

"That's settled then. In you come."

***

Viola Cleeve's cottage is as comfortable as her clothing, as welcoming as her smile. In the small low-ceilinged living room printed scarves hang from lamps, while shelves of books line the crooked walls. An ageing black Labrador lies in front of the orange glow of a wood stove. The dog slaps a tail on the rug as we walk in but doesn't get up to greet us.

"Don't mind Dara. He's very old and lets out the most tremendous trumps. I'll open the window should that happen."

"I have a terrier. He's called Rabbit."

Viola Cleeve flashes me a smile and I feel the tension in my shoulders easing. "I'm always suspicious of people who don't own a dog. Now sit! I will make us some tea and warm this bottle of milk. You can feed your baby and tell me how we might be related."

The baby sucks on my knuckles as we wait on the sofa, dribble running down my wrist and soaking my blouse cuff. I found this woman by concocting a lie, but how much of the truth should I entrust her with? I rake my nails over my sleeve. The wood in the stove crackles and spits, and my head is heavy with indecision.

Elderly Viola soon returns with a tea tray, a knitted multicoloured cosy warming the pot. "You made that?" I ask, accepting the baby's glass bottle and testing the temperature of the milk on my wrist.

"I'm a great believer in keeping my hands busy. Knitting, gardening, reading, flower arranging. My father used to say idle hands makes an idle person."

I look up. "It's your father, Emanuel, I'm here about."

The woman sits on the armchair opposite, gives me an expectant look. "Go on."

"I believe he lived in Arcadia House which is where . . . we live now."

She makes a face as she sips her tea. "Arcadia House. It's long time since I heard that name."

"Is it true, then? Your family did live there?"

"Yes. My father had the house designed and built. We lived there until he died." She shakes her head, lips thinning. "It wasn't a happy time towards the end."

Baby Viola rests her hand on mine, as if assuring me that my probing questions will be well received. "Would you mind . . . talking about what happened?"

Her eyes settle on me, her look knowing. "I can see what the reverend said about me being a distant relation of your husband wasn't the entire truth, then?"

"No," I admit. "It's your family's connection to the house which brought me here." I like this woman, want her to find me agreeable too. This means I can't entrust her with the truth that I'm looking after this baby left in my house by a man posing as her dead father. But I can press her on the things I found in the attic, so I tell her about Emanuel's initials carved into the rafter, the baby's thigh bone hidden in a handkerchief.

Elderly Viola's eyes widen, and she sits forwards. "A bone. How morbid . . . and curious."

I nod, not admitting my strange attachment to it. "Do you know . . . who it may have belonged to. Why it might have been hidden?"

"I can't believe that was my father's doing." Her expression changes, becomes softer. "Although he was an ill man towards the end, in a depressive state. He made poor investments you see, lost a lot of money. He would disappear for hours at a time, often into that attic. Do you know he had that place built for me? A space I could play. I never much liked it though. It became his domain."

I nod and my thoughts drift as I consider all the items belonging to Theo's family still stored up in the attic. The weight of other people's lives and choices pressing down on me as I lie in my bedroom below.

"My father said the cool and the dark at the top of the house helped settle his nerves. Except one day, he went up there and never came back down."

She looks stricken, and I feel a ripple of guilt that my being here is making her confront these unhappy memories. The baby dribbles milky vomit and I wipe her mouth with my handkerchief, wait for the woman to continue.

"My mother found him in the attic. Next to a bottle of rat poison."

"Poison," I echo. Dread tingles my fingertips.

She shakes her head. "He was allowed a burial, but Mother never got over it, insisted we sell the house. We moved here, to Grantchester. But a year later, my mother suffered from a bad bout of pneumonia. Then it was just me."

I place the baby's bottle on the table beside the tea tray. "I'm so sorry for your losses." *Emanuel, dead in my attic from rat poison.* I think of the hideous creature I found behind the trunk up there and bite the inside of my cheek.

"Sometimes I wonder . . . if she had a hand in it, you know." The woman's voice is tart, as if she's sucking on a jellied lemon sweet.

"Excuse me?"

Viola Cleeve turns to look out of the lead-paned window. "My mother. I sometimes wonder if she coaxed my father into taking his own life. She was so bitter at his lost investments; at the downward turn our life had taken."

My stomach knots. Theo never once mentioned any of this, and I wonder if he was aware of the terrible circumstances under which his father had purchased Arcadia House from the Cleeve family.

A bump and a scrabbling sound, from another part of the house. Similar to the noises I hear in Arcadia House at night. I stare at the door leading to the hallway.

"That'll be Dara wanting to be let out," the woman says. She gives me a curious look but doesn't question my jumpiness.

I hadn't noticed the dog has gone from its position by the stove, disappeared from the room like a ghost.

Elderly Viola turns her attention back to me. "May I ask *you* something?"

I nod.

"What led you here to my door? How did you find me?"

A man posing as your father in his top hat and tails, this small baby with your name concealed under his coat. Instead, I say, "A photograph. Of your parents, and a baby in a carriage. Taken at the rear of Arcadia House. I found the photographic records which gave me a name, then it was a matter of looking in the parish register. That led me to your father's grave."

Viola's head pulls up, as if she is marionette on a string. "That picture . . . I know of it. My father cherished it."

"Oh. I shall return it to you then," I say.

"Thank you. I regretted not searching for it before we left the house," Viola says, her voice thick.

"Searching for it?"

"My father would squirrel things away to the attic, small items he coveted. But after his death we couldn't bear the idea of going up there to hunt them out."

More bumping and scrabbling. The dog barks gruffly from another room and Viola disappears to tend to him.

While she's gone, I stand at the front window looking out at the winter-wilted garden, thinking again of Emanuel's carved initials in the wood, the hidden bone.

A man stands on the opposite side of the street in the shadows of a thatched house, his face shielded by a black umbrella. A memory tugs at me – the man leaving Arthur's bookshop after enquiring about a book on moths.

Laying Viola on the chair, I run from the room into the hallway and pull open the front door. My feet fly down the path to the gate. The man's already walking away, his shoulders hunched into his coat. "Wait . . . please, wait . . ." I call. He ignores me, turns a corner and is gone.

I make to run after him then pause and turn, see elderly Viola standing in the doorway of her home. She's holding the grizzling baby, her face scrunched in concern. *Or is it me standing there looking out?* My surroundings swim in and out of focus. I grind my palms into my eyes. No . . . no . . . it's an old woman I'm looking at holding a precious baby. I'm suddenly struggling to draw breath as I think again of our own loss. Tiny bones, thin skin and born too soon for an official burial. I find myself gasping and gasping, as if every glimmer of air has been sucked away.

The woman's face contorts. "Come inside. Please come back inside."

In the living room she sits me close to the stove. "My dear, you're shivering. Whatever is the matter? Who were you calling to out there?"

"A man. There was a man. Did you not see him?"

Viola Cleeve shakes her head.

I feel a portion of the truth nagging and needling its way out as I grip my knees. "Maybe I . . . maybe I imagined it. I haven't been feeling well. My husband and I . . . we lost our only child before it was born . . ."

Viola Cleeve's cheeks tighten in confusion as she glances at the baby she is still carefully holding.

"This baby isn't mine. I'm just caring for her. I did not lie about her name, though."

Her confusion softens, as does my breathing. She waits and watches, until I'm more composed and then seems to choose her words carefully, as if aware I may clam up and decide to keep my secrets close. "Why hide that fact from me?"

My throat is clogged, as if I've swallowed dirt. I am unable to tell her the house she once lived in delivered me this baby and other gifts too, the latest one containing a notice alleging I'll commit a heinous crime.

She waits again as I attempt to find something else I can share. "Things . . . are difficult with my husband." My next words tumble out in a rush. "I think he has taken a lover."

She arches an eyebrow, pats Viola's back. "I never married. There is much to be said for living alone and being in control of one's own destiny."

I cover my face to hide my tears. Why do I feel this need to lie, to not share the truth of my life? Because I'm ashamed of what I've become, and who I am. I'm often glad Theo and his secrets are gone. Yet I'm often not glad at the same time. So much was left unsaid between us, so many unanswered questions. *And yet I loved him. I miss him. I miss him.*

I wipe my face dry, then take the baby. A small silence settles between us. I feel a new alertness, an urge to tell Viola Cleeve everything and the truth about Theo. Then a familiar wave of warmth engulfs me. Reaching for the top button of my blouse, I run a finger around the inside of the collar, and it comes away wet. "I apologise. These warm spells . . ."

"Think nothing of it." She smiles. "Terrible nuisance. I occasionally suffer from them now."

Dismay drags my mouth downwards. "They don't ever . . . end?"

She tilts her head. "I suppose for some they might, but for my mother they continued until her death. Not that we ever spoke of it of course, but she always carried a paper fan, even in the winter months."

Pulling out my handkerchief, I dab at the beads of perspiration on my top lip. "I didn't expect to find this stage of life so difficult."

Elderly Viola nods. She's listening quietly, her face non-judgmental. It prompts me to carry on. "I've no friends and no longer work. I feel . . . dizzy often and muddled. I . . . sometimes wonder where I've gone. If I may eventually . . . simply slip between a crack in the paving one day and disappear."

The woman snorts, a surprisingly inelegant sound. "Oh, yes. The anxiety and aches and pains too. But all things pass. That is the tenet of life after all."

I adjust the baby on my lap, stroke her eyebrows. *All things pass. I have to keep believing that.*

Her intense gaze drills into me but offers no sympathy. "Remember . . . try and keep looking beyond your own reflection, dear. No good can come of dwelling on your aches and pains. Every phase of our lives is so short. Try and live each to the fullest."

"Yes. Yes, you're right," I agree. As I finish drinking my tea, I imagine this wise woman has infused it with her strength and sensibility, her determination and grit. That the liquid seeps into every part of me, into the tips of my fingers, coating my nails and every strand of my hair.

I must become the mistress of my life again, look beyond what I see in the mirror. There's a reason why a person believes I will commit murder. And I cannot help feeling that the answer to that question lies within the bricks of Arcadia House.

Chapter 24

In the afternoon I settle Viola in a nest of blankets on the study floor and commence another, and this time more thorough, search through my husband's things. Spurred on by my visit to Emanuel's daughter and her words of common sense, I sit in my husband's chair and glance out at the street. The building site opposite is still abandoned, tree branches twisting in the opaque sky. There's no sign of Arthur cowering amongst the bricks and planks and I am glad he heeded my advice to stay away, hope that he's now sitting around the fire with his family, reading a detective novel or playing card games. The man with the umbrella outside Viola Cleeve's house – was he real, someone who followed me there? Or just another figment of my unravelling mind? Neither option is good.

Shaking off my uneasiness, I pick up the scattered papers and letters I've already scrutinised for information about Arcadia House and tidy them away, wishing I could do the same with my thoughts. My attention turns to the box file of notes related to Theo's work at the Zoology department. Details of lectures and research proposals.

Most could be written in a foreign language for all I understand them, but a note headed *Confidential: Cambridge breeding programme* makes me sit up. The list of species is short, but I recognise *Lymantria dispar* – gypsy moth – immediately. It mentions egg colour and size, the embryo which is fully formed after lying for three weeks in paper boxes covered with cheese cloth. How the caterpillars are fed on lettuce leaves.

Here it is, then – this species that brought Theo and me together is being bred not far from this house. I've not visited my husband's place of work since he died. The few personal possessions he kept there were boxed up and delivered here by an anxious looking colleague whose name I can't recall.

Pushing back my chair, I walk over to the display cabinet where Bertie discovered the live gypsy moth. As I peer inside at the pinned, dead species that Theo devoted so much of his time and attention to, I steady my thinking. The eggs of this moth don't hatch until spring – April at the earliest, I seem to remember. Someone went to a great effort to obtain the moth and place it here in the cabinet. *This bringer of chaos and havoc.* It's a message, one meant only for me. Perhaps tomorrow someone in the department of Zoology can help me unravel it.

***

I am sick again when I wake the next morning, my head so thick it feels coated in resin. I study the list of ingredients on the back of the tonic bottle. Black cohosh, fenugreek seed, butterfly weed. Sugar syrup and preserving alcohol. The label tells me this is a safe and reliable remedy for female troubles. So why isn't it working? I take a sip, willing my insides to settle.

Making my way upstairs with Viola to bathe and dress,

I pause at the front door. Dread swills in my already unsteady stomach.

On the door mat rests a pair of my boots, the heels clotted with fresh mud. I've not worn these in months. My heart contracts as I see the bolts to the door are drawn back too. Viola frets and squirms, protesting at my tightened grip.

After falling asleep last night in the kitchen chair, did I wake, drift up here like a ghost and leave the house? Where did I go? I press a hand to my face. The thought I could have left the baby alone during my night-time wandering, and left the house unsecured, brings hot tears of fear and despair to my eyes. It's a small mercy that the imposter didn't return while I was gone. That thought has me picking up the toasting fork from the drawing room fireplace and checking the house top to bottom just as Arthur did. There's nothing to indicate anyone has been inside except me and the baby.

"I'm sorry. I'm so sorry," I murmur into Viola's ear. She settles again, forgiving me, I hope.

***

I refuse to look back at Arcadia House as I push the pram towards town and the university, not even once. I feel its pull though. A silent begging for me to tilt my head, admire its beige bricks, wide windows and black front door. A keening for me to uncover its secrets.

The pram wheels squeak as I walk around the side of St Mark's church to the side door I entered three days ago during the Christmas Eve crib service.

Tugging the handle, I find it locked today. Lifting the edge of the pram mattress, I pull out the parish register, carefully wrapped in oil cloth. To my right is the rectory, its windows glinting. If someone is watching, I'm unaware of it. I am almost past caring as I place my offering on the step. I glance back once at the package as I walk away; a stolen thing returned. A grim smile grazes my lips. There's a first time for everything, I suppose.

***

I press on to Pembroke Street, where tall, soot-stained buildings block out much of the sunlight. Under an archway, and then I'm faced with Theo's place of work. Within the small courtyard is the museum of zoology that sits below his lecture rooms. It's open, and a few studious young men chat at the entrance.

Parking the pram, I lift Viola out and she squirms. "This is where Theo worked," I murmur in her ear. Stepping inside, it's familiar yet odd to be back. The high-ceilinged room is home to heavy wooden cabinets housing shells, insects, birds and fish from faraway places that my husband used to tell me about as we lay in bed in the dark.

Exotic names and places with beaches of blindingly white sand, aquamarine waters and lush vegetation so thick that Theo took a machete to it on the exploratory trips he made in his youth.

His travels took him to South America and the jungles of Indonesia. Expeditions that filled me with both horror and wonder. It made my own life seem so narrow, growing up first in Suffolk then my move to Cambridge in search of something more. It was another trait that drew us together, his worldliness, and my lack of it.

A few steps away is the display cabinet Theo visited most often: the moths and butterflies. I, meanwhile, usually found myself searching out the skeletons in this small museum – a crocodile, a whale, fish even. Seeing the insides of a creature and their perfectly formed bones brought me a strange solace. We were all startlingly similar on the inside, no matter our differences.

Looking about, I see a young man tending to one of the display cabinets, tightening the screws on its top. I make my way over, adjusting Viola who is beginning to grizzle. "Good afternoon."

He looks up, blinks. "Mrs . . . Pemberton?"

I do not recognise him and wonder how he knows me.

"How are you?" His eyes stray to the baby, and I notice confusion brewing.

"Yes, well, thank you. I am sorry . . . I've forgotten your name . . ."

His brow creases. "Christopher Barns. I'm a research student, worked with your husband. A few years back I was invalided out from the front. When I'd recovered you were kind enough to invite me to your home for Sunday lunch."

"Of course. Yes. I'm hopeless with names and faces. It's nice to see you again, Mr Barns." I remember him now – a kind-eyed man with shrapnel wounds to the leg who chewed his roast lamb slowly. Theo's eyes twinkled when he'd gone, said it was a wonder we ever moved on to dessert.

Mr Barns stands looking at me expectantly and so I get straight to the point of my visit. "Mr Barns. I was wondering if you might have an idea of how someone may get hold of a live gypsy moth at this time of year?"

He places his screwdriver on the cabinet. "Um. Well . . . it's extinct as a species in this country. Your husband . . ."

"Yes, I'm aware of my husband's research," I say, and the man's eyes widen at my tone. Recoiling inwardly at my impatience, I offer an apology. "I'm sorry . . . it's just I believe I found a live gypsy moth in my home. Is that even possible?"

"In your home?" Mr Barns echoes, looking aghast. He shakes his head. "No. Not possible at all. For one thing the eggs do not hatch until . . ."

"The spring," I interject.

Mr Barns arches an eyebrow.

I clear my throat. "Did my husband . . . did Theo . . . breed them as part of his research? He never spoke of this, yet I found some notes . . ."

The man wets his lips, looks uncomfortable. "It was a rather confidential project, contentious in some circles. But yes. The breeding is done in the laboratory."

"You said 'is'. There is a breeding programme now, here in this building?"

"Yes, but . . ."

I touch Mr Barns lightly on the arm. "Please can you show me. I'd be so grateful."

Mr Barns looks about, a flash of desperation crossing his face. "There are only two of us manning the museum today. I'm not sure it would be . . ."

"It will only take a few minutes. As I said, I would be so very grateful." I give him what I hope is a winning smile, adjust Viola in my arms again and hope that she stays quiet.

***

The lecture rooms and laboratory above the museum look out onto the courtyard. The air is tinged with the smell of chemicals and something earthier too as Mr Barns unlocks the door.

As we step in, my eyes rake over the walls of this warm room which are lined with posters of colourful species of birds, circular diagrams of the life cycles of insects. Below these sit tables and shelves bearing weighty books, microscopes and all manner of scientific equipment.

"Over here," Mr Barns says, making for the far corner of the room near the tall windows and a heating pipe that runs from ceiling to floor. I follow.

On the table here are several brown cardboard boxes covered with white cheese cloth.

Viola grizzles and Mr Barns gives her an anxious glance. *A new species he's unfamiliar with.*

"This box houses the gypsy moth. One of my colleagues is continuing the research your husband started . . . breeding the species to find out the best methods of destroying it." He makes a face. "Sounds rather cruel when I put it like that." He removes a corner of cloth covering the box closest to us.

Peeping inside, I see a number of small, brown-bodied caterpillars with pale yellow hairs cupped in decaying lettuce leaves.

"These are at the sixth larval stage, have been through their moult," Mr Barns says.

"They're close to pupating then?"

He nods, wets his bottom lip, as he refastens the cloth. The same pinched look crosses his face as it did when we were in the museum. "Mrs Pemberton, may I ask you something?"

"Of course."

Mr Barns swallows. "Your coming here today. Is this about . . . the person who visited a few weeks back?"

"I'm afraid I don't know what you mean." My skin prickles with curiosity as I wait for him to continue.

His throat bobs again. "A colleague told me someone came into the museum a couple of weeks ago asking about this species of moth. They were a collector and breeder – said they were a friend of your husband. Asked if we had any caterpillars on the premises that were pupating."

"Would it be possible for me to speak to your colleague about this?" I can sense the beads of perspiration gathering on my forehead.

Mr Barns shakes his head. "He lives in Brighton – gone home for the holidays."

"There's nothing else you can tell me about this visitor . . . his name?" I press, as Viola begins to squawk, her small lips parting in hunger.

"Mrs Pemberton . . ."

"Please, Mr Barns. This *is* important."

Mr Barns throws an anxious glance at the door, draws closer and I hold my breath, certain he is about to confide in me. "I don't want to cause any bother . . . but . . ."

I shift position, give him a pleading look. "Please, just tell me."

Colour floods Mr Barns's cheeks. "It was a woman. A female friend."

Concentrate on Viola's perfect little face. Do not react. "I see."

"It's unusual to find a woman with an interest of this . . . sort," he says.

"Yes. I imagine so," I reply carefully.

He chews on his bottom lip. "I'm not suggesting anything improper, of course . . ."

"Of course you are not, Mr Barns," I soothe, pinning a smile to my face. Inside my stomach is a pit of writhing eels. *A female collector friend of Theo's. The woman he was disappearing to meet?* The baby squirms as my handle on her tightens. "What was the outcome of the meeting . . . with this woman?"

Mr Barns looks down.

"I appreciate your honesty. I really do," I cajole. Tears burn at the back of my nose.

The man seems undecided, but when he eventually speaks his tone is low, as if other people may be listening in rather than insects. "It was a bit irregular . . . and I'm still in two minds whether to report him . . . but my colleague was short of money and arranged to sell her a few pupae. They were around fourteen days from hatching, I believe."

Tears escape onto my cheeks unbidden.

Mr Barns clears his throat, directs his gaze away from me to the window.

This is her doing then? Is it the same woman Theo was entangled with; the person he was meeting in secret? But it's beyond me how this woman could have planted the moth inside the display cabinet without me knowing. This comes back to Emanuel Cleeve's impersonator and his key to my house. *Theo's house.* This man and woman are in cahoots.

Chapter 25

The bottle of infant milk I've brought with me is thoroughly chilled despite being swaddled in a blanket inside the pram. Shaky and wrung out, I stand in the shadows outside the zoology museum while Viola suckles the teat, wondering if this woman who bought the moth pupae is someone I know. Running through Theo's friends and acquaintances in my head, the list is short. My husband wasn't an especially social man, and he certainly had no female friends. Preferring his own or my company. *Until he decided he didn't.*

I walk on into town, purchase three more tins of infant milk. Each tin should last a week, take me into the new year and beyond. This thought soothes me, the act of standing in the busy chemist's shop and buying this milk – a ward against my supposed murderous future.

Lining the foot of the pram with the tins, the rhythmic beat of drums charges the air near King's Parade. Curious, I follow the sound and come across a huddle of people clapping outside the church, a small crowd gathering. The cheerfulness draws me near, and I stand and watch. After a while I find my feet tapping in time to the tempo.

Three men in the centre of the crowd are dressed in yellow and red costumes, bells on their pointed boots jangling as they dance about with their instruments.

Viola's eyes are wide, and I smile as I lift her from the pram, fold a blanket around her and hold her close. Putting on the pram brake, and leaving it to one side, I step through the throng to better see the spectacle, wanting, *needing* a moment of normality, to be cocooned in the smell and sight of strangers.

The tune takes me away from myself for a brief moment and I get lost in the claps and heat from the bodies around me. The urge to flee rises, yet I breathe through it, remembering Viola Cleeve's advice. I mustn't let my anxieties control my actions. They are not my true self, just thoughts and feelings I can let come and go at will.

The drummer man in the middle is spinning in a circle, and he stops and faces the crowd. His cheeks crease into a smile.

My stomach falls, as if I have taken a dive off a cliff. I stare. This man . . . his nose, his eyes. The darkness of his hair. *I've seen him before.*

Blinking, I push past a lady smelling strongly of violets, a couple standing arm in arm. Then I'm at the front, with nothing obstructing my view of these three men and their drums and the top hat people are tossing coins into.

His sideburns have been trimmed, but it's him, the man who let himself into my house with a key and left Viola. The man from the photograph pretending to be Emanual Cleeve.

I look about wildly, my mind unrooted, not understanding why the others watching can't see this too. This pretender. A man who abandoned a child. Stepping into the performers' circle, my heart pounds as I cradle the baby. *His baby?* I'm less sure of that now.

Curling my arms around Viola, my throat thickens. I cannot do it. I cannot give her up. This man doesn't care for her, came into my house a second time and left music playing without checking the child he abandoned was safe and well. But he's the only known connection to the baby . . . can help me solve the riddle of who she is. And perhaps the identity of the woman who brought a moth into my house.

"You!" My voice is thin. "You!" Stronger this time. "Emanuel Cleeve."

His gaze falls directly on me then, like a spotlight. He knows this name. Knows full well he is Emanuel's mimic. Jaw slackening, his eyes sweep over me and the baby. Quickly placing his drum on the ground, he turns to say something to the other two musicians, then he's pushing through the crowd and running.

"No. Wait!"

The two remaining drummers ignore me as they continue to beat their instruments, the noise swelling and echoing off the surrounding buildings.

"Let me through . . . please, let me through." The crowd tightens around me like a knot. It tangles us up as I push and heave, my arms protecting Viola from the crush. For a second I fear I'll be trapped in here forever like a butterfly in a net, and then we are spat out on the periphery and the pram is waiting just where I parked it.

I pivot on my heel, catch a glimpse of red as the man disappears between the market stalls. Placing Viola in the pram, I set off after him, the baby starting to fret as she jolts about, as my boots slap on the cobbles.

"Steady there."

"What's the hurry?"

People leap back, and I swerve to avoid hitting a woman and her small dog. There's no time to pause, no time to apologise. I catch sight of him again on Rose Crescent, and I follow the curve of the street, emerging onto Trinity Street. He could have turned left, and double backed to the market and King's Parade or turned right towards the colleges. I've no way of knowing and scream out in frustration.

"A man dressed in red and yellow? Has anyone seen him run by?" Disapproving looks are directed towards me, a woman shouting in public is obscene. But it's necessary. Two college porters in their black bowler hats gawp.

"Green Street," says a voice, and I look left, see a young girl with a basket of toffee apples pointing.

Setting off again, I grit my teeth. There he is, at the far end of the street, taking another right turn. He's leading us in a full circle and a bitter laugh flies from my lips at the irony of this. A never-ending circle of mysteries.

The pram bumps and squeaks and Viola is crying in earnest now. Her distress tugs at me, but I can't stop and tend to her. I must find this man for her sake if nothing else.

Halfway along Green Street I pause, my breaths short and panting. The cobbles are slowing us; I'll never catch him. Reaching into the pram, I whisk Viola into my arms and set off again. I'm thick with heat and anger, my feet skimming the ground in pursuit.

Spinning around the corner, I feel my right boot slide,

recognise in that instant that I will fall and take this precious baby down to the cobbles with me. I tighten my grasp on her, preparing for the worst. Then there are fingers on my coat sleeve, a firm grip on my arm.

"Steady there. You came around that corner at quite a lick." A man. With kind eyes, full of concern. They are eyes I recognise.

His kindness causes me to unfold, my knees to weaken. "I . . . I . . ." my words are gasped. I open my mouth again to speak, urge him to follow the man in yellow and red. But my vision dims, retracts at the edges.

The man's grip on me tightens and my ears ring. His voice is soft and shallow, a whisper. "Oh Lordy. I think she's going to faint."

***

The man who so sweetly broke my fall sits opposite me in the tea shop as I cradle Viola, a pot of tea for two and a plate of ginger snaps before us. He's just returned from Green Street to fetch the abandoned pram, has parked it outside the shop window which is dripping with condensation. "Thank you. I'm so grateful . . . for seeing me in here, ordering the tea and fetching the pram."

"Gave me quite a shock to see you go down like that," he says over the chatter of customers enjoying currant buns and slices of fruit cake. "It's Mrs Pemberton, isn't it?"

I smile. "Yes. You met with my husband Theo."

"Yes, that's right. I'm John. John Garland," he replies.

"An architect," I say, and he nods. I came home from work one day to find Mr Garland and Theo talking on the steps of Arcadia House. Theo took his advice on some home improvements.

"You are feeling better now?" he asks.

"Yes, thank you. The tea helped," I murmur. My fingers still shake as I pick up the dainty teacup mottled with purple irises and take another sip. As I inspect Mr Garland over the rim of my teacup, I see he is about my height, and of a stocky build. His brown hair curls around his ears and I should think he's younger than me by a good five years. My eyes drift to his paisley tie which is slightly askew, and I wonder if my rescue was the cause of that. He must see my gaze for his face colours, and he lifts a hand to straighten it.

"Um. . . you were in quite the hurry," says Mr Garland as he offers me the biscuit plate. "The pram was where you said it was. I've put on the brake." I sense he's inquisitive, but he doesn't press me on why I was running with the baby. I'm grateful for that. A gentle smile curves his cheeks as he looks at Viola. It fans the skin at the edges of his eyes. "Your baby . . . she seems none the worse for it all, thank goodness. She's a dear thing. You and Mr Pemberton must be very proud."

I return his smile, smothering a wave of guilt that I must lie to this kind man. "Yes. Very proud. Her name is Viola."

Mr Garland takes a sip of tea. "Viola. Pretty name, that." He shifts in his seat, fiddles with his tie again, smooths it in a single, long stroke.

"Please, don't feel you have to stay," I say, my cheeks warming. I've interrupted this man's day and I'm sure the last thing he wants is to be sitting here with me.

Uncertainty crosses his face. "Um . . . I'm not sure you

should be alone after nearly fainting like that. Is . . . is your husband nearby? Could I get a message to him so he can walk you and the baby home?"

I glance down at my wedding ring and swallow. Mr Garland won't know Theo died last year. The lie I've already told about Viola being our baby expands like rubber. "Theo's been away for a while. Visiting a sick relative."

Mr Garland's forehead furrows. "Oh. Oh, I'm sorry about that. He was away over Christmas, then?"

"Yes," I reply. "My sister and her family came to stay . . . which was pleasant."

His eyebrows tug together, perhaps detecting from my tone that the visit wasn't as pleasant as it might have been. "There can be a lot of pressure to be merry at this time of year. I'll be glad enough when the festivities are over. My wife . . . she . . ." His voice trails off and he shakes his head, reaches for his teacup again.

I sit watching him, note the sadness in his eyes and wonder about the missing part of his sentence.

***

While Mr Garland pays, I settle Viola in the pram outside. Our small talk was stilted and awkward and I drank my tea quickly, eager to get home and back to Rabbit.

Mr Garland comes straight over when he reappears. "You're certain you'll be all right walking home?"

I smile. "Yes. Quite sure. Thank you once again. I don't know what came over me."

Putting on his hat, he gives me a courteous nod and sets off towards town. I lift the pram brake, curl my gloved fingers around the silver handle, but see Mr Garland has turned. "If you don't mind me asking, where were you off to in such a hurry with your baby?"

I take a breath, preparing to trot out some other lie that will enable us to say our goodbyes and be on our way. But his enquiring eyes are patient and settled on me as he waits for a response. The gentleness in his expression reminds me of Theo then. The way my husband used to ask me about my day, always making room for me in a conversation. "I was . . . following someone."

His gaze is startled, still focused on me, quietly waiting for me to continue.

I begin to walk, and Mr Garland falls in step alongside me, the secret slowly spilling out of me about the man who came into my house with a key. I don't tell him the truth about Viola, or the other things. But I do tell him that I'm certain the drummer-man I was chasing was the intruder who came into my house.

Mr Garland stops dead in the street. "Mrs Pemberton, you must go to the police station at once and report this fellow."

Pausing, I turn a gloved palm to the sky. "But I don't know who he is, have no information to give the police." There's another reason of course why I can't return to the police station. If that same sergeant sees me back again making fresh claims, that will surely only bring more trouble to my door.

Mr Garland adjusts his neck scarf. "I . . . well this is only a suggestion, but should we go back, then? To the place you first saw the drummers. Perhaps they are still there."

***

As we approach King's Parade there is no echoing beat from the buildings. The spot the three men were standing in is clear of crowds, all evidence of them vanished, as if they were never there at all. *I didn't imagine it. I couldn't have.*

I push the pram on to a low wall separating the street from the manicured green lawns in front of King's College. Sinking onto the cold stone, I grip the curved edge of the wall.

Mr Garland wrings his hands together, his shadow looming over me. "Mrs Pemberton. I've . . . um . . .I've a feeling you're not as well as you say. Please . . . would it be all right if I walked you home? I believe it's what your husband would expect of me." He fumbles in his jacket pocket, pulls out a small card and offers it to me. "You can show this to your husband if he asks about me . . . he may not have kept the quotation I provided, and the card I gave him when we met."

John Garland & Co.
Architect.
Tunwell's Court, Trumpington Street, Cambridge

I look up. "I'm sorry my husband didn't engage you for the work to our house." Theo had sometimes spoken to me of extending the house downstairs, so it wasn't a surprise to discover he'd been seeking advice and quotations. But the idea of the work lost its shine as the country fell deeper into the darkness of war, his plans abandoned.

"Oh, please. Think nothing of it," says Mr Garland, waving a hand. "If there's a bright side to the last few years, there's plenty of work now for men like me. I'm planning a new neighbourhood at Fen Ditton – homes fit for heroes."

"Addison's Housing Act," I say. I've read about this in the newspapers, homes to meet the need of those returning from the war with nowhere to live. "That's very worthy of you."

He grimaces. "I was in the eleventh Battalion Suffolk Regiment. Was invalided out twice with shrapnel wounds. Luckily, I made a good enough recovery. After it was over, I wanted to use my formal training to do something more to help those who'd also survived."

I give him a small smile. John Garland is an earnest man. And he's right, if Theo was alive, he would be grateful that someone is helping me. The thought of my empty house and its secrets is also doing nothing for my wobbly legs. "Yes please, then, to accompanying me home. That would be kind."

The conversation as we walk is polite, quietly spoken. I learn that John rents the flat above his office. He doesn't mention his wife, and I do not ask about her. If he wishes to tell me about his personal circumstances, then he will.

He equally does not probe me about my own life or ask questions about Theo. His concern for us is apparent though as he helps manoeuvre the pram up and down kerbs, and I let it cloak me like a blanket.

As Arcadia House comes into view, I feel my heart quicken and worries march back into my head, a tight band around my chest bringing a sharp pulse of pain. Two men in suits stand half-hidden behind one of the larger stacks of bricks opposite the house. A black motor van waits at the kerb and two more men linger beside it in their police officer's uniforms. They look up as they see us approaching.

"I wonder what's happening over there?" muses Mr Garland.

I peer at them, wondering if one of these men is the sergeant from the station who accused me of being a drunkard.

The police officers converse quickly, then stride over to us.

"Is everything all right, officers?" asks Mr Garland, tipping his hat.

Some of my tension slips away as I realise I've never seen these men before; one with close-set eyes and the other with permanent furrows in his brow.

"Can I ask if you live here, in this house?" asks the furrow-browed officer, gesturing at my front steps.

"Yes, I do," I say, giving them a nervous glance.

Mr Garland clears his throat. "I'm just accompanying Mrs Pemberton home. She took a turn in town today and her husband is away."

The officers share a quick glance. "Ah, I see. Can I ask what time you left the house today, Mrs Pemberton?" the one with close-set eyes enquires, pulling a notebook and pencil from his jacket pocket.

"It must have been around nine-thirty," I admit.

"You didn't see anyone across the street when you left? Anyone lingering?" he continues.

"No . . . no one at all," I reply. "May I ask what this is about?" Across the road, I see the driver of the van climb out.

The close-set eyed police officer coughs, scribbles in his book. "Um. I'm sorry to tell you this, but there's been an incident. An accident on the building site over there . . . a young lad took a knock to the head. Looks like it happened last night or in the early hours of the morning. Unfortunately, he didn't . . ."

I stare at the bricks and planks, the tarpaulin-covered cement bags. The other two men are now inching out from between the stacks of materials with a stretcher. Upon it is a lumpen form covered in a blanket. As they turn the corner the blanket snags on a pile of bricks. It pulls back to reveal a coated arm, a pale hand at the end of it. *Dead. This person is dead.* I can't tear my eyes away as the van driver opens the rear doors, and the men slide the stretcher inside. The doors bang close, and I blink.

"It would have been a quick end . . . was the result of what looks to be a slip or a fall," the furrow-browed officer finishes quietly.

"Oh dear. Oh dear," murmurs Mr Garland, his cheeks ashen and his hat now gripped in his hands.

The officer's eyes sweep over my house and the one next door. "Unfortunately, there seem to have been no witnesses. Your neighbours are away?"

"Yes. Abroad. Not due back . . . not back until the new year," I stutter.

The close-set eyed police officer writes this down too.

A sudden thought strikes me as I look across at the black van which is now driving off. The inside of my mouth feels as rough as newly sawn wood. "Do you . . . do you know the identity of the . . ." I can't bring myself to finish the sentence.

"The lad's family own a bookshop." The officer's eyes pinch together even more closely. "They've no idea what he was doing this side of town, have of course taken the news very badly."

He pauses. "You don't know of him, do you? Seen a lad around here before?"

I push my gloved hands into my pockets, curl them into tight fists. *Arthur.* "No."

Mr Garland places a hand on the side of the pram. "I can see Mrs Pemberton is quite shaken by this news. I should see her and the baby safely inside."

"Yes, of course," the furrow-browed officer agrees, giving us a courteous nod.

We walk around the back of the house in silence, the pram wheels squeaking on the damp paving.

"This is . . . this such a terrible thing. Is there anyone who can look in on you? You really did take quite a turn in town this afternoon. And now this . . ." Mr Garland's voice is low and anxious as he trails behind.

I can't answer him. I told Arthur not to come here again. *And now he's dead.* What made him return? Then another wave of dizziness hits. My muddy boots on the doormat . . . I left the house last night, or in the early hours. Did Arthur and I meet? Did we exchange words before he hit his head? *Was I there when the accident happened?*

All I wish for in this moment is the weight of the baby in my arms, and the tonic slipping down my throat. For this all to go away.

Gathering myself, I turn and fix what I hope is a calm and collected expression to my face. I mustn't make Mr Garland any more concerned than he already is. "Yes, it's a dreadful thing, but I shall be perfectly all right here alone." I swallow. "Thank you again for your kindness, Mr Garland.

I do appreciate everything you've done."

He gives me a tremulous smile. "Well . . . um . . . I'm glad I could help."

As I'm about turn away, he calls over. "Um . . . Mrs Pemberton. I worry about you being here alone. Would you mind terribly if I stopped by tomorrow? I must drive out this way on an errand."

I see his eyes are hopeful as he carefully puts on his hat, tilts the angle of it until it's just right. It's a simple action that again reminds me of my husband.

"I'll . . . I'll come by around eleven o'clock then?" he asks when I don't reply.

Not trusting myself to speak, I give him a quick nod.

Chapter 26

Night closes in and I hunker down under a blanket, doze on and off in the kitchen chair. Each time I wake to feed the baby I think of Arthur, drag through my memories for a meeting between us the night of his accident and an explanation for his death.

Viola screams, her body writhing and twisting as I attempt to soothe her. Her forehead is warm to the touch. Is she sickening? I cool her with a damp flannel and her screams worsen. *Milk. She needs more milk.* The tin I find on the table is empty.

In the larder I search out a new tin, thinking about my muddy boots by the front door. *My missing memories . . . the accusation I will commit murder. My boots. My boots.*

I spoon the powdered milk into the jug of boiled and cooled water, stir it three times. "It's coming. Milk is coming. Milk is . . ." I drop the spoon I'm holding, the metal clattering to the floor.

Rabbit rises, trots over to sniff at it.

Not a milk tin on the table, but a tonic bottle. A new one brought from the larder; the screw uncapped. The boiled water in the jug has the hue of murky dishwater. *How can this be happening?*

Stumbling to the sink, I tip the concoction away, rinse

and wash the jug twice. This is the first time, the only time, I have made this mistake.

Isn't it?

***

When Viola is sleeping again, I creep upstairs and examine my muddy boots from every angle. Dried clots of soil pepper the floor tiles. I sweep them up into my palm, scrunch them to dust.

Baubles and paper chains dance on the fir tree as I push beyond it to the window. Across the road a tarpaulin on the building site flaps in the wind. I reach for missing memories of opening the front door, crossing the road and greeting Arthur over there. Was I angry to see him here again, watching me from his hiding place? Madness nips at my heels, and I squash a thought too disturbing to contemplate, try to outrun it as I breathlessly hurry back towards the kitchen and the baby.

The glint of the hall mirror catches my eye, and I pause to stare at it. *No . . . no it can't be.* "Arthur?" It's not a mirror, but a doorway. There the boy is, in his green hat. His hand reaching out to me. The same pale and lifeless hand I saw this afternoon on the stretcher. He gestures at his head, mouths something, but I can't make out his words.

Viola begins to cry. Or is it my baby Emily? Or did we have a boy called George. Yes, it's George crying. Our sweet baby George who grew up into this lovely young man standing before me now. I shake my head, thoughts tumbling as if I am doing loops on a trapeze. *Arthur. This is Arthur.*

I reach out to touch the boy and at the same moment

he pulls off his hat and turns. It reveals a deep, gaping gash near his temple, the creamy white of his skull lurking beneath. Blood dripping down his cheek and neck. He makes no attempt to wipe it away as it stains the collar of his shirt.

"My God. Oh, my Lord . . ." Lurching forwards, my hands meet a cold, smooth surface. I blink twice. My dull-faced reflection stares back at me. The mirror. I'm staring at myself. *There is no Arthur. No George or Emily.*

The floorboards creak above my head. The baby's cries, Viola's cries, pull at me from the kitchen. I let my hands drop to my sides, watch as my foggy handprints on the mirrored glass fade.

Chapter 27

Mr Garland's motor pulls up in front of the house at eleven o'clock sharp the next morning. I've done my best with my appearance, fished out from the wardrobe my Sunday best navy skirt and a cream blouse which still sits a little tight, despite my lack of appetite. I've twisted my hair up into a bun and silver filigree earrings dangle from my ears.

The man perches on a chair in my drawing room in his grey suit and waistcoat, his hands gripping his knees. His eyes dart about, taking in the fire I've coaxed into life, the fir tree with its glass baubles, homemade paper garlands and blue and red twinkling lights, the tea tray I've made-up with a plate of gingerbread warmed in the stove to disguise any staleness.

Viola lies on a blanket on the sofa wedged between two cushions. If he wonders why there is no baby's crib down here, he's too polite to question it.

"I must say, it's quite a relief seeing you looking better." He gives me a warm smile. "I was quite concerned yesterday."

"I'm sorry I gave you such a fright."

"A good night's sleep is the remedy for most things."

"Yes," I reply with a nod. After the mirror incident last night there was no more sleep to be had. I couldn't shake off the image of Arthur's head wound, the dripping blood and stain on his collar. *A memory or my imagination?* In Theo's study I sought out the butterfly book Arthur had given me, hoping for a jolt of clarity. But the book was gone from the desk. Thundering up and down the stairs with the baby, I turned out bookcases, drawers and shelves, searched under beds and down the backs of chairs. Where had I put it? The book was not to be found in any room of the house. *It was as if Arthur had never visited me here at all.* What I did find, though, was Mr Garland's business card. Tucked away in a file along with his quotation for the works to the house which Theo never accepted.

"Mrs Pemberton?"

Mr Garland's voice snaps me back to the present. Beside me is the photograph of Emanuel Cleeve and the notes I made about his death and his daughter's birth from the church register. Mr Garland was a kind shoulder to lean on yesterday. This man is almost a stranger, but there's also a familiarity that somehow eases my loneliness when I'm in his company. And there's his link with Theo of course. Maybe sharing more of my troubles will help me find a way out of this nightmare, for that is what it's become. "My apologies. Let me pour you some tea."

"When is your husband due home?" he enquires, as I hand him a cup and saucer.

"In a few days." I feel a curdle of guilt at continuing this lie, but it's safer to let him believe Theo is still alive. But Viola. The urge to tell him the truth about her and how she arrived at this house nips at me. Not the murder notice, though. I'm not brave enough to share that. No man will want to hear the woman he's taking tea with is considered capable of such a shocking crime.

Mr Garland nods and sips his tea, tells me about his errand, as I silently admire the cut of his flannel suit, his high collared white shirt. He's unaware that our conversation is about to take an unpleasant turn, move away from his purchase of cheap building materials to something much darker.

When I finish speaking, his teacup and saucer tremble as he returns them to the silver tea tray. His cheeks have taken on the same hue as the wintry sky outside. "I . . . I really don't know what to say." He directs his gaze to Viola. "This baby isn't yours?"

Dampness gathers in the hollow between my breasts, my brassiere and petticoat clammy against my skin. "Yes, that's right. As I said, the man who came into my house left this baby, and the photograph."

Mr Garland leans in and peers at the photograph, then his eyes graze over my notes. "This picture was taken in the back garden of your home, but the man in it – this Emanuel Cleeve – is dead? The woman you met in Grantchester. His daughter Viola. She confirmed he died in this house?"

Folding my arms around my middle, I pace the room. "I know this must all sound unlikely, perhaps impossible. But everything I'm telling you is true."

"But what man leaves a child in a stranger's home?" he blusters, colour slowly returning to his cheeks. "And for the imposter to name the child after a person who once lived here . . ." He pauses, shakes his head. "It's . . . preposterous!"

I stare at a patterned blue swirl on the carpet. "I've cared for Viola well, Mr Garland."

He stands up, his face strained as he walks over. "I don't doubt it. But . . . but as I said yesterday, you *must* go to the police."

My breathing accelerates. "I did. I just . . . don't think I can return there. They weren't much help. And . . . I worry what would happen to the baby."

Mr Garland glances at her small form on the sofa, awake but settled, her arms flung back behind her head, her legs kicking. A flash of understanding crosses his face. "You've become attached to her."

My nod is small, unlike my expanding feelings for this child. "No one has come forward to claim her. There are no reports of a baby gone missing in the daily newspaper. The man I saw in town, the one who ran away from me yesterday, left this baby here. Came back a second time and started up the gramophone in this room while I was downstairs. Yet there he was dancing about with a drum on the street as if he didn't have a care in the world." I pause and wipe my palms on my skirt. "Why? Tell me how that could be?"

Mr Garland gives me a long look. "You're absolutely certain it was the same fellow."

"Yes, it was him I saw!" My voice is shrill, and I see him wince. Curling my nails into my sides, I accept the pinch of reality this brings and take a breath. "I called out to him the name Emanuel Cleeve. He looked at me then, knew who I was. That's why he ran."

Mr Garland looks beyond the Christmas tree branches and out to the street. "You truly believe the man who left the baby wanted you to believe that he was this Emanuel Cleeve."

"It's the only explanation I have," I say, fiddling with my belt clasp and loosening it so I can breathe a little easier.

"Spiritualism. The supernatural, demons, ghouls, ghosts and apparitions. How about these as an explanation, Mrs Pemberton?"

Agnes? Her voice is clear as a bell from beside the tree. A glass bauble lies on the carpet where I must have knocked it off. Striding over to pick it up, I cradle it in my palms. My skin prickles, a feeling of being watched. The street is empty. Just Mr Garland's motor waiting at the kerb.

"Um . . . Mrs Pemberton?" Turning, I see Mr Garland's forehead is buckled.

Pulling in a breath, I clip the bauble back on to a branch, tilt my head in case Agnes has something else to say. *What is the matter with me? Agnes is not here.* Reaching for Viola on the sofa, I hold her close, feel the pulse of her heart beating, the vibrations of her snuffles and grunts. *She is real. I am real. John Garland is real.* "Sorry. I'm sorry . . . I'm fine. Please, carry on."

Mr Garland pulls at his tie, adjusts it even though it's already perfectly straight. "You say on Christmas Eve there was a delivery?"

"Yes. A crib that I didn't purchase. Although the warehouse docket suggests otherwise."

Mr Garland looks at the baby in my arms. "This is just a suggestion . . . but we could go to the warehouse . . . try and find out who the real purchaser is? See whether this sheds any light on your Emanuel Cleeve. Although, that may be too much for you . . . perhaps it's a bad idea . . ."

I feel a thread of hope. "No, it's not a bad idea at all."

"This is a difficult question to ask . . . but do you know of anyone who might have a vendetta against you, or your husband?" Mr Garland continues, looking a little pained.

I stand with my back to the fire, thinking of Theo's absences and lies as I sway from side to side with Viola. My husband's visit to the cinema in Huntingdon, the train journey to St Ives. The solicitor's letter. The woman at the museum asking about moths – maybe the lover I assumed him to have. Some secrets are too painful to share . . . yet. "No. I can think of no one. We lead very ordinary lives."

Mr Garland pats his tie. "I could . . . take you to the warehouse now, Mrs Pemberton? I can see this is troubling you and my errand can wait."

I glance down at Viola. "That's very kind, but I would need to bring the baby."

He smiles. "But of course. I'm a careful driver; well, I like to think I am. Perhaps you can tell me afterwards."

***

Mr Garland's motorcar is as black as oil, its canopy pulled taut, and the sides open to the elements. He holds open the door and I step inside, settle into the buttery leather seat cradling Viola. I adjust her hat and mittens, pull the blanket more closely around her to ward off the chill.

The wind whips my face as we motor along the Cambridge backs, the spires of King's College grazing the leaden sky. We skirt along the river, where a few boats are sculling through the water. Over the bridge, we slow to allow a family with three small children to cross. The mother in her dowdy grey coat glances at me and I sit a little straighter, hold Viola so that the woman can see I have a baby. She smiles at me, and I return her silent greeting with one of my own. Does she assume we are man and wife sitting here, that Viola is our child? This sudden thought is shocking, causes me to clench my toes in my boots. *I'm sorry, Theo. I'm sorry.*

Soon we are driving along Mill Road and over the railway bridge, and in no time at all we have arrived at the warehouse.

G. Warland's Furniture, shouts the garish wooden sign as we pull up outside.

"You found the journey all right? Not too cold I hope?" Mr Garland asks.

"Not at all. And yes, you are a very careful driver," I reply.

The man's eyes shine with the compliment. "Cambridge can be a tricky place to navigate . . . all the students and bicycles." He climbs out and comes around to my door, takes my arm to help me on to the pavement. "Does your husband have a motor?"

"No. No he doesn't." My lips brush Viola's forehead to test her temperature which is cool today. No telephone in the house, and no motor car. What other innovations would Theo have ignored if he were still alive? I like to think I'd have coaxed him into this new future in the end though, persuaded him of the benefits of a modern life.

Mr Garland stares at the baby, then blinks and looks back at the car. "I bought mine this year. If he's looking for a recommendation, I could certainly help with that."

"Thank you, that's very generous." I turn away for a short moment, straighten my hat and Viola's blanket, the lie about my absent husband twisting my stomach.

The warehouse is brick built, and its wooden door is wedged open. I've given Mr Garland the docket the delivery men left with the crib. He's offered to do the talking here, and that is a blessed relief.

Beds, wardrobes, sideboards and all other manner of items needed to furnish a home greet us as we step inside. I'm distracted by the sight of two cribs like the one that stands in my bedroom now, the white wicker light and airy against the other heavy oak, tropical hardwood and walnut pieces.

Mr Garland approaches a ruddy cheeked man in navy overalls to the rear of the building. The conversation seems to be quite animated as they hunch over the docket and a notebook. I gather fragments of the conversation as I draw nearer, notice Mr Garland's eyebrows are tugged together. He throws me a worried glance, then turns his attention back to the man in blue. "There must be some mistake here. Mrs Pemberton is certain she didn't order the crib."

The man in overalls shrugs, taps his book. "What it says on the docket, is what it says in here."

Closing the distance between us, I stroke Viola's back to stop her fretting. "I'm afraid your book must be wrong, then."

He gestures at the baby in my arms. "Why all this fuss? It's paid for and yours! It's a high-quality item."

Mr Garland's brow is furrowed. "May I enquire about the person who served the purchaser, then? Do they happen to be about today?"

The man sighs heavily, glances again at the book. "From the initials I can see young Tom served Mrs Pemberton."

"Is he here?" I ask.

"Yes. He's out back. I'll go and fetch him."

Mr Garland scratches his chin, as the man disappears to find his colleague. "Very peculiar business, isn't it? They seem insistent that their records are correct, and you're the purchaser."

"Well, they are wrong," I say hotly, which only causes the lines on Mr Garland's forehead to deepen.

The overalled man soon reappears with a young fellow I assume to be Tom. He's hurriedly pulling on his tweed jacket, straightening his shirt and waistcoat. His gaze flickers to Mr Garland, and then to me. He gives me a broad smile. "Mrs Pemberton. Is there something wrong with the crib I sold you?"

I shift position and the baby squirms. "But . . . you didn't sell me anything. We've never met before today."

Tom throws an uncertain look at his colleague and then returns his attention to me. "You came in last week. Said you wanted the crib delivered specially on Christmas Eve for your baby."

My skin bristles. "No. No, that isn't right. I've never visited this place before, would certainly remember if I had done."

Tom nods. "You were wearing the exact brown coat you have on now. I remember you as clear as day."

"You're mistaken. You're confusing me with somebody else."

Mr Garland places a gentle hand on my arm. "Um . . . Mrs Pemberton. Perhaps we should leave?"

My head reels, and I vaguely hear Mr Garland thank the two men for their time. He carefully steers me around the furniture and out of the warehouse until we're standing outside on the street, amidst the stutter of motor cars, the whistle of a train passing under the bridge, the air cold against my flaming cheeks. He leads me to the motor and opens the door.

As I sink into the seat, my pulse floods in my ears.

When we're both sitting, Mr Garland turns to me, his cheeks taut. "This is all my fault. It was a mistake to bring you here. I apologise. I felt this issue would be easily resolved."

My jaw clenches. "It was not me. I did not buy the crib." I cradle Viola against my shoulder, breathe in her milky smell in the hope it will settle my agitation.

Mr Garland runs his tongue over his lower lip. "When we met yesterday, you were . . . confused. You almost fainted. Then you tell me about this man coming into your house and leaving the baby, and the delivery of a crib." He pauses, his throat bobbing. "It must be unsettling, your husband being away. Perhaps his absence has . . . caused your nerves to fray, to imagine things that aren't true, and forget things that are?"

My skin bristles. "You believe I'm lying? That I've fabricated this?"

He raises his palms. "No, no. That's not what I'm suggesting. I . . . um . . . I just wonder if perhaps . . . you . . . you should visit a doctor, seek his advice."

"A doctor!" I exclaim.

Mr Garland looks away and a flash of embarrassment pinks his cheeks. "The baby. Viola. If you've recently given birth perhaps . . ."

"She's not mine!" Rain mists the windshield and I stare

hard at the droplets, willing myself not to cry. He thinks me a liar, that I've fabricated all of this, just as the police officer did. A bored and lonely housewife, craving attention. Prone to fits of fainting in the street as she chases an imaginary drummer who came into her house uninvited.

"My wife. She had some . . . troubles after giving birth to our son." Mr Garland's voice is quiet and thick with emotion. "It was a difficult time. I only wish to help you, Mrs Pemberton."

Mr Garland has a son. I turn my head away from him as we drive back to Arcadia House, thankful for the wind which steals the tears from my eyes. *He thinks Viola is mine. He thinks me mad; he thinks me quite mad.* Bile rises as the buildings whiz past in a blur.

Perhaps I am.

Chapter 28

Sitting in the kitchen feeding Viola that evening, I keep running over our awkward goodbye. Stilted smiles, and clipped tones. Mr Garland did not ask to visit again, and why would he if he thinks me deranged, a person who bought a baby's crib and then lied about it? Lied also about her own baby being deposited in her house by a stranger. A bubble of hysterical laughter rises, and I press a hand to my lips, smother it.

My throat then burns and I wipe away hot and angry tears before they spill onto the baby's face.

Perhaps I'm imagining it, but Viola's cheeks seem to be filling out, and she looks up at me with wide eyes, sometimes focusing in as if memorising the angles of me, the length of my nose and my unruly hair. A warm sensation rattles through me, a golden thread binding me to this child. She gives me a slow blink, an acknowledgement that she feels this connection between us too. When she's finished drinking, I lift her up, nuzzle her neck and breathe until the burn in my throat releases.

While the baby sleeps in her drawer bed, I fall into a fitful doze in the armchair, dreaming that Arthur is at the door snapping out questions about the photograph, the baby and the crib. He takes off his green hat, grips it in his hands when he speaks. It's stained crimson, shot through with his own blood.

The sickening image startles me awake and I reach for the tonic bottle jammed down the side of the chair.

Blinking, I somehow find myself facing the locked door to the hallway above. Rabbit sits at my feet, panting. In my hand is the baby's thigh bone that I've been keeping upstairs in the bedroom. I stare at it and blink again, see that I'm barefooted, my stockings hanging over the side of the armchair. My feet are mottled purple and chilled, and my toes curl into the tiles. *What am I doing here . . . how did this bone get into my hand? Did Emanuel place it there? No . . . no . . . he's dead. Dead from rat poison.*

Swivelling, I glance back to the baby's drawer bed. *Empty!* My heart thrumming an unsteady beat, I stride over to the drawer and turn back the covers as if I might find a miniature Emily entangled within them. *She's gone.*

"Where are you? Where are you? Where is my baby?" My voice is so unlike my own, croaky and thin. I am a bad mother, neglectful. A metallic sour taste creeps into my mouth.

Rabbit whines and twists around my legs like a question mark.

A distant cry then, from upstairs.

Hurtling back to the door, I find it unlocked. Bewildered, I take the stairs two at a time, the bone still tight in my fist, flying through the dark hallway above, up the stairs again, and then again. My knees weaken as I pull open my bedroom door and see the baby's legs kicking in the crib, her breathy cries reverberating. *Not Emily. Not my dead baby. This is Viola.*

"Oh . . . oh," I say, dropping the bone on the carpet and scooping her up. Her knitted stockings are damp, the sheets too. Her back arches in unhappiness. For Viola's sake I need to get a grip. I must pull myself back from this chasm I'm tumbling into. *How did she get here?* My head whirls as I drag through my memories, but I'm met only with blank space. I rock the baby back and forth until she settles, until she quietens and understands she's not been abandoned for a second time.

***

Later, when the house is still and the baby is dozing safely back in her drawer bed in the kitchen, I lay out several items in a circle on the table.

Twelve o'clock is the photograph of Emanuel Cleeve, his wife Sophia and their baby Viola in her carriage.

Three o'clock is the book of nursery rhymes.

Six o'clock is marked by the baby's thigh bone.

Nine o'clock is given over to the newspaper notice telling of the murder I'll commit in three days.

The answer to the riddle of Theo, the woman at the museum and Emanuel Cleeve's mimic lies somewhere in these items, or the spaces in-between. An answer that will also prove to Mr Garland I'm not mad, or a liar.

I place my hands on my lap, pick at the loose skin on a thumbnail as I think again of Arthur.

***

I wake at dawn to Viola's hungry cries. My neck is cricked, my mouth parched. While the milk warms on the stove, I pace the kitchen with the baby, Rabbit's eyes following our slow circles around the table. My final dream of the night was about Mr Garland. The three of us motoring along a country lane where cows and sheep grazed in the gloaming light. In the distance the sea arched blue to the horizon.

Dreaming about another man, as innocent as it was, feels like a betrayal of sorts. It has me selecting and wrapping a slice of gingerbread from the tin, bundling up the baby and making the short trip to the bottom of the garden.

My knuckles hover above the wooden door of the groom's lodgings in the half-light, the baby squirming and grunting. She's filling the nappy I have only just changed.

What am I doing here? Standing barefooted in my dressing gown on the soggy ground trying to gain this man's confidence and trust with the offer of biscuits. Shoving the parcel under the door, I turn back for the house.

I glance back once, see the glow of a lamp, the twitch of the curtain and know he's watching. Gritting my teeth, the visit to Emanuel's daughter freshens in my mind. I'll not be like him in the lodgings, cowed and hiding away from my own life. I must set an intention and stick to it. This morning, I'll return to town and pound the streets until I find this drummer who mimicked Emanuel Cleeve. Prove to Mr Garland that I'm not mad. Prove to myself those things too.

A trowel sticks out from one of the vegetable beds. I pause beside it, then look to the back door. Keeping Viola and Rabbit safe is my priority. If someone is getting into the house around the back, I need to know about it.

Bending, I scoop some soil into the trowel and carefully carry it to the back door. When I next leave the house,

I'll set a trap, sprinkle the earth just thickly enough to capture a footprint, but thin enough not to be noticed.

***

In town I make casual enquires in many of the shops close to where the drummers stood performing. Half of the people I speak with were unaware of them, or not working on Saturday. The others don't have any useful information about who they were, or where they might be now.

In the chemist's the girl behind the counter is a little more helpful. "Travellers, most likely." She sniffs. "There are some caravans parked up on Midsummer Common. Try asking there."

***

Arcs of fog rise from the river as I stand with the pram on the edge of the common watching the small group of brightly painted caravans from a distance. Slithers of smoke rise from thin metal chimneys, children kicking a ball about on the grass while grazing cattle roam. There are no instruments, no drums or flashes of red and yellow. Viola cries, my stomach groans with either nausea or hunger – I can't tell which – and I turn back to town.

***

I'm in the same teashop Mr Garland and I sat in after my near fall. A different table this time, a mother and daughter sitting where we did. The daughter must be around ten, has plaited hair the colour of roasted chestnuts.

Glancing down at Viola I touch a wisp of hair on her crown. It's fair now, but that's likely to change, of course. Will I be around to witness that change? Could I instead be locked up and convicted of murder? Tears spring to my eyes. *I'm not capable of it*, I think fiercely.

Some years ago, I recall reading about Mrs Swann and her lover in the newspaper. Mother of eleven. Found guilty of the murder of her husband. She and her lover went to the gallows together, were hanged side by side. Their appeals to the king for clemency were ignored.

Taking a bite of my cream bun, I allow the sugary dough to slide about in my mouth until thoughts of the gallows are replaced with sweetness.

I have an errand to run before I head for home. Turning down Post Office Terrace with the pram, my heart clenches as I approach the secondhand bookshop. There are no lights on inside, a closed sign is hanging on the door. The bookbinders are also shut. There's nobody about, no children playing today.

Taking the stolen teaspoon from my coat pocket, I push it through the shop's brass letterbox. It clinks to the floor on the other side. "I'm sorry, Arthur. I'm sorry," I whisper through my tears.

***

Mr Garland's motor is parked up outside Arcadia House when I arrive home. My heart quickens and so does my pace.

He waits at the bottom of my front steps, takes off his hat, gives me a pensive smile as I draw near. "Mrs Pemberton . . . I owe you an apology."

I wait for him to continue.

"I was quick to make assumptions yesterday. I'm sorry for that." He swallows, then takes a deep breath. High spots of colour stain his cheeks. "I . . . um . . . I haven't been entirely honest with you. My . . . my wife has left me, you see. Taken our son Harold. She and my former business partner . . . they . . . they took a liner to America in the summer."

I cannot help staring at him after this frank admission. "How terrible."

Mr Garland runs a hand across his mouth, as if trying to wipe away his confession. "Yes, it's been terrible. More than terrible."

I've a peculiar urge to touch his arm, console him somehow.

He clears his throat. "Mrs Pemberton, I think my own worries clouded my judgement yesterday. I said things that offended you. I never intended that. You see, my wife was ill after Harold's birth. Quite unwell, in fact. She spent time in hospital." He swallows. "My wife imagined things. That Harold had a twin. That the nurses took him when he was born." His cheeks pink. "It was hogwash, of course. But she fully believed it for a while."

I let out a long breath. *Here is his story, then.* This is the explanation for the sorrow stooping his shoulders and clouding his eyes. "I'm sorry. But she recovered well enough?"

"Yes." He sighs. "Whatever I may think of my wife for taking off with Harold, she's a good mother. Wants only the best for our boy."

I nod, believing him and appreciating the effort he's made in coming here today. And for what he's told me about his wife's betrayal. That must have taken some courage.

"I'd . . . I'd very much like to hear your story again about the man and this baby he left in your house. I'd like to help, if I may?" he continues.

His tone is gentle and tentative, and I feel a surge of heady relief. "Thank you, Mr Garland."

"Please. Call me John."

"And you must call me Della." He looks at me expectantly, is waiting for an invitation to come inside. Tea and biscuits in the drawing room again. But then I remember the clock face of mysteries still arranged on my kitchen table.

***

I lead John around the back of Arcadia House to the kitchen, past the dripping drainpipe and to the outhouse where I park the pram.

John looks to the end of the garden, the smoke curling from the chimney of the groom's lodgings. He doesn't offer up a question or comment, and neither do I. The truth of that situation will come out soon enough and it's time for me to match John's honesty with mine.

"It's a grand old house, all right," he says, puffing out a breath and turning to gaze up at the glinting windows.

"My husband was born here," I say, staring at the sprinkled mud trap by the back door.

John smiles. "Yes. I remember him telling me when we met. It's nice when a home stays within a family." He says this wistfully, and I have an urge to know more about where he lives now. Did his wife take some of his furnishings and possessions as well as his son? *What a cruel woman.*

There are no footprints in the mud, no signs of disturbance and entry, and my shoulders loosen. Holding Viola in the crook of my arm, I reach for my door key in my bag, gesture at the paving. "Sorry about the mess, you'll need to step over it.

No footprints mean no intruders." My attempt at a laugh is hollow.

John shakes his head. "I . . . I didn't appreciate how bad things had got. How frightened you must have been living here. I will help in any way I can."

My smile is grateful as I unlock and open the back door, but I feel a pinch of dismay at the mess waiting for us inside. I should think John's flat is practical, and well-designed. Modern and in keeping with his profession, appearance and car. "Do you own a telephone?"

John arches an eyebrow at my question, as he follows me inside. "A telephone. Yes. I use it mostly for business, mind. They're quite the thing nowadays, aren't they?"

"My husband didn't care for them, preferred to write letters." I watch a flare of understanding cross John's face at my deliberate use of the past tense.

Taking off his hat, he looks on in confusion as I place Viola in her drawer bed, and I steel myself. "I haven't been entirely honest with you. Theo died in the war. November last year."

John blinks, follows me to the table, hat still gripped in his hands. "Della. You said your husband was . . . away."

My legs feel suddenly weak, and I reach for the back of a chair. "I know. I'm sorry I misled you. It's . . . difficult to talk about."

John shakes his head, his eyes sorrowful. "He died just before the Armistice, then?"

Do not weep, do not. I direct my gaze to the clock wheel of items on the table. "The day before," I confirm. But as the words leave my mouth, I notice something.

Placing a hand to my lips, I skirt around the table until I'm standing directly in front of the circle. The order of the items has changed, rearranged just like the insect sketches upstairs on the study wall.

Twelve o'clock is now the baby's thigh bone and at six o'clock lies the photograph of Emanuel and his family. The nursery rhymes remain in their original position, but the murder notice is missing altogether.

My eyes sweep around the kitchen surfaces. I check the dresser, the waste pail, even inside the stove. A shrill ringing in my ears begins. John watches me in silent alarm. *Did I do this?* I think of finding Viola gone from her drawer bed in the early hours, discovering her tucked up in the crib in my bedroom. I've no memory of taking her there, or of doing this. But there was no sign anyone entered the house around the back, and the front door is bolted.

"Della?" John's voice is dim behind me as I stand in the cool larder rummaging behind and under the tins, bottles and tubs as I search out the notice.

Turning, I see John still looking at me with tight-lipped concern.

My hands tremble as I return to the table. "John . . . please, will you sit? There are some things I must tell you."

***

I use mugs today for our tea, not the white and blue china. It seems more fitting as we perch on our chairs among this melee of curious objects and the truths I have told. I've been more honest with this man than anyone of late, and my body feels strangely light, as I might float to the ceiling at any moment.

John now knows about Theo's death, about the arrival of the fir tree and the book of rhymes, the fox and ham incident. The live gypsy moth in the display cabinet and the woman who bought pupae from Theo's place of work. I tell him more about my visit to Viola Cleeve in Grantchester and how her troubled father most likely hid the photograph in the attic before he died. But not the bone. *Emanuel's daughter didn't think him responsible for hiding the bone.*

When I speak about the noises and disturbances I sometimes hear at night, the misplaced and moved items and my lapses in memory, John doesn't spring to his feet and claim me mad or incoherent. He just quietly listens, his attention on me and me alone.

Finally, finally, he speaks. "Honestly . . . I don't know what to say. Aside from . . . this is . . . this is outrageous. You're being terrorised in your own home."

"Yes . . . yes, I am. And I don't know why," I admit.

John's eyes are hooded, a muscle ticking in his jaw.

It takes some effort to steady my shaking hands enough to lift my mug and sip my tea. "You believe me, then?"

"Yes. Yes, of course." John traces a finger over a scratch in the table. "But . . . you can't be alone in this house, Della. Not after this."

I watch his finger press into the pocked wood, forever marked by mine and Theo's lives, and his parents' lives before us. "This is my home. There's nowhere else for me to go," I say.

John stills his hand. "What about the sister you mentioned . . . you could go and stay . . ."

"No. Not Mary," I interrupt. "We didn't part on good terms after her visit."

"A friend then, or a neighbour?" he suggests.

I shake my head. There's another admission I must make. "My husband . . . he . . ." I pause, wipe my damp palms on my skirt. "Theo was keeping secrets from me."

John watches me silently. Viola grumbles in her bed and I reach across and pat her stomach, her breaths anchoring me to this moment.

Despite the burn of embarrassment, it's a relief John will know all of it.

Apart from my thieving and the murder I'm supposed to commit.

Apart from me knowing Arthur, the boy who died across the road.

Apart from my muddy boots being by the front door the morning the boy died.

"Theo would disappear for whole afternoons, lie about where he'd been. A solicitor was involved too, although when I contacted them, they'd tell me nothing." I look down. My meaning, my thoughts on this are clear enough and I feel a curl of shame.

"A woman?" John suggests softly.

"Perhaps," I say. "Maybe the one from the museum. I'm thinking she and the man who came into my house could be working together. Seeking revenge for something?"

John's eyes widen. "Revenge for what, though? I have to say when I met Theo he seemed the honest sort."

I grimace at that. I believed him to be honest too.

"Even if your husband behaved badly, I presume you've

been living a quiet life here since his passing. Bothering no one," John continues.

My gold wedding band glints in the low light. John is right of course, but someone does know about my thieving, has been watching me. Knows I have a darker side. I gaze at Viola, at this baby who has delivered me this exhaustion but also quiet moments of stillness and peace. "Theo and I . . . we had a child. It was our greatest loss."

Another silence settles between us, and I see John stare hard at the baby's thigh bone in the circle of objects. He slowly, so slowly, reaches across the table for my hand, says nothing at all.

I quietly weep then, for this gentle and caring gesture, for the warmth of his touch, for all my losses, for all the things stolen from me, for this life that no longer feels like my own.

Eventually he pulls away and passes me his handkerchief. Clean and pressed. A man who takes care of himself as well as others.

My eyes are still damp. "I know Viola isn't mine, but what if she's unwanted?"

"Della . . . I . . ."

"I could provide her with a good home," I say quietly.

John glances at the window. A ragged leaf has become trapped in a spider's web and flutters at the glass, like a waving hand desperate for attention. "I understand your becoming attached. My own son – Harold. I miss him badly. Sometimes so much it takes my breath away."

This man. He's suffering, just like me. The handkerchief clenches in my fist. "When will you next see him?"

"Perhaps never," he says with such open and honest sadness my heart ties into a knot. John wipes a hand across his face and the hopelessness of it all sits between us, until finally he clears his throat. "The place at the end of your garden. I saw smoke from the chimney. Someone lives there?"

I blow out a long breath, sit back in my chair. "Theo's younger brother."

John frowns.

"He'd been on the front for more than a year when Theo enlisted. He was injured the same day Theo was killed." The shock on John's face is clear. Two brothers, one dead and one wounded on the day before the fighting stopped. I swallow. "His face is . . . well, it isn't the same. He isn't the same."

"Do you see much of him?" John asks quietly.

I resist the urge to scratch my itching arms. "No. He works on a small holding during the day. Digs the vegetable beds in the garden here too. Our paths rarely cross. He avoids me, refuses to talk. I want us to be friends, but, well . . . it's a difficult situation."

Rabbit ambles over and John bends to rub behind the dog's ears. "Difficult that he survived and Theo didn't, you mean."

"Yes. Exactly that." Feeling understood in this moment is like a ray of long absent sunshine on my face. I swallow. "Oliver. His name is Oliver."

John's smile is soft, as if he understands the effort of my admissions. "This might seem like an odd question," he continues. "But might Oliver know something about what's happening here?"

"It crossed my mind, but I honestly don't believe him capable."

"But he must have a clear view of the house, see folks coming and going," John suggests.

I think of the flicker I thought I saw at the attic window while down the end of the garden and suppress a shiver. "He might . . . but he keeps his curtains drawn."

John drinks his tea, wipes his lips. "I suppose he uses the side passage when he leaves, walks past the house then?"

"No. He never comes this way. There's a back gate leading to a lane."

"Of course, the lane," John muses. "So, it's entirely possible someone could get around the back of your house unnoticed?"

I shake my head. "Rabbit would bark at a stranger in the garden. And Oliver is here at night, would also hear an intruder."

John gestures at the teapot, offering a refill. I shake my head, nausea nestling under my ribcage. He handles the pot delicately, the tea pouring into his mug at just the right angle. He glances up as he uses the milk jug. "Apologies if I'm stating the obvious, but you're sitting here in this magnificent house, while your brother-in-law lives at the foot of the garden in a . . . stable."

My fingers worry at the edges of John's damp handkerchief on my lap. "It's the groom's lodgings. And I invited him to stay in the house, but he refused."

I think back to the stilted conversation Oliver and I had the week before he was discharged from hospital last winter. He'd let go of his rented room in a shared flat close to his place of work in London. I offered him his childhood room here. Told him it was his for as long as he needed. He refused, said it wouldn't be right. Asked instead if he could live in the groom's lodgings, just until he was back on his feet. Whenever that might be.

I'd no hesitation in agreeing to his request, was wrung out with grief and loneliness in the months after Theo's death. Oliver and I had only met a handful of times, and always with Theo. I liked the man, found him reserved and quietly spoken, younger than Theo by five years. He seemed in awe of his elder brother's academic achievements, a little self-conscious of his own work as a bookkeeper.

But when we were together Theo and I would draw Oliver out of himself, his eyes lighting up as he amused us with tales of his colleagues' quirks. I hoped I'd be able to draw him out this time too, that he could be a friend.

John takes a sip of his tea. "Again . . . I'm sorry for suggesting it . . . but do you think it's possible Oliver wants the house for himself, is trying to . . . scare you out of the place?"

My first instinct is to protest. Oliver might have suffered mentally and physically, but that did not make him dangerous. But was it *him* who found the photograph of Emanuel Cleeve in the attic? Has he found some way of getting into this house unseen, intent on making my life a misery? Is he responsible for the fir tree and the book of nursery rhymes? Moving the sketches around on the walls upstairs?

My thoughts about my brother-in-law are scattering and rearranging, thinking of his nightly terrors, the written apologies in that tin. *I'm sorry. I'm sorry. I'm sorry.* I quickly tell

John about that discovery.

"Sorry for something that happened during the war, do you think?" asks John, concern knitting his brow.

"Perhaps." It's a possibility. What happened to Oliver on the front has left its mark both mentally and physically. There's still a tremor in my fingers as I straighten Viola's blanket.

"We should pay Oliver a visit . . . together?" John suggests, his voice slow and unsure.

"Now?" I say, looking up.

"Um. Well . . . yes, if you think it's a good idea?"

Chapter 29

Viola grizzles in my arms as we approach the groom's lodgings, the grey sky beginning to darken. I know Oliver is inside, from the sliver of light bleeding between the curtains.

John knocks on the door loudly and we wait. And wait. He knocks again. "Um . . . Mr Pemberton? May we have a word? I'm here with your sister-in-law."

There is no response. I gesture to the stone by the threshold. "He keeps a key there," I whisper, determined that whatever it takes we will get to speak to Oliver today. John is about to reach for it when I hear footsteps. *Oliver is by the door listening.* Placing a hand on the gnarled wood, I take a deep breath. "Please. This is important."

Viola begins to shriek, and perhaps it's that, or maybe it's down to the urgency he hears in my voice, but the door unlocks and opens a crack.

John steps forwards, but Oliver remains out of sight behind the door. "Um . . . hello, old chap. My name's John Garland. I'm a friend of Mrs Pemberton's. May we come inside for a moment?"

"What's this about?" Oliver's voice is small.

John gives me an uncertain look.

"Please, Oliver. Just let us in." My tone is firm, and after a second of consideration, he pulls the door wider, still concealing himself behind it.

I watch John assessing Oliver's living space with a keen eye, the open newspaper on the table, the strings of onions tacked to the wall, the grey blanket on his neatly made bed. The room smells earthy, of woodsmoke and vegetables. It's a shambolic place to live, and I wonder if I should have tried harder to make him move into his old bedroom in the house. Whether this is another failing on my part.

Moving to the table, Oliver cannot look either of us in the eye. But I force myself to focus on his face. The ricocheted bullet he took to his right cheek caused it to sink, the pink scar tissue bubbling over what remains of his nose. The painted copper mask he wears to disguise his injury sits on the shelf; an uncanny likeness for the man he used to be with its matching skin tone and dark eyebrows. A permanent memory of the brutal and unforgiving war. *But still . . . he came back while Theo didn't.* I sway from side to side with the baby, breathing through the unfairness of it all.

John clears his throat. "Della . . . Mrs Pemberton has had a spot of trouble up at the house. We wondered, might you know anything about this?"

Oliver picks up a packet of woodbines, pulls one out. His hand trembles as he strikes a match, lights the cigarette. The tip glows orange as his eyes lift to me. "What sort of trouble?"

John throws me a beseeching look as if he doesn't know where to begin. *He's right. This is my story to tell.* "A man had a key to the house. He came inside and left this baby. There was a Christmas tree too, and a book of rhymes for the child – with a dedication inside written by Theo."

Oliver takes a long drag on his cigarette, smoke clouding the already fuggy air. His eyes pinch together at the mention of Theo, then dart from me and the baby to John. I watch him for any glimmer of guilt, but there's no reaction aside from the deepening bead of orange at the tip of his cigarette as he inhales again. "No. I know nothing about any of that."

John takes a halting step over to Oliver, until there's no more than an arm's length between them. He struggles to hide a wince as he glances at Oliver's cheek. "Are you certain? I'm sure things must have been hard . . . the war . . . and now living here."

Oliver refuses to meet John's scrutinous gaze, gives a swift shake of his head. "It wasn't me. None of what you just said was down to me." He glances up. "Why would I do any of that? And my brother's dead . . . how would he have written inside a book?"

John and I exchange a quick glance. It's my turn to press Oliver again and I swallow my unease. "Have you seen or heard anyone around here at night, or at any other time? Seen anyone other than me or Agnes enter the house?"

Another shake of his head. "I keep my curtains shut; you know that. My hearing isn't as good since . . ." He pauses, gestures at his scars and his ear.

I know from my time at the war hospital that his wounds are not as severe as many I came across, but his loss of identity, the hidden injuries you can't see and the need to wear a mask. I could weep for him.

Taking a step closer to my brother-in-law, the scent of stale sweat and hard work pinches in my nose. His nails are encrusted with dirt and his dark hair hangs in lank, greasy strands. But beneath all of this I still see echoes of the man he was when he worked in an office, wore a suit and tie, shined his shoes each Sunday night. There are also echoes of my husband here too and that makes it suddenly hard to breathe. "You're still working for Mr Greengage at the small holding?"

Oliver nods. "Most days. My hours aren't regular, though."

"Good. Being occupied is good." Then I think of seeing him heading off towards town the day Arthur visited last week. The same day someone came in and started the gramophone. "Someone was in the house the day before Christmas Eve. Was that you?" My face heats at the frankness of my question, but it's necessary.

John shifts position.

Oliver's marbled flesh ripples and tightens. He doesn't meet my gaze. "No."

Exasperation rattles through me. I'm unable to see how this broken man can possibly be responsible for any of the things that are happening. But might he know something about Theo's secrets? "When Theo left things were . . . strained between us. Did you know that?"

John looks instantly uncomfortable, but Oliver more so. He turns to the curtained window, his shoulders taut as wire.

Tentatively I reach out and touch his shoulder, but he flinches and moves away. "Theo was hiding things from me. Speaking with a solicitor. Did he ever mention this?" My cheeks flame at the thought I wasn't enough for my husband, that he may have had someone else. I trust Oliver will have picked up on my meaning without me having to say these words out loud.

A guttural noise comes from Oliver's throat. My heart thunders as I wait for his answer and I realise to hear the truth from him, to have it confirmed that Theo had a lover, and was perhaps planning to leave me, will be a relief.

"You should go," Oliver says curtly, glancing once more at John, then at the door.

I reach for him again, but he twists away. "But Oliver . . ."

"I said go!" His voice is a stern warning. He will not speak about anything, and the frustration of it overwhelms me.

Viola begins to fret in my arms, sharp breathy cries. Clicking my tongue, I bow my head and make for the door. John follows, his face tight. We will get no answers here tonight.

***

"You may not like hearing this, but I don't think you should stay here alone. Not with him living there," says John once we are back inside. He paces the kitchen, as I change Viola's nappy at the table. A stream of yellow urine immediately soaks the new cloth I place under her and John looks away.

"Oliver didn't admit to anything," I say over the baby's wails, her screams punctuated by hiccupping coughs as I set about cleaning her up.

John folds his arms. "Maybe not, but I worry he's not all with it. Don't you think his reactions were off, as if he wasn't taking in what we were saying . . . what you were saying?"

I shake my head. "Oliver's been damaged by the war, but I don't believe he'd intentionally hurt me." *He has unintentionally though, ignored all my attempts at friendship.* Fastening the nappy and easing on Viola's knitted stockings, I soothe her and dab away the wetness on her cheeks with my thumbs.

John sighs. "You're too gentle . . . too kind to understand. I hate to say this, Della, but I fear you're viewing him through the wrong lens."

Am I? I clean the table, wash up the tea mugs, wonder if I've been blinded by a sense of family loyalty, the urge to befriend and care for my brother-in-law. He's my final connection to Theo, and how can I walk away from that? Oliver's reactions to me asking about the solicitor were off, and I wonder if that's because he knows something, or whether it was just because he was too embarrassed to contemplate his brother would have been capable of such a betrayal. That Theo is now dead and can never explain himself, that we'll both be left frustrated by the unanswered questions we have about a man we both loved.

"You can't stay here. I can't go home and leave you and the baby alone knowing that man is living in such close quarters," says John in a low voice.

I turn to see John tapping a finger on his jacket sleeve faster than a ticking clock. His brisk statement and agitation startle me.

"You could stay in a hotel perhaps, or a guest house? If money's an issue I could . . ." he begins.

"John . . . that's kind, but I've the baby to think of. And it's getting late," I interrupt. This man has been helpful enough today and I must not abuse that kindness. And the thought of packing a bag and leaving . . . it's too much to contemplate. The basement kitchen is my cocoon, a place of safety. I throw a quick glance at the baby's bone on the table, in its new position on the clockface. *I must believe it's safe.*

"We need to talk more about this – find a solution," urges John. He walks over to me at the sink. "Would you . . . would you let me take you out for the evening, away from here?"

I look at him blankly, wipe the soap suds from my fingers. "Away . . . where?"

"Dinner. Somewhere in town. Somewhere your feelings and decisions won't be affected by this house." The look he gives me is full of worry. "If you're certain you don't want the police involved, we could try and come up with a plan for the best way of dealing with the situation," he ends.

By the 'situation' I'm assuming he still means Oliver. John smiles at me then, a tentative but full smile which curves his lips, and it does something strange to my insides. Something I've not felt since first meeting Theo.

I think again of my dream about driving with John in his motor, leaving Arcadia House and my troubles far behind. Shaking that thought away, I'm left with a pinch of anticipation at the thought of eating somewhere other than this kitchen. A place where I mostly survive on one pot meals. "Yes, dinner then. That would be nice."

He smiles at me again, nods. His hand brushes against mine, as he reaches for the dish cloth. "You're exhausted. Sit. I can finish this."

Standing back from the sink I dry my hands, watch John's shoulders round as he bends to wash and rinse each item. A strand of his dark hair falls out of place, a rebellious act. I fight the urge to smooth it back into place.

Chapter 30

John watches over Viola in the kitchen while I change upstairs. I feel strangely peaceful knowing he's here, that he's so intent on helping. Stepping into an emerald-green dress, I fumble with the mother of pearl buttons as I look at the crib, thinking about my rash suggestion we visit Agnes and ask her to mind Viola for a few hours while we dine out.

I frown at my reflection in the full-length mirror, feel a longing for the slimmer curves of my thirties. For clear unblemished skin and defined jowls. Sparkling eyes that aren't hooded with tiredness. Taking a long sip from the bottle of tonic I'm holding, I put these thoughts to one side, smooth a hand over my rounded stomach and search for a kernel of acceptance for the way I am now. My body might have betrayed me, might not have fulfilled its natural function and nurtured a child, but I am still here. *I am alive and have a baby and a dog to care for.*

After inspecting my nails, I pin up my hair. I pluck a few strands of grey from my hairline and grimace. My cheeks are sallow, and I pinch them. With a tut I walk to the chest of drawers, pull out the stolen things I hid up here after Bertie's discovery. I take out the salmon pink pot rouge and carefully apply it to my cheeks. The shade looks better than I thought it might – *a good theft after all.*

As I return the rouge to its new hiding place, something else catches my eye. An envelope sticking out from beneath my folded underwear. Pulling it out, cold skitters across my shoulders. It's the notice missing from the clock face on the kitchen table. It's Monday evening now and New Year's Eve is on Wednesday. If this note is telling my future, I've one more day of normality. One more day to uncover what is happening here before somebody believes I'll commit an act that will change my life forever. *Who would I kill, though?* I cannot wrap my mind around this hideous thought.

Picking up the tonic bottle I take another sip. The notice is folded twice and back inside its original envelope. I quickly slide it under a petticoat; glad I had the foresight to take this note from the clockface of items downstairs and hide this terrible accusation. Even if I don't remember doing so.

***

Agnes peers at me as I stand outside her family's front door, Viola cradled in my arms. "It will just be for a couple of hours. I'd be most grateful." I glance back at the motor. John is waiting by the passenger door, his hat in his hands. Feeling dizzy, I lift my head, tip my shoulders back. "I'll pay you, of course."

"What're you standing there for? Take the baby," I hear a voice hiss from inside.

"Good evening, Mrs Hatter," I call to Agnes's mother.

The woman peeps around her daughter, gives me a friendly smile. "Evening, Mrs Pemberton."

"Who's he?" Agnes asks bluntly, gesturing at John as I pass the baby over.

"A . . . friend."

"You don't have any friends." Her voice is suspicious, but also shot through with worry. I see the girl's mother deliver a swift kick to her daughter's ankle.

Ignoring her barbed, but accurate, observation, I thank Agnes and her mother, the pang at leaving Viola gnawing at me as I return to the motor.

***

John takes my arm, guides me beneath the portico of the ivy-clad University Arms Hotel. Rain taps on the glass above, but we are shielded from the elements as we walk up the steps, through the doors and into the warmth.

I trail my fingers over a potted palm, vibrant green, like the lush vegetation Theo spoke of seeing in the jungles he'd visited. My heart clenches uncomfortably.

A fire crackles in the grate, and the hum of voices from the other patrons fills the air as John enquires about a table for two in the restaurant.

We're soon seated in the bay window overlooking Parker's Piece, although the large square of grass outside, once home to troop encampments in the war, is invisible in the dark. All I see is my own ghostly reflection as the waiter pulls out my chair, lays a starched napkin across my lap.

I have a burst of longing for the bottle of tonic concealed in my velvet evening bag. Having only just been seated, it would be bad-mannered to excuse myself and visit the ladies powder room. I must wait a reasonable amount of time, perhaps until after the entrees have been served.

John insists we have three courses from the dinner menu, despite my appetite being small. The thought of plate after plate of food arriving makes my stomach roil and I stamp down on my nausea. I want to be here, I do. *So why do I now feel like bolting, running until I reach the Hatters' home and Viola?*

"Della? Have you made a choice?"

The words on the menu blur in and out of my vision and I run my tongue across my dry lips.

"Perhaps . . . I could order for you?" John suggests, his voice muffled by the ringing in my ears.

"Please. Yes, please," I croak, my skin crawling with phantom insect-like feet. I press my hands into my thighs under the table.

"How about the prawn cocktail and then the lamb chop? Shall I order wine as well?"

"I . . . don't often drink," I admit.

John flushes. "I'm sorry. That was presumptuous of me."

This man is so thoughtful. I think of the red wine that slipped down so nicely while we dined on bread and potatoes on Christmas Day. "It's not presumptuous at all. Yes, wine would be nice, thank you."

My muscles begin to unwind as I sip from my glass of claret, as John talks of his business, the growing list of men who seek employment on his building site. I tell him the same is happening at William's jam factory.

There's a lull in conversation as our entrees arrive, silver dishes of delicate pink prawns on a bed of crisp lettuce, a roundel of lemon. Elegantly presented. Unlike anything I've eaten in months.

John leans across the table when the waiter is gone. "Della, are you all right? You're very quiet."

"This is lovely. Really. I . . . haven't been out in such a long time." I gesture around the restaurant. "The food, surroundings. It's a . . . little overwhelming."

John's cheeks hollow. "I'm sorry. I didn't think. This is too much after . . ."

I shake my head. "It is I who should be apologising."

He is crestfallen, his neck sagging into his shirt collar.

Pulling in a breath, I pick up my fork, spear it into a prawn. It's soft and perfectly boiled. "Thank you for your kindness . . . for bringing me here tonight."

He smiles, his shoulders pulling back a little.

Another sip of wine. My stomach unfurls, and so does the conversation. As we eat our main courses, we talk about his wife who left him in July taking five-year-old Harold to California with a man he considered a friend and colleague. His devastation at no longer being in his son's life. At another man taking on the role of the boy's father.

"That was a horribly cruel thing for your wife to do," I say. From the corner of my eye, I see other couples dining in this restaurant tonight giving each other tender glances and looks, their feet touching under the table. These things seem more acceptable than ever since the war.

A thought tickles my mind of what it might be like to tuck a stray lock of John's hair behind his ear, feel the warmth of his skin. Heat builds in my midriff, the satin of my dress straining and clinging to my petticoat. I imagine perspiration bleeding through the glossy fabric, John's eyes widening in horror. Placing my napkin on the table, I stand up. "If you'll excuse me for a moment."

John's chair scrapes on the wooden floor as he stands too. "Of course."

At the entrance to the restaurant, I glance back, see him watching me. He lifts a hand of acknowledgement, gives me that familiar attentive look. His cheeks arch into a smile. I grip my bag, feel the outline of the tonic bottle and hurry on to the ladies' powder room.

***

When I return, desserts have arrived. Preserved strawberries for me and an orange pudding for John. "Everything all right?" he enquires.

"Oh, yes," I say tightly, omitting to tell him about the young woman who came across me sipping from the tonic bottle. It was quiet in the powder room, and I'd assumed I was alone. But she emerged from around a corner where I later saw there was a vanity mirror and stool. Her eyebrows lifted, a flash of judgement at me there with the bottle in my hand. She'd apologised for intruding; I'd apologised for startling her.

"Did you and your husband dine out often?" John asks, spooning a piece of pudding into his mouth and chewing slowly once I'm seated.

I take sip of wine to wash down the bitterness of the tonic's herbs. "When we first met, yes. But later . . . Theo preferred the two of us dining at home. We had a housekeeper until the war began – Mrs Finch. He adored her cooking."

"Lucky fellow," says John, and for a moment I'm uncertain whether he's talking about me, or the food and my neck prickles.

"What about Oliver? Did your husband see much of his brother?"

Forking a strawberry into my mouth, my gums ache from the sweetness. "Not really. Oliver lived in London. Because of their age difference, he and Theo weren't particularly close growing up."

"That's a pity. I'm not especially close to my own family either." John bites his bottom lip, looks stricken for a second and I sense it's not the time to press him on this.

"Families can be complicated," I offer.

"And then some," he counters with a small smile. John's expression darkens then. "We haven't yet talked about your situation and what must be done."

"No." *And I don't want to. I don't want to sully this beautiful dinner with thoughts of what I must return home to, the concerns that will clamour and crowd my head.*

"Della . . . you can't ignore this or let it continue."

I grimace. "I know. I know that."

John's next words are low and urgent. "We need to make a plan, decide what you'll do about Oliver, where you'll go."

"You still believe this is down to Oliver?" I say, placing down my fork.

John rubs his face. "Perhaps. I can't stop thinking that . . . well . . . he has the opportunity, and the motive."

"The house. You truly believe he wants the house," I whisper. The house Oliver grew up in. A house that belonged to his father. *I am the interloper here, after all.*

His shoulders lift into a half-shrug, and I know then that John does truly believe it. That my brother-in-law is behind the noises, the items being moved, the arrival of Viola. That he's attempting to drive me from my home in a twisted and cruel manner. I fear that if Mary were here, she would readily agree.

But even if that's the case, there's a part of this which will never make sense to me. "The noises I hear . . . the items sometimes moving from one place to another, or going missing, when I'm at home . . . they can't all be down to Oliver. He gets night terrors, so I know when he's in the lodgings. Sometimes I'm quite alone in the house when . . . things happen."

"Can you be certain of that?" John probes.

My fingers worry at the napkin on my lap. "That I'm the only one inside?"

John nods and I think hard about what I've been asked to consider. "If someone *has* been inside the house causing this mischief while I'm there, where would they hide?"

"Your sister said your nephews heard the sound of someone walking around at night," John says quietly.

I bunch the napkin into a fist. "It was just us in the house for the whole of my sister's visit. There's nowhere an intruder could hide in that house undetected."

John tilts his head, his eyes full of shadows. "Oliver might have found a way to get in. What about the oak tree? He could climb it. Perhaps gain entry via an attic window?"

My laugh is verging on hysterical, and I ignore the curious glances from a neighbouring table. "No. That would be impossible. My bedroom is at the back of the house. I'd have heard or seen him." Folding my napkin, I lay it beside my dessert bowl. It will be a risk voicing what I wish to say next, could bring this dinner to a swift close. But I sense I can trust this man. Like me, he's been lonely, wounded, grief stricken. "Perhaps some of this is down to . . . me."

John opens and closes his mouth, seems to be struggling to summon the right words, any words, as he twiddles his dessert spoon in his hand.

Taking a deep breath to disguise my discomfort, I wonder if I've made a terrible mistake. My palms moisten as the fear I've done my best to quash rises. *I'm going quietly insane.* The arrival of a baby so soon after my urge to steal one from a pram outside the stationery shop – just a happy coincidence, or something darker? Finding Viola in the crib upstairs when I'd put her down to sleep in the kitchen. My lapses in memory. The items that begin in one location and end up in another. *My muddy boots by the front door the morning Arthur was found dead.* Did Arthur have an accident, or was it more than that?

"You mustn't think like this," John berates eventually, shaking his head.

Lightheaded from the wine and rich food, the thought of my petty thefts and the murder I am supposed to commit, my throat closes.

John turns to summon the waiter, requests the bill.

We sit in silence at the table as we wait, as I wonder if it's possible I typed the notice announcing I will kill someone on New Year's Eve. That I then placed it in the crib which I purchased. The moth in the cabinet – the woman at the zoology department who came to buy pupae. *What if that was me too?*

What if I did steal a baby? What if the intruder is a figment of my vibrant imagination after I discovered the photograph in the attic. That I felt some sickened urge to place a baby's bone in the eaves. That Arthur didn't fall . . . but was pushed by me during my frustration at finding him back again.

What if I'm the mischief maker here?

What if I am already a murderer?

Chapter 31

John starts the motor outside the hotel, and the engine stutters. It's a little after nine o'clock – we are late picking up Viola. I don't voice my concerns that perhaps we should leave her with Agnes, that she'll be safer away from Arcadia House. *Safer away from me.*

A downstairs curtain twitches as we pull up outside the Hatters' home. John comes around and helps me out. His grip is light, and I lean into him a little, my head hazy from the wine.

Agnes's cheeks are taut and pinched with worry when she opens the door and sees us both. Viola sleeps in her arms. Seeing the baby brings tears of gladness to my eyes and I'm full of apologies at our lateness.

John introduces himself. "It's my fault," he says, his hat in his hands. "I lost track of the time." He looks their terraced cottage up and down. "This is a nice part of town. Close to the amenities, but quiet too."

The girl hands the baby over without comment, and her gaze rakes over John, assessing and appraising him. I sense she likes what she sees for her face softens.

"Thank you, Agnes. See you . . . I will . . ." I pause and lick my lips, try to summon the right words in the right order. Holding the baby to my chest as I open my bag, I pull out my purse and pay her, generously, I think. "I'll see you after New Year."

She doesn't reply and her look becomes closed as her eyes drift to my bag. I see the neck of the tonic bottle sticking out and I fumble to push it back inside. Risking a glance at John, he's looking down the street and hasn't noticed.

"Goodbye, Mrs Pemberton," says Agnes. "Look after yourself and the baby. Take good care, won't you."

Unease curdles her words. Before I can reply, her front door closes and then it's just the three of us again.

***

John pets Rabbit by the kitchen stove when we return, the dog rolling onto his back and exposing his tummy. His tail wags furiously against the tiled floor and I steal the occasional glance in their direction as I change the baby on the table.

Dropping the dirty nappy in a copper pot, and balking at the smell, John offers to set some water to boil to soak the cloths overnight.

When the baby is asleep upstairs in her crib, we explore each room of Arcadia House together, switching on lights to extinguish shadows, opening wardrobes, checking every nook and cranny for evidence of an intruder.

I stand on the attic threshold with a lamp as John searches the place, looking at each trunk and piece of furniture. I sniff. The smell in here today isn't sweet, but rancid. More dead rodents? *Rat poison.* I imagine the crunch and sting of it, slipping down Emanuel's throat. The painful burn in his gut.

John turns his attention to the windows, the night as black as onyx beyond. They have no locks and, with my consent, he takes a hammer and nail to them to seal them shut, the steady thumps dampening my agitation. When he's finished, he turns. "You must believe you are safe here, Della. There's really no need to be afraid."

I smile and thank him. Having an ally in John makes me bolder, certain that tonight Viola and I will sleep well in our own beds.

When John makes to leave, he presses on me to bolt the basement door after him, and that under no circumstances should I confront Oliver again. He tells me he has business to attend to in the morning but will return here later in the day. We will then discuss what must be done over tea.

"I wonder if . . . you should think of letting this house go. Whether you'd be happier living somewhere else?" he suggests quietly as we stand at the open door, the thickness of the night leaching in.

"Perhaps," I reply honestly. This is what Mary wants for me too. A fresh start, a place where I can dance towards my future rather than stumble.

Without warning, John leans in and tucks a strand of hair behind my ear. The graze of his fingers against my skin sends a shiver scuttling through me, the feeling of being startled awake after a long, deep sleep.

He smiles, his hand falling to his side.

Again. Please do that again.

He shuffles his feet, gives me a shy look. "I think that . . . two people alone can be company for one another, don't you think?"

"Yes," I reply. "I do believe they can."

***

Later, I sit on the edge of my bed in the silent house staring at Viola in her crib. Her tiny mouth moves in her sleep, and her arms are flung behind her head. I disappear into the image of her until my back aches and my feet prickle with pins and needles. My head thrums with the start of a headache and I drag myself back to the present and lift the bottle of tonic to my lips.

I try and summon the strength that infused me as I drank tea in old Viola Cleeve's home, but dizziness spins my head, and the room becomes so soft around the edges it feels like I am sinking into a pillow. Thoughts come and go, images from the night bleeding into one another as I apply cold cream to my face, swiping away the remains of the pot rouge.

The feel of John's hand in the kitchen as I cried.

John's care and attentiveness in the restaurant.

His skin brushing against my cheek as he touched my hair.

Two people alone can be company for one another.

Yet how can I accept his company and his help when at least part of what's happening in this house must be down to my own actions?

The thought of Emanuel hiding his family photograph in the attic nags at me. If it was me who discovered it, did I come across anything else of Emanuel's up there?

My climb up the attic stairs is unsteady, the oil lamp in my hand swinging and jolting against the wall. The waves of dizziness still come, and my chest spasms in pain. The richness of the food and wine, I suppose. Approaching the door, I place the lamp down, rub at the spot above my heart until the pain dims enough for me to insert the key in the lock.

Cool air rushes out to greet me as I open the door. I linger for a second or two, summon the new courage I felt when I was in here earlier with John. *There's really no need to be afraid.* Forcing my leaden feet forwards, I place the lamp down and move past the old pieces of furniture jammed against the wall.

I feel behind each rafter, run my fingers around the skirting boards. *Nothing.* My eyes stray to the trunks. Opening the one nearest, I root around in Theo's clothes, the textures stinging my sensitive fingers as I hunt for items belonging to Emanuel Cleeve that may not even exist. *I can't help myself.* A woollen jumper, trousers, shirts. The sight of my husband's garments brings back memories I've done my best to keep buried. There's nothing to be found of Emanuel's here, and so I turn my attention to the next trunk, and the next.

Frustration wells inside me. Wiping my damp palms on my dress, streaks of perspiration and dust stain the fabric.

A sudden tapping, and I whirl around. The spindly branches of the oak tree flick at a windowpane. Another movement then and fear grips me by the throat. A man lies curled like a comma between two trunks. He holds up a translucent hand, his lips moving, his eyes wide and seeking something I don't understand. *Emanuel.*

We stare at each other, my heart thudding. *It's a vision like before. Not real.*

A scrabbling, scratching sound then, the noise I hear in the walls and in the floorboards. Emanuel's vision flickers and dims, but his finger still points at me, his lips still speaking words I cannot hear. I want to close my eyes and blink him away, put a stop to my eyes playing this wicked, wicked trick. *The man who came into my house promised he'd return . . . and he has.*

The touch on my foot is light, and I gasp, half expecting to see the blur of Emanuel's pale hand gripping it, but it's a rat, its tail flicking as it scuttles towards this vision that's still pointing and speaking silent words.

Scrabbles and scratches come from above and below and my mouth arches into a scream as a plethora of rats spill from the walls, dropping from the rafters until they surround Emanuel in a writhing grey jumble of legs, bodies and tails. And then they are under him and picking him up and carrying him away to the opposite side of the attic, passing through the travelling trunks, the fairground horse and a boy's tricycle, as if these things were no more substantial than clouds.

I collapse to the boards, my chest heaving. "What do you want? What do you want from me?" Weeping, I think of Emanuel's lonely death up here. The same must not happen to me. *There's a baby downstairs who is depending on me, a small dog I love fiercely.*

The rats deposit Emanuel before a child-sized wooden wardrobe and dissipate, their tiny feet scuttling them off to the four corners of the attic and back to their hiding places in the underbelly of this house.

My limbs are heavy, moving without choice or action. It's as if I'm standing outside myself as I watch my dress drag across the boards, my fingers clawing at the wood. "No! No!" But my lips are being stitched shut, a silver needle and the thread I stole from the drapers doing the job nimbly.

Arching my back in pain, I kick out my legs, scratch my nails on the wooden floor. The fight rises and rises in me and then I'm upon this vision of a man, and a ferocious light blinds me until I see nothing at all.

***

Blinking my eyes open, I find myself lying in the attic on my side, hands resting under my head as if in prayer. My mind is comfortably blank. Did I fall? Stretching out an arm, I circle my wrist. It's stiff, as if I've been here some time. My ears strain for the sound of Viola crying, but it's silent beneath the sound of my rapid breaths.

Then images flood into my head with the ferocity of a hailstorm, and I scrabble to my feet. It was a nightmare. And yet I'm here, on the opposite side of the attic. There is no rancid smell of rat now, no scratching in the walls as I grind my palms into my eyes.

Pulling my shaking hands away, I inspect my nails, remembering my crawl across the boards. They are their usual stubby selves. I touch my lips. Not stitched shut.

Turning, I notice the wardrobe pressed against the wall behind me. The dark and ugly black painted wood, the single panelled door and the slim drawer beneath. It stands almost at head height, is built for a child. It's a simple piece and doesn't match the other furniture in this house, the rich mahoganies, and walnuts with their intricate cornicing. I'd never paid it much attention, had supposed it belonged to either Theo or Oliver when they were small. It's then I notice the swatch of grey fabric trapped in the door.

My eyes are drawn to the key in the lock. Somewhere in

my missing memories did I open this door and root around inside? Is this where Emanuel hid his precious things?

A click of the key and the door unlocks and swings back without even a creak. I'm faced with a rack of coats, the scent of musty wool. The garments are made for an adult, folding in on themselves as they scrape the wardrobe's base. Running a hand over the wool, I do not recognise any of these coats as belonging to my husband.

My fingers tremble as I gently part them, then I feel a whisker of cooler air tickling my cheeks. Frowning, I part the coats further, until they reveal something that makes me stop dead. A rectangular hole cut in the back of this piece of furniture, a yawning, dark space.

I fetch the oil lamp, take a steadying breath, and fold myself small as I prepare to crawl inside.

Chapter 32

The oil lamp quivers in my hand as I hold it out ahead. My senses are heightened, fully aware that if it drops in this confined space it could set it alight. Forcing my hand to steady, I push forwards, the fabric of the coats prickling at my hair and cheeks.

I stare into the void at the back of the wardrobe, the wick flickering in the lamp's glass shade. My breath hitches. It's an extension of the attic – the width between the two walls about the same as my arms if I were to hold them out wide. As far as I can see, this room runs the length of the house from front to back, has been separated off from the rest of the attic by a false wall.

The lamp illuminates a few wooden crates, tins of food and a metal pail with a lid. A mattress, pile of blankets and pillow. A stack of magazines. Holding the lamp higher, the rafters above my head gleam. They are whitewashed, and on closer inspection the small blue dots peppering them are delicately painted flowers.

Do you know he had that place built for me? A space I could play. Emanuel's daughter's words about this attic echo in my head. I hadn't paid attention to them at the time. Is this what she meant? A private place designed by her father – by Emanuel.

Blinking, I try and make sense of what I see before me.

A secret room where someone has been living?

Bewilderment drives me on, clambering through the gap and into this hidden room. While it smells musty, the air in here carries the scent of sweeter things too.

Turning to the first crate, I see it contains a few apples. Poking them, their skins are soft and dimpled. Tins of evaporated milk and peaches sit alongside tins of ham. The single mattress on the floor is flattened, dented by the person who last lay on it. There's an army issued flashlight beside it, an oil lamp and box of matches too. A pile of Adventure Magazines, a whole stack of them. Illustrations of men in canoes, carrying pistols, climbing the rigging of tall ships adorn the covers.

I huddle over them, seeking a clue from their pages. A man's been staying here, then. The noises I've heard, the scrapes, scrabbles and creaks. An invasion of my house, my privacy . . . *my sanity.* Then I see something else . . . wedged behind the mattress.

My fingers tremble as I tease it out, this familiar green woollen hat. *Arthur?* Blinking, I stare at the Adventure Magazines. Think of the boy watching me and this house. His death. My boots at the door – a possible sign I'd spoken with him the night he died.

The hat is stiff in places and holding it to the lamp my heart clatters. A large stain. *Blood.* I press a hand to my lips to quieten the moan. Stuffing the hat back where I found it, my fingers are so tainted by this discovery I can barely look at them. I think of Arthur's family, how hard up they are and how much they've suffered already. Their devastation at his death.

Trying to quieten my noisy breaths, my attention is drawn to a small book sticking out from beneath the lumpy pillow. I ease it out. The book of butterflies Arthur gave me. *I searched for this book. I left it on Theo's desk.*

My thoughts slowly clear. The man who's been living in my house. This is all his doing. I place the book with Arthur's hat, biting back my nausea.

Moving away from the mattress, I'm drawn to another crate and the curious metal funnel resting on top. I angle the lamp to better examine the bottles beneath the funnel.

The first is small and brown with a cork stopper. My heart thuds as I read the label. *Opium tincture.*

My fingers trace over the bevelled writing on the front of the green bottle beside it. *Gordon's Special Dry London Gin.*

I recognise the curved shape of the other glass bottles in the crate instantly. *Tonic for Female Disorders.*

Selecting a bottle of my tonic, I shake it, find it near empty. Taking out the stopper, I sniff its familiar smell. Earthy herbs and water with a little preserving alcohol. *Or is it?* When I sniff again, I catch a different, sharper scent.

The sergeant's accusation at the police station he could smell liquor on my breath. Mary's quips about me turning to drink.

The glass bottles clink together as I quickly remove and examine each in turn. The funnel, the gin and opium.

Someone's been filling my tonic bottles with a different remedy.

One that could quite easily do me harm. *Or kill me.*

My stomach swoops. The urge to flee rises as if a fire has

been lit under me.

A wavering and clear cry drifts up through the floorboards and I startle, almost knocking over the lamp. It's as if Viola is right here beside me. Staring at the floor, I try and place myself in this house, see that I must be above my bedroom.

A foot beyond is a circle of light the size of a penny, a wad of cotton stuffing beside it. Shivering, I kneel and press my eye to the spy hole. I find myself peering through the cornicing above a ceiling light in my bedroom.

There's the baby in her crib, legs kicking, face crumpled.

My pink quilt on the bed, the waterglass on the table beside it.

The cream cotton nightdress. My slippers and gown.

I can't breathe. There's no air. I grab at the neck of my dress, gasping. This person living up here has spied on me. Poisoned me. Made me feel afraid and fearful for my own life. They are responsible for all of this, leaving Viola here with me, the noises I've been hearing, the rearranged pictures on the wall, the gramophone, the moth, the fox. *And Arthur.* The arrival of the crib and newspaper notice announcing I will murder someone here tomorrow, on New Year's Eve. They want to drive me insane or to my death. Perhaps both. The drummer in yellow and red, the man impersonating Emanuel. *It's him who has done this.*

Get away . . . I must get away from this house. I'll pack a bag and go. As soon as daylight comes, I'll leave, taking the baby with me. And if I'm not here tomorrow, murder is impossible; the prophecy in the notice cannot be true.

***

When Viola is settled once more, my feet fly through the house as I gather up each and every tonic bottle. I find them in my bag, in the larder, under the bed, jammed down the side of chairs, on tabletops and around the bathtub. I didn't purchase all of these, I'm sure of it.

I unscrew each cap and empty each one down the bathroom sink. The brown liquid glugs down the plughole, this bitter concoction I've been taking for months.

As well as the stomach cramps, a tight band of pain now laces across my forehead. The nausea, aches, pains, cramps and sickness. The ferocious sweats. The foggy head and muddled words. How much of what I've been feeling, saying and doing is down to this rotten liquor?

When every bottle is emptied, I place them in the bathtub. All nine of them. I grind my palms into my eyes. This tonic is the first thing I think of in the morning, the last thing at night and often in between.

I lay a towel over the bottles, then fetching and pulling on my boots I stand inside the tub. Grabbing at the wall for balance, the glass splinters and cracks as I stamp my feet over and over again.

Panting and out of breath I catch a glimpse of my reflection in the bathroom mirror, my wild eyes, sallow cheeks and limp hair, my emerald dress dusty and sweat stained. I lift my hair from the nape of my damp neck, teeth chattering, wondering about the woman I used to be. The one who worked for a living, could hold a conversation and laugh. I feel a flicker of hope she might still be in there, waiting to be found.

***

In the morning, I move from room to room with Viola in my arms, shuttering the windows, closing the doors. Returning to the kitchen, I glance at my suitcase packed and waiting by the back door. The photograph of Emanuel and his family is inside, sealed within an envelope addressed to Viola Cleeve and ready for posting.

Rabbit sits on his rug silently watching, he knows something is afoot. The baby grizzles, she can also sense my unease. John Garland's business card is tucked inside my coat pocket; he'll know what to do, how this must be dealt with.

The front doorbell trills upstairs. Rabbit barks gruffly. Perhaps it's John come early, not having to go out on his errand after all. Placing Viola in her drawer bed, I hurtle upstairs, boots clattering to the door.

Flinging it open, I blink at the sight of Mary and William on my front step. An elderly man with greying whiskers stands beside them, and someone else. Agnes. The girl looks to her shoes, does not meet my eye.

"Mary! Agnes? What . . ."

My sister's eyes sweep past me, along the gloomy hall. "Where's the baby, Della?" I see a muscle twitch in William's jaw. He places a restraining hand on my sister's arm as if she's revealed the purpose of their surprise visit too soon.

The man with them is carrying a brown leather case. Its brass handle gleams in the early morning sun. "Good morning, Mrs Pemberton. May we come inside?"

I swallow, dimly aware that I must look a fright. I've changed into a skirt and blouse, but my hair's unwashed and unbrushed, dark smudges stain the skin beneath my eyes.

"What is this about? Agnes. Why are you here?" My voice is thin and high with confusion.

Agnes looks up, her cheeks pinking. "They turned up on my doorstep wanting answers. They said you told them Viola was my sister. I've been so worried about you, Mrs Pemberton. I had to tell them . . ."

"That's enough," commands William, giving the girl a sharp look that makes her shoulders tip inwards.

The man with the case gives me a sickly smile that I suppose is intended to put me at ease but instead curls my insides into a knot. "My name is Doctor Broughton. If we could have a word inside, Mrs Pemberton . . ."

My sister's hands shake as she clasps them. "Bertie's told us everything. The stolen things . . . your book of drawings. Agnes told us about the baby and the tonic you've been taking. Going out with a man you've told us nothing about. You're unwell and we're here to help, not cause trouble. A short spell in hospital will . . ."

I don't let Mary finish, see the startle of surprise on all their faces as I slam the door closed, turn the key and throw the bolts across. Agnes has told them the truth about how the baby arrived in this house. About the bottles of tonic she disposed of and saw in my evening bag last night. They know about my thieving. *They've come to lock me up and take Viola.*

My feet trip over themselves as I stumble down the stairs and into the basement. The bell upstairs in the hallway rings and rings, then a persistent thudding on the door begins.

Whisking Viola into my arms I fling open the back door, glance down at my suitcase. I'd planned to take it with me in the pram, but there's no time for that. Any minute and they'll come along that side passage and accost me, take Viola and I'll never see her again. They'll make me vanish, just as poor Mrs Holway did. *Not fit for society. Not right in the head.*

My eyes skim over every bush and tree, seeking out a small hiding place for a woman with a baby and a dog. Any remaining leaves on the shrubs are thin, and we'll soon be found, Viola and Rabbit revealing us soon enough with cries and barks through no fault of their own.

Smoke rises from the chimney at the end of the garden. Oliver is at home. Grabbing my coat from the chair, I set off at a run towards the building, fully aware that the imprints of my footsteps on the damp grass are leaving a ready trail. John made me promise not to talk to him, but this is the only option, the only hope I have of saving her. *Of saving me.*

My feet charge as fast as a hare being chased by a fox, my muscles tense and throbbing as Rabbit struggles to keep up. My urgent thumps on the door are answered quickly today, then Oliver is listening open-mouthed to my garbled words. "They've come to take her . . . and me. We need to disappear."

Casting a look back towards the house, he nods, his jaw twitching. Asking no questions he picks up the dog, and takes him into his home, settles him by the stove with a bowl of water.

I swallow. "No! I can't leave Rabbit."

"You must," he says gruffly, coming out and locking his door. Inside the dog whines and begins to yap.

Oliver hurries us to the back gate. The lane behind is muddy and cool under the mottled shade of the tall trees.

We stand silently for a second as he reaches up to latch the gate closed.

I hear every bird call, every thud of our boots as we turn left and quickly walk along the backs of building sites, where scaffolding looms. Past the rear gates of houses already built, where people will be having breakfast, conversations with loved ones as a new day begins.

Oliver throws a quick glance behind. "I'll keep you safe, Della." His eyes are bright with this spoken promise.

Chapter 33

The lodging house is on a side street off Mill Road. The housekeeper demands an overinflated price for one night in exchange for ignoring her rule of no infants. There was no time for Oliver to put on his face mask before we left. Perhaps she was persuaded by his injury, for I couldn't help noticing the glances she kept throwing at his rippled skin, his eaten away nose.

To her we are Mr and Mrs Pemberton, a lie but not a lie, as I stand beside my brother-in-law looking at the double bed with its olive-green counterpane, the hardwood chest of drawers and washstand with cracked porcelain bowl. Vibrations from passing steam trains rattle the grimy windows.

Oliver turns to lock the door behind us, and I sink on the bed, placing Viola beside me. My arms are rashed with goosebumps, yet my skin is blazing. My side twinges and a headache thrums. My heartbeat is too quick, from the lack of sleep, the appearance of my sister at the door. Sweat beads on my forehead and I wipe it with the back of my hand. How I long for a spoon of that tonic, anything to ease the sharp edges of this moment. *Don't think of that, do not crave it.*

"You look sick, Della." Oliver's voice is low as he lights a cigarette.

I begin to shiver, teeth chattering. "Tired. And the . . .

the shock of it, I suppose. I need to tell you . . ."

"Rest first. We can talk after that." Smoke puffs from Oliver's lips, his voice thick with concern.

Glancing at the baby, I feel a throb of despair. "I've nothing with me. No tin of infant milk, no feeding bottle." My purse and bag. The suitcase. Everything I own is back at Arcadia House.

"I'll fetch what you need later," Oliver replies. He comes over, gestures for me to pick up Viola and then draws back the counterpane.

Slipping under the covers with the baby, I curl onto my side, stroke her soft cheek. She blinks, maybe wondering at these unfamiliar surroundings. Her eyelids flicker closed though and, as I listen to Oliver's steady breaths, so do mine.

***

I wake with a start to Viola's cries. Oliver is standing at the window with her, humming quietly. His large hands cradle her head as if she's a precious artefact from a museum.

The creak of the bed springs makes him turn. He gives me a thin smile. "You went out like a spark." He touches his own cheek. "You've more colour. Were white as a ghost before."

My shivers have stopped, but the pain in my sides and head is worse, as if I'm being stabbed by a tiny army wielding knitting needles. Easing myself up and walking over, I massage my temples. The baby smacks her lips together. "She's hungry."

Worry flits across Oliver's face. "I'm out of money."

My heart sinks. Oliver paid for one night here. I can't go back to Arcadia House. They will be there waiting. Taking

Viola from him, I let her suckle at a finger and know I'll do anything to keep her safe.

"You love her. This baby that appeared in your house."

I swallow. "Yes. Yes, I do."

"But she's not yours."

Viola slurps and sucks. "That doesn't change things," I say.

Oliver sighs, tugs at his ear.

"John Garland. The man you met the other day. He's out on an errand this morning but was going to stop by later. He'll help us." Taking John's business card from my coat pocket on the bed, I hold it out.

Oliver's expression is blank as he examines it. "I'm not sure about him."

I shake my head. "You can trust him. He's a good man. He's building homes for people like you."

The windows shake as another train steams past, the blur of people in the carriages all travelling somewhere with purpose. Viola arches her back and whimpers. I sway with her, but the whimper soon turns into a deafening screech. A person in the next-door room raps loudly on the wall and Oliver and I share a look of dismay.

Gently swaddling the baby, and passing her to Oliver again, I see there's something I must do if I'm to meet her needs right now.

Oliver looks at me in confusion as I shrug on my coat, head to the door. "Watch the baby. I'll be quick." Holding a hand to the pain in my side, I canter down the stairs, pass the communal bathroom, steam curling under the threshold. Fly past another closed door behind which two women are having a low but heated conversation.

Out on the street, I lower my head, don't meet anyone's eye. But I needn't worry, this isn't a place of casual greetings and ready smiles for strangers.

No one knows me inside the dispensing chemist. Swiping the tin of milk while the owner's back is turned is as easy as falling from a log. I'm a middle-aged woman in an old but well-made coat; I'm beneath anyone's suspicion. The theft of this item boldens me and I slip two apples from a crate into my pocket as I pass the grocers, my feet barely losing their stride.

***

Oliver uses his penknife to open the tin of milk, does not ask how I came by it for we both know the answer to that. I heat some water on the hot plate in the communal kitchen, and make up the milk in a handleless mug I find at the back of a cupboard.

Viola takes it by spoon hungrily; her eyes fixed only on me as I perch on the edge of the bed dribbling it into her mouth. "That's better. What a hungry girl you are."

"Tell me then. Tell me all of it," Oliver says quietly, sitting at the other end of the bed. He cuts an apple into slivers, shares it equally, chewing carefully on the good side of his jaw.

I speak quietly as we eat, as Viola drinks and dribbles. Tell him every single thing that has happened, like I'm a child repeating the alphabet from A to Z.

When I reach the events of last night, the discovery of the hidden room behind a false wall in the attic, Oliver's breaths quicken, and he stands. He paces the room, to the window and back again, his eyes stormy. "Someone's been living in the house. The person responsible for all this? A person out to . . . poison you?"

"Yes. They fairly well succeeded too." I begin to shiver again as I tell him about the hallucinations I've been having, my lapses in memory. The occasional euphoric highs and terrible lows. When I tell him about the spy hole into my bedroom Oliver's fists clench.

"Della . . . this is . . ." He's as sickened by this as I am. He becomes quiet then; his shoulders hunched as another train rattles past. "You thought this was my doing?" His voice is small as he slumps back onto the bed.

Tears build behind my eyes. Viola finally turns away from the spoon, and I place her against my chest, her head nestled into the curve between my shoulder and neck. I gently rub her back. "Truthfully, I didn't know what to think."

He lowers his head. "Maybe that's all I deserve."

"What do you mean by that?" He doesn't respond but I sense that here, in this room that holds no meaning to either of us, we'll finally be able to talk. And that most important of all I should open this conversation with honesty. So I admit to my betrayal – letting myself in to his home uninvited and finding his written apologies in the notebooks.

Oliver looks stricken, presses his fingers to his eyes.

"What did those apologies mean?" I press gently.

He shudders out a sigh.

"You can tell me . . . whatever it is . . . I'll help you through it, just as you're helping me now," I say, watching him carefully.

He shakes his head, won't meet my eye. "You've been kind.

Checking up on me and the parcels of biscuits. But you don't know what I . . . what I've done. You wouldn't come near me if you did."

"Tell me, then. Let me make up my own mind about that."

A prism of noise emits from his lips, a keening that causes me to blink. His fingers drop from his face, and he gives me a pained look. His bottom lip wobbles. "The truth is . . . I was with Theo when he died."

My hand stills on Viola's back and the baby gurgles. *My husband and his brother. Together at the end.* Tears spill onto my cheeks.

Oliver's eyes drop to the linoleum floor. "Theo's patrol was fired upon crossing a bridge. He was badly wounded."

My arms tighten around the baby. The letter I'd received from Theo's commanding officer told me he'd died in action, a swift and painless death. I knew from my work at the war hospital that the reality was likely to have been so much bleaker and unkind.

"My battalion was attached to one of the Canadian Divisions," Oliver continues. "We were advancing on Mons . . . the pitted roads crowded with gun carriages, lorries and ambulances. Northeast of the town we arrived at the bridge just as it was getting dark. The bridge was twisted, almost destroyed. But some of the men ahead of us had tried to cross it and had come under artillery fire."

"Theo's battalion," I whisper.

Oliver nods, drags in a breath. "The wounded men lay on the verges. We had two ambulances, horse transport as well. We offered to help. Theo . . . he was lying apart from the others."

His shoulders rounding, he places his head in his hands.

Settling Viola on the bed, I kneel before Oliver. "Why keep this from me?" I see in his hooded eyes there's more to this, that the reason for his apologies is connected to this time and once out in the open is something that can never be unheard.

"You misunderstand. He died because me. I killed him. I killed my own brother."

My hands tremble as I sit back on my heels and stare, desperately trying to understand.

There's the sound of laughter from the corridor, the hum of pipes in the wall as the lavatory flushes.

Oliver swallows. "Theo was in a bad way. Shrapnel wedged in his stomach. It was clear nothing could be done."

"Oh, Oliver," I whisper, wishing I could wash the pain from his eyes, the horror spearing at my own throat.

"He was awake . . . knew it was me. He was . . . crying. Asking me to take him home, asking for you. Again and again, he asked for you."

My nails bite into my palms. *He asked for me.*

Oliver's pale cheeks crumple and his eyes are faraway, as if he's back near that Belgian bridge on that terrible day. "Theo's commanding officer came over." He pauses, drags in a ragged breath. "He asked me to finish him off – said it was better than one of his own men doing it. He didn't know we were brothers. He didn't know . . . we were brothers." Tears run freely down his face, settling in the hollows of his scars.

My heart feels as if it's being cleaved from my chest. "Did . . . did Theo know? Did he know what was happening?"

Oliver nods, the memory clouding his eyes. "I could've . . . I could've walked away. Let someone else do it. But . . . my brother was dying, Della. The fear and pain in his eyes . . . he was screaming, asking for help. I couldn't . . . I couldn't take it."

I shudder at his words and the image they present of my husband's final moments. Tears drip onto my skirt, the room blurring as I gulp in breath after breath.

"I . . . I gripped Theo's hand," Oliver continues. "He was deathly cold. I told him I loved him. That you loved him. He seemed calmer then. He knew what I was going to do. 'Do it quick,' he said. 'Just do it quick.'"

Oliver wipes his nose with the back of his hand, and my tears keep falling at these images of the blood, the gore, the pain and fear. And the love too. In his final moments, Theo was with someone who loved him. When all else ends, perhaps that's as much as any of us can hope for.

"It was quick. Over in an instant. I'm so sorry . . . I'm so sorry," Oliver finishes with sob.

A weary calm loosens the knot in my shoulders as I openly weep. This terrible secret Oliver's been hiding explains his nightly screams, his hiding away. His inability to communicate and his rejection of me. I understand it now. I understand *him*. "This wasn't your fault," I gasp. "It was a . . . kindness. It stopped his suffering. Thank you . . . thank you for sharing that with me. Thank you." These are perhaps the most truthful words I've ever spoken.

Oliver looks up, his face broken and stricken. But perhaps tinged with hope too.

Taking his hands, I squeeze all my warmth into his palms.

These poor men. So much suffering. Gathering Oliver to me, he rests his head on my shoulder, the weight of him and his laboured breaths mooring me. "I thought . . . Theo didn't want me," I murmur.

Oliver's voice is gruff in my ear. "Theo loved you. Would never have betrayed you."

My beliefs fall and scatter like leaves. Theo was distant and secretive in the final months before he left for the front. I was angry at the way we'd grown apart, blamed him for it. But I'd changed too. Become withdrawn and consumed with my worsening health and lost child. Our marriage was complicated towards the end, but I still loved him. *And he still loved me.* The clock was ticking, though. We ran out of time to find our way back to one another to make things right.

Oliver shudders, and I stroke his back. My fingertips moving firmly, long strokes to soothe away his distress. His arms tentatively arch around my body, and we cry together, for all the things we've both lost.

Chapter 34

That evening as I lie in the lodging house under the bed covers with Viola, my head pulsing, I wonder what was waiting for Oliver when he returned to Arcadia House. My sister? The doctor with his medical bag? The police? Oliver thought any of those things unlikely, promised me he'd be cautious and make sure he wasn't followed when he returns here tomorrow.

We have a plan of sorts, hastily cobbled together. He's to stop at John Garland's place tonight, give him the address of this lodging house and the telephone number. I pressed on Oliver again how certain I am that John will help us, but he remains unconvinced, wonders why a man I barely know would want to help me out of this bind I am in. There's also the fact that John is mistrustful of Oliver, but I must believe that these two men can put their differences aside.

It was too difficult to explain to Oliver the betrayal that John has suffered which is perhaps making him want to help another. The tender feelings that the man is beginning to rouse in me, the small ache inside when I think of him touching my hair.

A little after eight o'clock there's a knock on my door. "Telephone call for Mrs Pemberton."

Viola sleeps, and I leave her on the bed, careful to lock

the door behind me.

I jam the receiver to my ear. "Hello?"

"Della. Thank God. Oliver told me everything."

Relief rises inside me at the hum of John's voice. "You believe me now . . . that Oliver has played no part in this?"

"Yes, yes of course. He wants the best for you, as do I. The hidden room . . . I can scarcely believe it. The man who's been staying there . . . I could murder him. You must go to the police this time." His voice is tight with urgency. "Do you want me to drive over? I could take you now?"

I'm quiet then, running through different possibilities in my mind. Of course, the police must be told, and this devil of a man brought to justice, but there's still the question of Viola. Even if I manage to explain and wheedle my way out of my petty theft – for Mary will make sure I confess to that – the baby will still be taken away.

If I'm to keep her, the only option is to lie low somewhere – with Oliver too. John can help us with that – his knowledge of the town and the new homes he's building. He'll know a place we can go, giving us space to think and plan.

But I can't explain that here over the telephone while other lodgers may be listening in. It's a conversation to be had in person. "Visitors aren't permitted, and the baby's sleeping. Tomorrow. Come tomorrow." There's a short pause, and the line clicks and whirs. "John? Are you still there?"

"There's nothing I can do to persuade you?"

I sigh, rub my eyes. "I'm so tired myself. Will feel more able to deal with things tomorrow. There's a matter I'd like to broach with you then."

In the short pause that follows I sense his curiosity. "I don't like this, but all right. I'll come tomorrow. You're sure . . . you are sure you feel safe where you are?"

"Yes. We're safe. Oliver is returning in the morning to bring me some things from the house. Can you come after that?"

John is quiet again. "Yes. Yes, of course. Take care of yourself and the baby, Della. Sleep well."

***

After the telephone call, my headache worsens, as does my longing for a long draught of my beloved tonic. *Not beloved. It was poison.*

I creep to the small, shared kitchen with its butler's sink and hot plate when I assume most people are asleep, root around in a cupboard and find a tin of biscuits. They're stale, but I cram them into my mouth anyway, wash them down with handfuls of water from the tap as my teeth chatter.

As I lie here in the dark listening to Viola's small breaths, my mind continually returns to the hidden room in Arcadia House. It's a space Oliver had no knowledge of, and he's convinced Theo didn't know about it either. Oliver's never heard of Emanuel Cleeve and doesn't remember seeing the man's carved initials on the rafter. But he said he and Theo rarely went up to the attic when they were boys.

It gets me wondering and thinking . . . if that secret room has been there from the time the house was built, how long have I been watched and observed? Since Theo died, or before then? While the two of us were still sleeping together in that bed? A voyeur and sadist, watching me undress. *Watching us.*

I pummel the saggy pillow into shape. As my fist meets the fabric, I feel a new violence rising inside me. Before I leave Cambridge, I must find this man. Make sure he does not do to somebody else what he's done to me.

***

Before dawn the next morning, I stand at the window watching the trains, waiting for Oliver to arrive. My eyes are gritty and swollen after pacing the floor with the baby for the latter part of the night. Arcadia House drifts into my mind. It's New Year's Eve – the day I will supposedly commit murder there. Forcing the sinister thought aside, my hold on Viola tightens, the fast flutter of her heartbeat matching mine.

Sneaking into the bathroom before others in the lodging house wake, I wash Viola in the sink, rinse out her only nappy. Hanging it to dry over the heater in there, I wrap a pillowslip around her bottom and hope for no ungodly explosions.

The baby naps between spoonfuls of milk and still Oliver does not come. Perhaps he changed his mind about helping me? Or maybe the police were waiting for him at Arcadia House, have taken him in for questioning. Are asking about the baby, and my whereabouts. They could be on their way here this very minute.

I listen to the other lives in this lodging house continuing in an ordinary fashion. The acrid smell of burnt toast, the two women still arguing. The bathroom always, always occupied.

There's a knock at my door. "You need to vacate the room. You only paid up for one night."

"Yes . . . yes, I'm sorry. I'll . . . we'll pay for tonight. My husband will pay when he gets back." *Where are you, Oliver?*

"Make sure he does," the housekeeper mutters, and her feet thud back down the stairs.

When the two o'clock train passes, and neither Oliver nor John appear, I make a decision. My legs are weak; I must venture outside and find some food.

Mill Road is quiet today, many of the shops closing early on New Year's Eve. The bakery is still open though, and I step inside with the baby hidden within my coat, tears springing to my eyes at the smell of freshly baked bread. The aproned man behind the counter looks up. "I'm just about to close. There isn't much left, I'm afraid."

My lips tremble. All the remaining bread is behind the counter. There's no option to steal today. "I don't have any money."

His eyes soften as he sees the top of Viola's head. He must see the desperation on my face, for he slips a loaf into a brown paper bag. Then thinking for a moment, he reaches below the counter, passes me a currant bun caked in icing. A perfect glistening glace cherry on top. Perhaps it was one he was keeping for himself.

"Thank you. Thank you." I am breathless with thanks, for this stranger's small act of kindness.

He smiles. "I hope the new year brings the both of you better fortune than the last."

Outside his shop, I eat the bun quickly. Licking the icing from my fingers, my eyes skirt over the posters pasted to the wall across the street, settle on a flash of red and yellow. I blink, wondering if I am imagining this, but it's still there when I look again.

I step around a pile of horse dung, am careful to avoid the motors as I hurry across the road with the baby. This particular poster is advertising a Christmas production at the New Theatre in St Andrew's Street. Men in the illustration are dressed in red and yellow costumes, banging on their drums. The group I saw performing on King's Parade, they were part of this theatre group.

He's an actor. The man posing as Emanuel Cleeve is an actor.

Chapter 35

I am not foolish enough to think I should confront this actor on my own. I find myself outside John's place of work and his home, a building on Trumpington Street given over to businesses on the lower floor and flats above. His motor is on the street, the wheels mud flecked.

My hands fizz as I ring the bell and wait expectantly. No one comes. I stamp my feet to ward off the cold, then duck behind a nearby tree when I spy a police officer cycling past.

Five minutes later a woman coming out of the communal door to the flats smiles as she sees me waiting with Viola. "Who are you after?"

"Mr Garland."

She gives a nod of acknowledgement. "Saw him heading out earlier. No idea when he'll be back though."

My shoulders dip with dismay at the thought we've missed each other. He'll worry when he arrives at the lodging house and finds me gone. Thanking the woman, I set off into town, seeing there's no time to return to the lodgings and find John. I must deal with this actor, this imposter, myself.

Rage simmers with every stride as I consider everything this man has put me through. *Why, why, why?*

A sly thought begins to germinate as I pass the Catholic Church and take a left turn into St Andrew's Street. I could proposition this man; demand he lets me keep Viola. It's clear he doesn't want her. And there's still been no word of a missing baby – nothing from the newspaper sellers calling out headlines around town. In exchange I could offer to keep quiet about his crimes. Oliver and I could leave Cambridge, sell the house from afar with John's help.

There's a sharp pinch at the base of my throat at the thought of leaving Mary and William, and the boys. But it won't be forever. I will be Viola's mother, and Oliver will no doubt be her devoted uncle. Surely my family will be accepting of that when they understand no one else has a claim over the child.

***

Outside the theatre, people are already arriving for the afternoon's matinee performance. Men in their best hats, women in long, luxurious coats. A few people give me sidelong glances, and I can understand why. Gaunt complexion, limp hair unbrushed, stale breath and a small baby tucked in her coat. Not the usual clientele. I'm not even good enough for the cheap seats today.

The foyer is thronging, the spirals of laughter and chatter worsening the band of pain around my forehead. I pin myself to the wall, follow it all the way around until I see a sign to the stalls and the refreshment salon. It's too early for people to take their seats, so they stand in clusters, sipping champagne or mulled wine, completely unaware that there's a criminal in their midst. That he will take to the stage and fool them too with his performance.

There's no one at the door to the stalls ready to take tickets.

With a quick glance about, I push the door open and slip inside. I can't help but draw a breath at the magnificence of this grand space. Claret coloured carpets, Corinthian columns, and a ceiling that goes up and up painted in marine-blue and gold. My feet hurry towards the stage and the orchestra pit, aware that I do not have much time.

"Excuse me, Madam? You shouldn't be in here yet."

Swivelling, I see a man carrying an armful of programmes, a leather purse attached to his belt.

"I'm so sorry. I had an urgent message to get to one of the drummers in the performance." Thinking quickly, I gesture at Viola. "Our daughter is sick."

Predictably, the man takes a step back. "Oh. I see."

Wrinkling my brow, I prepare to adjust the timbre of my voice, take on the role of a pitiful wife. "It was so crowded in the foyer, and I don't know this theatre, or where the dressing rooms are."

The sympathetic nod I receive is the perfect reward. "The performance starts in twenty minutes. You'll find the drummers in dressing room four, I think. I'll tell you how to get there."

***

He directs me to the steps at the side of orchestra pit, says if anyone questions me to tell them Jack Parker said it was all right for me to be here. I hold his name on the tip of my tongue, this golden backstage ticket.

As I reach the top of the steps and prepare to slip into the wings left of the stage, I glance back at the auditorium. This place must seat over one thousand. People coming here for entertainment and light relief, a chance to forget about their worries about money, health, relationships, what to cook for supper. Maybe in another life I might have sat in this audience too, with Theo by my side.

Following Jack Parker's directions as well as I can remember them, his name works like a charm when I'm questioned – people are so helpful here in their brightly coloured costumes, the scent of grease paint and expectation all around. The baby helps too of course. Everyone admires a baby.

And then I'm in the corridor of dressing rooms, pushing open the door with the painted number four on it. I don't knock and announce myself; there's no time for niceties.

Two men turn as I walk in. Dressed in red and yellow, their drums sit by the door. Neither are the man I'm looking for. "The other one, the other drummer. Where is he?" My question is curt and to the point.

I see them exchange an uncertain look. "Billy?" one of them says.

Billy. His name is Billy. "Yes, that'll be him."

Viola starts to fret. She's been as good as gold, but she must be hungry again.

"What do you want him for?"

"It's a personal matter."

I watch them both eye the baby. Opening my coat a fraction, I reveal Viola. "Is this his child?"

My question is met with the scratch of a chin, the dropping of a jaw. A burst of laughter from them both. "Billy? I think you've the wrong man, love. If you get my meaning?" More laughter.

"Where is he?" I demand.

The men quieten at my steely tone.

"He went for a smoke in the alley – the door at the end of the corridor."

With a nod of thanks, I leave and continue on past the other dressing rooms where people are emerging in gaudy costumes, dripping in frills and flounces. Pushing through the tide of them, I see the door to the outside is slightly ajar. I pause and peer around it.

There's Billy at the end of a gloomy alleyway, a cigarette dangling from his lips, his head leaning against the wall as if he doesn't have a care in the world.

I open my mouth to call out, but as I do a figure approaches from the opposite end of the alley. Blinking the confusion from my eyes, I stare hard. *John Garland.*

Billy looks up at John. "You're late."

John gives him a curt nod, takes an envelope from his pocket and passes it over.

Billy and John.

John and Billy.

My legs buckle, and I retract my head back around the door like a turtle into its shell. I press a hand to my lips. Viola begins to cry, her breaths sharp and jagged.

Pressing my heels to the floor, I gather myself, wonder what to do next. The decision is taken from me. A clatter of feet along the alleyway, then the door is pushed back, and John is there staring, eyes wide. He runs a hand through his hair.

"Della?" He reaches out a hand to take my arm, but I twist

away and run back along the corridor. I hear John set off in pursuit, calling my name.

"Stop that man. Stop that man," I cry, as I stumble through the huddles of performers.

Hearing a shout, I risk a look back and see that someone has John by the arm. He's throwing me a confused look.

Finding my way back to the street, thoughts clamour and chime. Were they working together? John thought we could be company for one another. The touch of his hand as he tucked my hair behind my ear. *I wanted more of that.* He's kind and gentle, grieving his absent son and intent on helping me. *But why was he meeting Billy?* My head spins as I push on through the crowds. I think of Oliver then, our bodies curved around each other as we shared our grief last night. I know I can trust him. But that means going back to Arcadia House.

Chapter 36

Viola exhausts herself crying as we walk, eventually falling into a shuddering sleep while I crouch among the building materials opposite Arcadia House. The light has faded and my head thrums as I wait and watch and wait and watch for any sign of Oliver, Mary, or the doctor. The police, even.

I think of Arthur, dear, sweet Arthur who loved books and wanted to be brave. Who hid in this spot and came unstuck as he tried to solve my mystery. His hat that lies upstairs in my house. I think of the murder notice too. The claim I will kill someone here today. A wave of sickness has me bending forwards, bile mixing with the mud at my feet. My throat aches with wanting for my tonic. Just one small sip. *How foolish to tip it all down the sink.* If I was asked to choose between food and this tonic there'd be no hesitation in my answer. This thought frightens me. I frighten myself. The baby stirs, her movement pulling me back. *No good will come of thinking like this. Think of the baby. And Oliver and Rabbit.*

The shutters are all closed just as I left them yesterday, and as the sky darkens further, the wind picks up and the temperature plummets. I know I've no choice but to act. Crossing the road, I slip along the side passage unnoticed. Almost unnoticed. Rabbit comes hurtling along to greet me, yapping and yapping. With a burst of relief, I bend to fondle the dog's ears. He jumps up at my calves, then turns and retreats to the garden.

Around the back of the house, I see the door to Oliver's lodgings is open, banging against the bricks in the stiff breeze. The basement door to my house is also ajar and there's a light on in the kitchen.

Peeping in, I see a trail of muddy footsteps on the tiles. My suitcase and handbag stand where they were yesterday to the left of the door. Something's happened here, something to prevent Oliver from bringing them to me. There's no sign of forced entry, a broken windowpane, or scattered glass. Rabbit's now in the kitchen standing at the internal door to the stairs and hallway above, shivering and barking. This small dog is telling me something is wrong, something I must attend to.

Dropping a kiss on top of the baby's head and willing her to remain quiet, I pick up the metal poker from beside the stove.

"Shush, Rabbit. Shush," I whisper, and the dog quietens for a moment and licks his lips, whines.

Tightening my grip on Viola, I head up the stairs, but arriving at the top I see the hallway is just as I left it. Creeping along to the stairs leading to the first floor, I look up. I hear a faint sound. Swallowing the dryness from my throat, I tentatively call out. "Oliver? Is that you?"

"Della! Thank God."

The poker slides in my sweaty palm as I see John emerge on the first-floor landing. I clench my fingers around it.

"Why did you run from me?" he asks. His cheeks are pink,

his eyes wide. "What were you doing at the theatre? I was there trying to help you!"

I take a step back. My head swims with uncertainty. *How did he get here before me?* "A poster . . . a picture of the drummers led me there. Billy Hall is his name. You were with him in the alley. Why?"

John hurries down the stairs to greet me. "I've been asking around town for the past two days, finally found out this afternoon this drummer you saw was performing at the theatre. An actor. He wanted paying to admit the truth. That's why I was there."

Retreating again, I find myself backed against the front door. I let the information he's just told me settle. John was investigating too, trying to extract the truth from this actor who posed as Emanuel Cleeve. The thought should be comforting, but for some reason it's not. He should have told me about this. We had dinner together and not one word of this was mentioned.

John's face softens, his eyes beseeching. "Della. Please put the poker down. I'm your friend."

I ignore his request. "What did Billy tell you?"

A slight lift of his shoulders, and a shadow flits across his face. "He scarpered with the cash before I could get the whole truth out of him."

"Did he say why he did it . . . why he's been staying here? Who Viola belongs to?"

John gently takes my arm. My head reels as he leads me into the shuttered drawing room, switches on the lamp and directs me to the sofa. Easing the poker from my hand, he lays it down in front of the cold fireplace, then flicks on the Christmas tree lights. They twinkle red and blue.

"Why are you here . . . at the house? I don't understand . . ."

John turns, shakes his head. "I chased Billy. Ran all the way here. It was obvious where he was heading."

"Here? He was coming back here?" Dread thickens in my chest, as I place the baby on the sofa next to me.

John nods. "I told him I knew about the hidden room . . . that we'd go to the police. He threw a punch, winded me. He was quick, must have taken a back route and I arrived after him. He'd already let himself in the basement door."

My stomach drops. How many times has Billy Hall come in and out of my house uninvited?

Kneeling at my feet, John takes my hand. He strokes my fingers, long soothing strokes that only causes my chest to constrict further. "I found Billy in the attic. I assume he'd come to clear out that room. We fought again . . . then he ran. We know who he is. We can go to the police station, and they'll find him." He reaches up and gently, so gently, traces a finger across the curve of my cheek. *Why do I now want to shrink away from his touch?* "Della, it's all right. You're safe now. It's over . . . this is all over . . ."

My teeth chatter as I remember the reason I came back. "But . . . but where's Oliver? The door to his lodgings was open. Rabbit was in the garden."

"You're cold. Put this rug over you." John tucks the checked fabric over my knees, glances at the ticking clock on the mantel. Unease sits heavy in my stomach as Rabbit's barks still echo up through the house.

Something is not right. The two open doors, the muddy footprints. "Water. I need a glass of water please," I croak.

"Of course." John smiles and I listen to the thud of his feet along the hall, then down the stairs to the kitchen. Flinging off the rug, blood pounds in my ears.

Picking up the baby, I hurry from the drawing room and upstairs, treading as lightly as I'm able. Looking up the final set of stairs to the attic, I can see that the door is ajar, that this must be the place where John and Billy fought. A creak then from above, a low moan.

Billy did not flee. He's still here in this house.

I glance down through the balustrade, prepare to call for John. But something makes me pause. Why would Billy Hall choose to come back here when he was about to perform on stage? When he'd already been paid? What would he have to gain?

Quietly opening the door to my bedroom, I settle Viola in her crib, then softly, softly make my way up to the attic, mentally steeling myself for what I'll find there.

Another low moan comes from inside, breathless with pain. I recognise that timbre from my time at the hospital, the sickening sound of men incapable of holding in the suffering inflicted on them in war.

I approach warily, knowing with every fibre in my body that tremendous care is needed. But I must also see the truth for myself, understand the part of this story that John is keeping from me.

A pile of blankets lies in front of the open wardrobe door that leads to the secret room; a hunched form concealed beneath. My head buzzes as if an electric current is flowing through it. I remember John's words on the telephone last night. *"The man who's been staying there . . . I could murder him."* He hasn't . . . he wouldn't . . .

Tiptoeing over, I bend and tentatively lift one corner of the covering. Gasping, I drop to my knees with a thud. *Oliver.* Flinging off the blanket, I take in the irregular crimson stain on his shirt, faded at the edges. Beside him is my silver letter opener, tarnished with blood. His eyelids flicker and his breathing is unbearably shallow.

"Della."

Startled, I whip around to the sound of John's voice, take in his narrowed eyes. "Help . . . Oliver needs help . . ."

Turning back to Oliver, I hear John step inside. "Billy . . . he did this?" I gasp. Oliver groans quietly. His face is leached of colour. *The man is dying.*

"Not Billy." John's voice is low. I blink and turn, not understanding. He's haloed by the light spilling in from the attic landing, and he sweeps a hand through his brown curls. "This was all *your* doing."

Chapter 37

My head thrums and I look at John blankly. "My doing? No! I do not . . ." I pause, noticing the key to the attic door in his hand.

"The police will be here in the morning." John gives me a small smile, and his next words are spoken in a considered tone. "Poor Della Pemberton. Addicted to opioids and liquor. A thief – a stolen child. Arrested. Tried for murder. Sentenced to death."

The note in the crib. *Murder in Cambridge at New Year.* My bowels feel like they may loosen, and I drag in a deep breath as I stare at John. *Two people alone can be company for one another, don't you think?* All traces of the diffident and gentle man who spoke those words is gone. This man's eyes are glazed and cruel, his lips curling into a snarl as he stares right back at me.

"Please . . ." Oliver's wheezed whisper is faint.

Summoning all my focus, I lift Oliver's shirt. Two knife wounds; one in his side and one to his chest. The blood loss is slow now, but the wounds are deep. My fingers come away sticky. I think back to my nursing training, desperation rattling through me.

John's gaze is not filled with horror at this scene, at the slashes of claret-red across Oliver's shirt and on the floorboards.

His eyes have drifted to an attic window and the dark sky beyond. "The baby'll go back to the orphanage. Frances. That's what her mother called her, not that she was much of a mother. I've made sure my name isn't on the birth certificate . . ."

My body stiffens. *Viola. He is talking about Viola.* "She's *your* child?"

His eyes are still faraway, and he doesn't reply, his fingers twisting around the metal key like it possesses him.

I think of Viola downstairs in her crib and a sharp pain flattens the breath in my lungs. John's baby . . . his own child. The thought should turn my stomach, but all I feel is an intense desire to hold the baby close, feel the tickle of her breath on my neck, the beating of her heart against mine.

Taking off my cardigan and wedging it under Oliver's head, I try to assess the blood loss, all the while turning over possible means of escape. John's intention is clear enough. To lock us in here until tomorrow. For me to be arrested for the murder of Oliver Pemberton.

Oliver is too sick and heavy to be moved from the attic. From his pallor and the crusts of dried blood on his clothes, he's been here some time – since yesterday? Was John here waiting when Oliver returned for my suitcase? "It was you tormenting me? All this time it was you!"

John's cheeks tighten into a granite-cold smile. "You had a hand in some of this yourself, Della. Thanks to the concoction you drank so readily."

Some of this was me. Tears prick at my eyelids, but I turn my attention back to Oliver, only Oliver. I will not weep and unfold in front of John.

"I had a little help with some of it. People will do anything for money," John continues. "A struggling actor paid to impersonate a dead man. The warehouse lad happy to make a few bob when I asked him to lie about having seen you buy the crib. A neighbour persuaded to pose as an insect collector."

I dip my head. John has lied, bribed and misled me. Oliver's eyes flicker open and closed. Then this – the attack on my husband's brother and John's intention I take the blame. "Why. Tell me why . . ."

John's curt laugh interrupts me, and he spreads his arms wide, standing before us like a demonic angel. His eyes shimmer. "For Arcadia House, of course. The place where my life began."

Oliver murmurs under his breath, words too quiet for me to catch. I silently wait for John to continue.

Arms dropping to his sides, he steps back, leans against the door jamb. "My father – Mr Pemberton senior – was a kind man, although not so kind to my mother as it turned out."

My head spins with this new knowledge. "*Brothers*? You, Theo and Oliver are brothers?"

He tilts his head. "Half-brothers. I'm the youngest."

"Theo never . . . he never . . ." I say thinly.

"Theo didn't know about me for a long while and Oliver never did," John snaps. He takes a breath, steadies himself. "I was allowed to visit Arcadia House from the age of five each year on Christmas Eve, when Mr Pemberton's two sons were taken to church by their dim-witted mother. The lights on the tree, the gifts. They should have been mine. The wealth . . . it burrowed into me. I was twelve when I stole my first key, slipped from a hook in the kitchen. And then I could come and go whenever I pleased."

My throat feels as if it is being threaded shut. I eye the letter opener next to Oliver, and slowly, ever so slowly inch my hand towards it.

"It was a game, slipping inside the house while everybody was out or sleeping," John continues, his eyes dream-like as they flit about the attic. "Pretending that I lived here, that I had my own room of toys and books."

"The hidden room in the attic... you stayed up here," I croak, the idea of it both bewildering and horrifying. The thought of him spying and watching Theo in his bedroom below, hungering for a life that wasn't his. "But that's impossible. You would have been heard... or seen."

John sneers. "Did *you* see me, Della? Did you know about the room? None of the Pembertons did. They weren't interested in exploring the attic, saw it as a place to store belongings they no longer cared for. Quite fitting it became mine, wouldn't you say?"

I close my eyes momentarily just to erase his cruel smile.

"It isn't difficult to watch and wait, learn the ins and outs of a family's, a person's, routine. *Your* routine. There were ample times for me to come and go unnoticed."

Revulsion claws up my spine, and I flick my eyes open. "You're wicked... you've done a wicked thing."

A muscle in his jaw ticks. "Mr Pemberton enjoyed his family holidays on the Suffolk coast. Gave me plenty of time to explore the place and discover Emanuel's hidden photograph. I was pleased to see you follow my trail. The initials on the rafter, the baby's bone – easy to come by if you know who to ask."

My fingers curl around the opener, feel the pinch of its sharp blade. "But why use Emanuel . . . what do you want from *me*?"

John smirks. "To make anyone close to you believe you were losing your mind. That you were obsessed with the death of Emanuel Cleeve, and your own dead child. Make them believe you could commit murder. I want the house which will rightfully belong to me when I become the eldest Pemberton. Pick any one of those answers and you'll have the truth."

Arcadia House. My home. He's driven me half mad with his desire for it.

"I must say," he continues with a tilt of the head, "you helped me better than I'd hoped. Your thieving and your visit to the police station. The boy in the bookshop and Emanuel's daughter in Grantchester. Your trip to the Zoology museum. You've feathered your own grave, have given me plenty to help incriminate you."

John has followed me about town as I've gone about my business, quietly observing and plotting. I've admitted small parts of myself to the people I have met in my attempt to learn the truth. Information that when reported to the police will make me appear deranged and incapable. It's all been about John creating a clear path to get what he believes is rightfully his.

I think of Arthur then and the blood-tinged woollen hat found in the secret room. "The boy found dead across the road. Arthur."

Looking up, I see John's eyes glint with malice. "I understand that was an unfortunate accident. Although I believe if examined closely your boots are caked with mud from that building site, and the hat the boy was wearing is now in your chest of drawers, along with the butterfly book he so helpfully dedicated to you. Questions will be asked."

"You killed him . . . *you* killed him." I can barely get the words out as the room spins around me.

"He was a thorn in my side. Watching the house and sticking his nose where it wasn't wanted," John spits.

Viola. Little Viola. I must keep her safe. I'm struggling to pull in each breath, the air so thin it's as if I'm climbing a mountain. John's eyes flicker to the key in his hand and in one swift and silent action, I slide the letter opener under my skirt. "Take the house. The baby . . . I'll care for her." It's a vain attempt to give him what he wants, and what I desire too.

His laugh is bitter. "I'd rather she lives out her days in the orphanage than with *you*."

This man is deranged. If I'm convicted of Oliver's murder, sentenced to death, is it possible he'll get this house? I remember Mary's insistence that I make my own will after inheriting the place from Theo. Regret surges through me that I didn't listen. "You'll not get away with this . . . I'll tell the police what you've done . . ."

John shakes his head. "And who'll believe it? The police will find in the house the crate of opium and gin, your stolen things. A notice saying you'll commit murder which they'll assume *you* typed up in a fit of madness. A baby's bone. You even have Emanuel's photograph in your suitcase downstairs – proof of your obsession. I'm just the half-brother to your dead husband. Someone who's tried to befriend you, help and advise you. I've clawed my way up from the gutter to get where I am now. A man with a good and honest profession."

A hot horror winds around me. *Foolish, foolish, Della.* Why didn't I dispose of all the things that could be used against me? *Because I never for one second believed it would come to this.* "No . . . there are people who will stand up for me, vouch for my character . . . my sister . . ."

"Yes, Mary," John cuts in. "The sister who believes the child you're caring for is stolen . . . a sister who thinks you're partial to a drink, who believes poor, war damaged Oliver Pemberton is out to do you harm. She'll have no trouble in thinking it was too much for you. That you murdered the man."

He's truly thought of everything, played me like a puppet. There must be someone whose advice I can seek. *His wife.* The story he told me of the circumstances of her leaving could be untrue. If she's aware of his cruel character, the child he's fathered with another woman, then she may be prepared to help me. The words spill out like a fishbone being pulled from my throat. "Your wife. I'll find her and . . ."

"There is no wife," John interrupts with a lazy smile. "It amazes me, Della, that you can't see through another's lies when you tell so many of your own."

John is a man who takes what he wants and will not stop until he gets it.

Oliver's forehead is beaded with sweat, and I wipe it away with my palm, stroke his damp hair from his wan cheeks. "This is your brother. He needs you."

John's laugh is shallow. "He doesn't need me. Neither did Theo, despite my efforts to convince him otherwise."

I blink and look up, readjusting my thoughts. "He knew who you were?"

John nods. "War makes you realise life is short. When I was invalided out, I decided to introduce myself to Theo, wrote to him at his place of work. He never replied. So, I turned up at the house and he couldn't ignore me then. He was angry to hear his old man had fathered a bastard, refused to believe it at first. But I had my birth certificate – the one thing my mother did right."

"I saw the two of you. Talking on the steps of this house. Theo never . . . he never . . ." I stutter.

"You're as gullible as any woman." John laughs. "Readily accepted Theo's lie that I'd come to talk to him about home improvements. It gave me great pleasure to sneak in and place my quotation in his files. I hope you found it."

My hands curl into fists. The absurdness and horror of John prowling around the house unnoticed. Moving and rearranging items. Making me believe I was slowly losing my mind.

His expression darkens. "Theo and I met regularly after that. Although never again at the house. We'd never meet in Cambridge. Always had to be a train ride away. He didn't want you or his brother knowing."

Theo's trips to St Ives.

The cinema in Huntingdon.

The afternoons he went missing.

This was to meet John.

Why didn't he trust me with the truth? *Because of our loss. My health. My withdrawal from him.*

What a mess. What an unholy mess.

"If you care for your brothers, if you wanted to be a part of their lives, why betray them like this?" My voice shakes with rage and desperation, with grief at Theo's inability to confide in me, at my own inability to see that my husband's actions were an attempt to shield us from the hurt he was feeling. That his own family was not all he'd thought it to be.

John's eyes are full of fire. "Theo let me down, just like my father. Just like my mother. Your husband decided *I* was too messy. Too complicated. He had a reputation to uphold at the university, was worried how you and his brother would take the news. He wanted a legal arrangement, to pay me off so I'd stay away. A grubby secret to be swept under the rug."

The solicitor. Theo sought his advice for a way to cut John from his life?

"It's unfortunate both brothers weren't killed in the war – it would have made things simpler. Just as well your child didn't live too – your son. Did you know it was a boy, or did Theo keep that from you as well?"

Blood rushes in my ears and with a roar, I'm on my feet clutching the letter opener and stumbling to the door quick, quick, quick. But John is nimble and slams the door in my face, the key turning once. Locking me and Oliver in the dark.

Chapter 38

A silvery pool of moonlight illuminates Oliver where he lies prone on the attic floor. Kneeling beside him, I drag in deep gulping breaths. The slam of the door, and my shouts, woke Viola and her distant cries fill me with misery. What will John do with her – and with Rabbit? *We had a son. Theo and I had a son.*

Trembling with fear and frustration I turn my attention to the man lying before me. Even in this low light his face is pale as ash in a grate. I glance at the letter opener in my hand, stained with Oliver's blood. John didn't leave it here by accident, this was intentional. My fingerprints are on it now. *More evidence to convict me.*

Stifling a scream, I fling it to the floor, hear a faint and spiteful chuckle from outside the door, then footsteps retreating down the stairs. *Stupid, naïve, foolish Della.* The dinner and my growing desire to touch and be touched by John. My flesh crawls.

Giving Oliver a little shake, I lean over his body, the smell of sweat and blood mingling in my nostrils. "Please wake up. Please."

His lips parting, a low moan gurgles in his throat. His eyes open a smidgeon then close again.

"It's me. It's Della. I'm here," I say, bending to his ear, stroking his hair from his face. His lips are chapped and dry.

He needs water.

The wardrobe door leading to the secret room is open and I remember the crates of tinned food. A thin vein of hope rises as I push past the thick coats, the darkness pressing down on me as I claw my way in.

Bands of moonlight spill through thin gaps in the rafters, but there's little light to see by. On my hands and knees, I cautiously feel my way to where I remember seeing the crates. Then I recall John saying the police will find the bottles of opium and gin in the house. It's quickly obvious this room is empty. John has been in, cleared out any evidence and replanted parts of it to help send me to the gallows.

Viola's cries are louder in here, and the spot of light from my bedroom below draws me over, my heart pulsing. Pressing an eye to the spyhole, I see John lying back on my bed, arms folded behind his head. Viola wailing in the crib. He's doing nothing to comfort her – *his own child.*

We had a son. Theo and I had a son. Why didn't he tell me? Why didn't he tell me? The fact Theo is gone, and I'll never be able to speak with him about any of this, causes a deep ache to pass through me. What I'd give for one more moment together, so we could speak our truths and find a way back to our marriage.

I've an urge to call out, to scream and shout and shriek through the spyhole as I watch John languishing on the bed, but instead I clamp my lips closed. To give him attention is to give him power. I must hold back.

My eyes adjusting to the darkness, I skirt around the entirety of the room, my hands groping and feeling for any small useful item left behind. But there's nothing.

***

The clothes from Theo's trunks I make into a mattress for Oliver, padding it out with jumpers, trousers, linen shirts and twill trousers. I've torn a shirt into strips, wrapped a make-shift bandage around his ribs. The wounds are deep, and I imagine Oliver's shock as John went for him with the letter opener. What lured Oliver up here?

I roll Oliver onto the mattress. The bleeding may start again, and I might be unable to stop it. But I can't leave him in his current position, must do everything to keep him comfortable. He groans and his eyes open as I settle him on the padding, tuck around him two blankets I found, like you would a sickly child. His look at me is bewildered, taut with pain and I know I must be brief and to the point.

"John Garland is your half-brother and Viola's father. He planned all of this. He wants the house."

Oliver swallows. "I know," he rasps.

Sparks fly at the corners of my eyes. "Did he tell you?"

Another swallow, and Oliver's face crumples as he nods and tries to sit.

"No. Lie still."

He takes a few slight breaths, his chest barely moving. "I went to his flat yesterday like you asked . . . told him everything. Then I came back here. Later . . . I heard a noise. Saw your door open, a light." He pauses, wets his lips. "Rabbit was barking. Went in . . . found John . . . up here. He . . . he told me all of it. Then he . . . went for me . . . stabbed me . . . locked me in . . ."

The weight of everything that's happened tilts me forwards. "I'm sorry. So sorry."

A touch on my arm, his fingers reaching for my hand. Oliver's skin is cool, and I rub his fingers, try and instil some warmth into them.

We had a son. Theo and I had a son. You would have been a wonderful uncle.

Oliver's eyes slip closed and my heart tugs. His hand is limp, and I carefully slip it beneath the blanket. Sitting back against the wall, I listen to his shallow breaths and the beat of my own heart, fast and irregular.

Wiping my damp cheeks, weariness overcomes me. There's no way out, nothing that can be done. All I can hope for is that Oliver's death is peaceful. That Viola finds a family who cares for her, that Rabbit lives out his remaining years with someone kind. That my arrest for this man's death, my hanging for a murder I did not commit, is swift.

***

Dawn light presses at the attic window above, casting a blue hue over Oliver whose breathing is so faint now I fear it may falter at any moment. Viola's occasional jagged cries accompanied me through the long night and twice I crept back into the hidden room to quietly observe her from above.

John was absent, but he'd left a lamp on and there was an empty feeding bottle on the bed. I worry endlessly he didn't measure the correct quantity of powder to water, that the baby's arching back was a sign of colic and her discomfort. I presume now he intends to keep her here so he can inform the police I stole her. *Lies, all of it.* How can he so carelessly discard this small life, use her in this tortuous game? We had a son, but he didn't survive. But this baby lives. A baby I've quickly grown to care for. To love. *I love her . . . I need her.* Just as she needs me.

Oliver stirs. Lightly, I rest a hand on his chest and inspect the wounds. Blood began seeping through the bandages again in the thickest part of the night, viscous and wet beneath my fingers as I applied pressure to stem the flow. There's nothing more I can do now except hope. Keep him alive as my friend, my family. And my witness.

He mumbles an incoherent sentence, and I tilt my head to his lips. "Say it again?"

This time I understand him fully. "Don't. Let. Him. Have. The. House." He wheezes and coughs, pink bubbles of spit forming at the edges of his cracked lips.

I shake my head in despair. "We've no choice. He's planned this too well, will get what he wants. He's made me appear mad – even my sister believes it." *Mary.* My throat constricts at the thought of her, William and the boys. My name dragged through the gutter. The taunts the boys may face at school, the shame they will all feel. *Your aunt is a murderer!*

"Let. It. Burn." Oliver's three croaked words are spoken so softly I wonder if I misheard. His eyes dance behind his closed lids, as if he is dreaming. With a pinch I remember his cigarettes, the flare of a match when we were together in the lodging house. *His jacket . . . where's his jacket?*

Crawling across the boards, I find it in a heap behind an open trunk of clothes. He must have taken it off after John left him up here. My fingers tremble as I check the pockets and I soon find what I'm looking for. Curling my hand around the matchbox, I look back at Oliver. *Let it burn.*

A feeling ignites within me, the beginnings of a plan. John wants this house, and the only way I'll lure him up here and possibly escape is if he thinks there's a chance the bricks and mortar he covets so dearly is in danger of slipping out of reach.

Chapter 39

Mr Pemberton senior was a hoarder of curiosities and for that I send him silent thanks, as I quietly and oh so carefully set about making a pile of kindling. The wooden acrobat sand toys and music boxes. These things taken apart and, in a jumble, piled up to the right of the attic door. Tearing up strips of cloth, I add these as well, along with paper I've peeled from the insides of the travelling trunks.

Rain freckles at the window, Rabbit barks in the garden. Hurrying over, my throat parched and my stomach groaning with hunger, I stand on tiptoes, see John leaning against the oak tree having a smoke. He kicks out at the dog, rubs his eyes and yawns. Glances at his wristwatch. Has he sent an errand boy to the police station – are they on their way?

I touch a finger to the nails John hammered into the window to keep me safe. *To keep me his prisoner.* I stood there watching him do it. How he must have laughed. Rage tightens my ribcage and I realise I must be quick.

Crouching by Oliver, I shake him until he wakes. "Look at me . . . you need to understand something. I'll do it. I'll let the place burn. John will never have Arcadia House. I promise you on my life that'll never happen."

His eyes half-open, are glazed and vacant. I wipe away the pinkish foam bubbling around his lips. Gently caress his scarred and dimpled cheek. His skin is clammy, his breaths further apart now. I lean over and whisper in his ear. "Rest now, Oliver. Theo is waiting. Tell him . . . I love him."

A ghost of a smile, and Oliver's eyes close.

It doesn't take long.

A sudden stillness, the absence of rattling breaths.

Pressing my lips to his forehead, I feel a new energy shimmering through my veins as I reach for the box of matches.

***

All fires begin small, a flicker of a flame hungry for fuel and oxygen. The match I strike has both of those things up here and I fan the fire with Oliver's jacket, smoke billowing and smarting my eyes. That is my intention of course; this smoke curling under the threshold and down the stairs, a warning to John that something is amiss. A thing that requires investigation.

Binding one of Theo's shirts around my mouth and nose, I wait and wait as the smoke thickens. It sticks in my throat, and I stifle my rising coughs.

Then the sound of feet on the stairs and a curse.

I'm waiting to the left of the door as he inserts the key in the lock, the letter opener tight in my fist. A sense of calm overcomes me as the orange flames take hold, licking at the base of the trunks now, securing a path of devastation that will not be stopped.

The door flings back and I hear John's yell of surprise, see him step in.

My head is clear and free from any thought as I launch

myself at him, the silver opener sinking into a tender spot in his upper thigh.

He screams in pain, but rather than dropping to his knees as I'd hoped, he swivels and grabs at my blouse, the fabric ripping. I arch back onto the small landing at the top of the attic stairs, twisting away, but his grip is firm.

"Bitch," he bellows, the smell of his breath hot and sour through the cloth binding my mouth and nose.

Pulling the shirt from my face and taking a gulp of air, I risk a glance back; see the stair treads. Gritting my teeth, I grasp for John's shirt collar and hurl myself backwards, see his eyes widen in horror as we tumble down together, a mass of arms and legs.

My arm twists behind me and I shriek. And then we are still, and I'm coughing from the smoke, winded from the fall. John's bleeding from the temple, his body splayed across mine.

Panic races through me and I scrabble and push my way out from beneath his weight, my back bruised and aching, my arm throbbing. I heave myself to my feet, stand panting over John who is lying with his eyes closed, blood beading down his cheek and on to the carpet. Red oozing from his thigh too. His breaths are short and sharp. *Not dead, then.* It was never my intention to kill him. I am defending myself, nothing more.

My head thuds, and waves of dizziness blur my surroundings as I hurtle into my bedroom and scoop Viola into my arms. I feel her body shudder in relief as she nestles into me. "Oh, my darling. My sweet, sweet girl. I'm here to keep you safe. You're safe now." Rabbit is barking downstairs;

any minute the police may arrive and now there are two men in my house; one dead and one injured. Both wounded by an object belonging to me.

I glance back at John, a dark fury sprouting inside me for all the hurt, all the terror he's caused. In five breathless steps I'm standing before him and the action of my boot meeting his face is involuntary and satisfying. I kick him a second time and a bruising swell blooms across his cheek. His eyes flick open and in an instant his hand is gripping my ankle, tight, tight, tight and I swallow a scream as he tugs me forwards.

Curling myself around the baby, I land hard on my knees, pain roaring up my thighs and spine. Then I'm gritting my teeth and staring John in the eye. "The house is on fire. It's burning. It'll never be yours unless you put it out."

His eyes widen, and he twists his head to glance up the stairs to the attic, his grip on me loosening for a fraction of a second. Then I'm free from his grasp, stumbling to my feet with the baby and hurtling down the stairs, the smell of smoke licking at my heels.

***

Outside, Rabbit dances around my boots and I look up to see flickers of orange through the attic windows. The dog sticks to my side as we hurry along the grass to the back gate, my limbs pulsing with pain as I loop my bag over my shoulder and grip my suitcase, the baby cradled in my good arm.

I throw one last quick glance at the house, its tall windows, a place of secrets and lies. The police will arrive, and I'll be blamed for this fire and the events that took place here. I'll be deemed insane; people will search for me. But it's a price worth paying to protect this small and innocent life in my arms, this unwanted child of his. Not unwanted by me though. *I have a son who died, but I also have a daughter who lives.*

Latching the back gate, I hurry through the early morning light, past the building sites where bricks and planks will be used to build homes for neighbours I'll never meet. Birds hidden within the twisted tree branches twitter and clamour at the arrival of this new day, and Viola's snuffles and Rabbit's pants anchor my boot heels to the muddy lane as we press on. It is just the three of us now and finally, finally, my heart begins to lift.

Ten Years Later

I stand by the railings of Great St Mary's Church watching my daughter linger at the market stall, this child with bobbed hair the colour of cork. She stands there chewing on her bottom lip. I sense her hesitation, but she's been instructed well enough by me. *You can do it*, I urge her silently as she eyes the man again.

John's hair is more grey than brown now and he's holding the hand of a boy of five. In his other hand he grips a walking cane. The child hops from foot to foot by his father's side. Vi has no idea, of course, that this boy is her half-brother. Andrew is his name and I swallow back the sudden ache in my throat as I note their similarities – their rounded pink cheeks, the wayward curls to their hair.

John and Andrew are buying vegetables and fruit; apples, onions and carrots with green fluffy tops. Vi's favourite type of vegetable. I tickle the greens under her chin before we cut them off, always making a game of things in our Highgate apartment.

Vi sidles closer to John. She's nimble in her task, well-practised. Her small hand darts into his jacket pocket and then she's skipping back towards me, the metal prize in her fist, braids bumping on her cardiganed shoulders on this cool autumn day.

She runs up to me, beaming. Grabbing her hand, I pivot and we hurry towards King's Parade. "I did it just like you asked, Mummy."

I hold out my palm, a proud smile curving my lips. "Well done, darling." She passes me the door key, and I slip it into my handbag, click it closed.

Vi tilts her head. "It's different from the usual things we take."

Arching an eyebrow, I adjust my headscarf as we walk. "Different, yes. But it'll come in useful."

Vi knows that there's little point in asking why it will be useful. I won't elaborate on why we take the things we do. She knows stealing is wrong, of course. But it's important to have the skills to be able to obtain food and drink if we're forced to flee without money or, heaven forbid, if we're parted.

"Are we going home now?" Vi asks brightly.

Nodding, I glance at my wristwatch. "The next London train is in an hour. Perhaps we can buy a bun from Fitzbillies to eat at the station while we wait?"

"There's no time to visit Great Aunt Viola then?" Vi asks.

"No. Not today," I say with a smile. My daughter often says how much she's enjoyed our recent trips to Cambridge and the visits to Viola in her cosy Grantchester cottage. Not an aunt by blood, of course, but the help that woman's given us these past years, the money she loaned us to start a new life in London, the way she believed my version of the events without question. That makes her the truest family I'll ever have.

Viola Cleeve's health might be failing her now, but her mind is still as sharp as a brass tack. She instilled in me the confidence to trail John Garland (not Pemberton, he'll never be a Pemberton) at a distance from Arcadia House. Noting where he always pocketed his house key.

Vi once asked me what Arcadia meant. "A place of quiet pleasure," I'd told her. For a time, that house lived up to its definition for both the Cleeves and the Pembertons.

The Cambridge spires tower above as Vi skips along the street. Her sunniness brings a swell of joy to my chest. Passing the stationery shop on King's Parade I risk a glance in. Under different ownership now, and of course no sign of Lottie.

Thinking back to that day it all began, my theft of the paint roundel and the urge to take the baby in its pram, the arrival of Viola in my house, I wonder at who I'd become. Living in a grey half-world, neither alive nor dead. Addicted to the potion John fed me and with only a small dog for company. A dog that lived beyond his years and who Viola and I miss deeply.

But we have Cleo waiting for us at home now, a bundle of white fluff who covers Vi in licks when she returns from school and who will sit quietly with me on the occasions I feel blue. My own health waxes and wanes and my hot spells still occasionally strike, but as Emanuel Cleeve's daughter once said, all things pass. When you think like that almost anything is bearable.

Vi waits for me to catch up. "Why are you smiling like that?" she asks, slipping her hand into mine.

"Oh. I'm just thinking about dear old Rabbit. And how much you love Cleo."

"Can't we get another dog . . . please?" my daughter begs.

Reaching down, I trace a finger across Vi's cheek, smiling

at this familiar question. "I've told you before, I'm not sure Mr Benson from across the hall will be willing to watch *two* dogs on the day's I work."

"You can take it to the art gallery. Sylvie won't mind," Vi pleads.

My employer wouldn't mind, but I don't tell Vi that yet. I've already planned to surprise her with a puppy on her birthday this November. If it's her actual date of birth or not, I'll never know, but it didn't take long to find someone in London who was willing to falsify birth certificates for her and me. Her surname is Lovett now, the name I've taken too. Picked from the telephone directory at random and it suits us, I think.

I took any work I could get in London at first. Sweeping taverns and cleaning shop windows in the early mornings, Viola swaddled at my chest. Then I met Sylvie. She would arrive early at the art gallery I cleaned, cooing over the baby and seeking my opinions on the pictures she was selling. Opinions that eventually led to her employing me to search out new stock; rooting through attics and dead people's belongings to find hidden gems. She says I have a talent for it.

"Do you think *he's* noticed his key's missing yet?" Vi whispers, as we wait in the queue at Fitzbillies, the smell of rising dough and sweet things softening my breathing.

"Perhaps," I murmur, lowering my head, hoping for invisibility as we stand here. Just a mother and daughter buying a sweet treat. It's always a risk coming back, but as the years pass, I grow bolder.

It was three years after the fire that I first plucked up the courage to return to Cambridge, leaving Vi in London with Sylvie who dotes on my daughter as if she's her own.

Borrowing a bicycle, I headed out to Newnham, risking only a quick glance at the house that had once been mine. The window shutters were gone, replaced by thick brocade drapes. That was the only difference, aside from the fact John had married and now lived there.

There was of course a lot of public interest in my alleged murder of Oliver Pemberton. The papers made much of the half-brother John who'd befriended me, only for me to turn against him and try and kill him too. I kept those newspaper clippings for a while in a tin under my bed, but as Vi grew older I disposed of them. Couldn't risk her coming across them and asking difficult questions.

But the articles written about me dwindled when I wasn't found. Some said I'd drowned myself and the baby in the river, others said I'd fled the country and was living abroad. The only person still looking for me now is Mary. I've seen the advertisements my sister places in the notice sections of the national papers each New Year asking me to contact her. The postal box address which I assume she checks regularly in case of my response. The temptation to write is sometimes all consuming, but I'll never succumb to it.

Vi tugs on my arm now. "Mummy. Look."

She's staring around the people in the queue behind us to the shop window. John Garland holds Andrew's hand, and his son is pointing out a tray of Chelsea buns. The man leans heavily on his walking cane, and I feel a pinch in my side at the memory of the letter opener sinking into his thigh.

It brings me satisfaction to know he has a permanent reminder of that night.

I turn Vi away, shield her from view. My daughter stiffens, and I take her hand, give it a reassuring squeeze. We wait in silence, and I pay for our buns, neither of us glancing back. Vi's palm is sweaty in mine. Finally risking a look over my shoulder, I see that they've gone.

The rage is still there, simmering and burning in my stomach. I've nothing against little Andrew, or John's wife, will be sure they're out when I finally make my return to Arcadia House. I don't know when that will be. This month or the next, perhaps?

Maybe John will have had the locks changed by then, will have a sense that his key isn't lost that a small and nimble hand could have slipped into his jacket pocket and taken it.

I made a promise to Oliver that I intend to keep. No matter what happens, I'm still coming for you, John Garland. I will strike a match and let Arcadia House burn. It will never be yours.

ACKNOWLEDGEMENTS

Having published seven historical mysteries for children, it was nerve-wracking telling my agent I had the urge to pivot my career and write an adult historical thriller about a woman who discovers a baby left in her house. Thank you to Clare Wallace at Darley Anderson for always believing I could do it – working with you on early edits for *Stolen Things* was an absolute joy.

Thank you to Fox & Ink for all your support and for loving this story from the start. Thanks to Kathy Webb, Hazel Holmes and Jasmine Dove for the considered and thoughtful edits. You helped me get to the heart of Della's story and the book is all the stronger because of your input.

The cover design is beyond anything I could have imagined, and a huge thanks to Amy Cooper from Fox & Ink and Ami Smithson for the inspired and glorious illustrations.

A huge thank you must go to my readers. Many of you have been asking what I've been working on, and this is it! Thank you for all your book blogging, reviews and for recommending me far and wide. You enable me to keep doing this job I adore.

Finally, thank you to my friends and family. I often write at home ensconced in a world of my own for hours at a time. Thank you for giving me the space to do this and for listening when I get stuck. To Jeremy, Jack, Ed and my mum – you are my world and I love you all.

AUTHOR'S NOTE

While the early years after the Great War were a time of hope for many, for others life was an ongoing personal struggle. It was this aspect which inspired me to write about those in society who had lost something, or in their view had something stolen, be that a person, relationship, good health, or employment.

The impact of war was horrific; men so badly wounded they were unrecognisable and shunned by society. In personal war diaries there are accounts of mercy killings, soldiers so badly injured there was no option but to end their suffering on the battlefield. This was of course illegal, but sometimes necessary. Everything I learned in my research helped inspire the war experiences of Della's husband Theo and his brother Oliver.

Theo's work at the University of Cambridge, and his interest in Gypsy Moths, is based on my own research which took me down many fascinating rabbit holes. Any mistakes here are entirely my own.

An important aspect of the book was writing about Della's experience of menopause, something I'm going through at present. There is little first-hand documentation to give us clues as to how women coped back in 1919. However, it is known that some women in their forties and fifties back then were deemed insane and sent to asylums. Others took their own lives or developed a reliance on alcohol. Some took herbal tonics for female disorders (which in the nineteenth century even contained opium).

While we are getting better at speaking up and seeking help for women's health issues today, there's still a long way to go in terms of being listened to by health professionals. Information and truth is power and brings agency, and while women may not have had this at the time of my historical thriller, that is something we all now deserve.

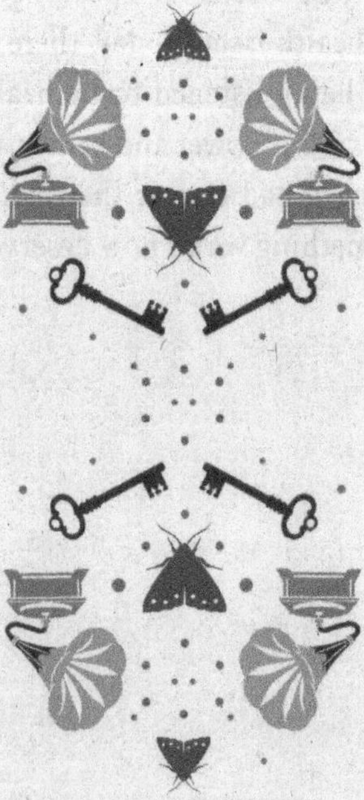